The

Spirit of Deadwood

(A Paranormal Snapshot)

By Sherry A. Burton

Dorry Press

The Jerry McNeal Series

Spirit of Deadwood
By Sherry A. Burton

The Jerry McNeal Series: Spirit of Deadwood
Copyright 2023

By Sherry A. Burton
Published by Dorry Press
Edited and Formatted by BZHercules.com
Cover by Laura J. Prevost
@laurajprevostphotography
Proofread by Latisha Rich

For more information on the author and her works, please see www.SherryABurton.com

Dedication

I will forever be grateful to my mom, who insisted the dog stay in the series.

To my hubby, thanks for helping me stay in the writing chair.

To my editor, Beth, for allowing me to keep my voice.

To Laura, for EVERYTHING you do to keep me current in both my covers and graphics.

To my beta readers for giving the books an early read.

To my proofreader, Latisha Rich, for the extra set of eyes.

To my fans, for the continued support.

Lastly, to my "writing voices," thank you for all the incredible ideas!

Chapter One

To most, a dream is merely a dream – a movie in one's mind often lost with something as simple as repositioning one's head. Psychic Jerry McNeal had learned from an early age that dreams were not to be dismissed until he'd taken the time to thoroughly sift through them to see if they were perhaps a message or warning sent from beyond to be acted upon as needed.

Jerry quickly learned that dreams are different than nightmares. Dreams hold messages; nightmares contain warnings – at least they had before his time with the Marines. Now Jerry's nightmares held not only predictions, but sometimes succeeded in unlocking a compartment within the recesses of his mind. They taunted him with memories of the brothers he couldn't save. His therapist had passed the nightmares off as PTSD – post-traumatic stress disorder. But Jerry knew they were more, as sometimes the spirits of his lost brothers visited him even while he was awake.

Not this time. While Jerry couldn't recall the nightmare, he knew it wasn't a visit from any of his Marine brothers. Being with April seemed to have somehow eased his burden, as he hadn't had one of those nightmares since moving in with her and her daughter Max several months ago. Jerry often found himself lying awake at night, not because of the nightmares that had plagued him so often in the past, but because it comforted him to lie there listening to April's soft, easy breaths. They were so soothing that he often remained in bed long after waking just to listen to her breathe.

Still, the nightmare had left him unsettled, and that was the reason Jerry now stood staring out the kitchen window a little after four in the morning, trying yet again to recall the specifics of the nightmare that had awakened him.

Gunter stood next to him, his dark muzzle resting on the windowsill. His ears stood tall – ghostly antennas twitching as he stared out the window. The old house sat on a half-acre lot that backed to the neighbor's yard. Both yards were filled with mature trees, which helped with privacy.

Jerry felt the dog stiffen and looked to see what had captured the K-9's attention. He got his answer a second later when a black squirrel scampered down a nearby maple tree.

Gunter snorted.

Jerry reached to pet the dog's head, and the K-9 wagged his tail while looking at him as if asking permission to give chase. Asking permission was unnecessary, as Jerry had no control over the dog. No one did, as the dog was, in fact, a ghost, the spirit of a K-9 police officer killed in the line of duty who had come back from the dead and attached himself to Jerry.

Jerry chuckled. "I'm fine. Go do dog stuff."

Gunter disappeared and reappeared three feet from where the squirrel was digging in the backyard. There was a short standoff as the squirrel debated the likelihood of the ghostly K-9 catching him. Gunter lifted a paw, and the chase was on – the black and tan German shepherd gathering his legs beneath him as the squirrel scurried for the tree. Just before reaching the tree, the squirrel cut to the right. Gunter slid to a stop and then caught up with the critter just as he scampered out of reach.

Gunter jumped after the wayward squirrel several times. On the third jump, the dog disappeared into thin air. Jerry stared at the tree for several moments, half expecting the dog to appear on one of the upper branches. When Gunter failed to show himself, Jerry turned from the window and saw him standing in the middle of the kitchen, smiling a K-9 grin.

"You almost had him."

Gunter wagged his tail.

Jerry walked to the counter, refilled his coffee cup, then pulled a legal pad from the drawer and went to the kitchen table. Opening the legal pad to a blank page, he sketched a rough outline of April's house. On the next page, he etched out a fair resemblance of the inside lower floor floorplan, detailing the large eat-in kitchen, dining room, living room, and bathroom. He leaned back in his chair and studied his handiwork while drumming his fingers on the table. He tore the paper from the pad and drew a square. Next, he drew the same floorplan, cordoning off some of the kitchen that lined the back side of the house. He roughed in some counters and cabinets and added two boxes into the small space before picking up the outline he'd drawn of the house and adding a large room off the back. Once again, he sat back, staring at his handiwork.

Jerry felt the hairs on the back of his neck stand on end and looked up as his grandmother's spirit appeared across the table from him. Jerry always enjoyed the woman's visits from beyond, mostly since she usually appeared wearing one of the simple dresses she'd often worn when working around the house and looking much less frail than she had in the years prior to her death.

Gunter hurried to where she sat and greeted the woman's ghostly form.

Granny smiled a heavily wrinkled grin as she

ruffled the dog's fur with age-spotted hands. After a moment, she gave the dog a firm pat and reached over the table to turn the paper so she could see it. "Do you think April will go for it?"

Jerry furrowed his brow. "You don't like it?"

"Of course I do. But it's not my house. I know you've done a lot of updates since you moved in and that April loves having a handyman in the house, but have you ever asked her if she wants to stay here?"

Jerry leaned back in the chair. "Do you know something I don't?"

Granny shook her head. "No, Jerry. I haven't been listening in on April's conversations. But I also know enough to know you shouldn't assume. You are used to taking charge and doing things on your own, but that's not how relationships work." She glanced at the paper sketch he'd made of the proposed mudroom on which he had detailed everything from wall color to the style of the washer and dryer, and clicked her tongue. "Women like to have a say in things, especially when it comes to designing kitchens and decorating."

Jerry crumpled the paper and redrew the floorplan, leaving out the finer details. He turned the tablet for her to see. "Better?"

Granny smiled and nodded her head. "Much."

Gunter plopped to the floor with a sigh.

"He's had a rough morning chasing squirrels," Jerry said by way of explanation.

Granny pulled an apple out of the pocket of her dress and took a bite. "You're up early."

"Nightmare."

Granny raised an eyebrow. "Anything I can help with?"

"Only if you can help me remember it. It was gone the moment I woke."

"But it bothered you?"

Jerry nodded. "Yes."

"If someone's trying to tell you something, they will keep trying."

"I know."

"But?"

"No buts. Just the same old wish – you know, for the easy button," Jerry replied.

"In my day, there wasn't any such thing as an easy button. None of those computers either. I wished for a filing cabinet. I had a vision once, but the image cleared before I had time to decide what to do with it. It was pretty too. A cherry-red file cabinet, floating about yea high." She stretched her arm to show him. "I knew without opening it that all of life's answers were tucked inside, and all I needed to do was open it to see them."

"Why didn't you?"

"I wasn't expecting it, and it kind of took me by surprise. I blinked, and the vision was gone, never to return. Probably for the best. Can you imagine having the answers to all of life's questions?"

Jerry smiled at the woman who had practically raised him. "I always thought you did."

She laughed. "Hardly."

"You made it seem that way. I don't recall you ever telling me you didn't know something." He smiled. "I do recall a lot of 'let's figure it out'."

Another laugh. "That was my way of stalling until I could think of a suitable answer."

"Yeah, well, it worked." The floor creaked overhead, and Jerry looked to the ceiling and smiled. "April's awake."

Granny reached over and patted his hand. "I like seeing you so happy, Jerry."

Jerry looked at the hand resting on his and sighed. "If I had access to that file cabinet, I know the first thing I would look up."

She met his gaze. "What's that, Jerry?"

He nodded toward her hand. "I'd want to know how I am able to feel the warmth of your hand on my skin."

She grinned. "Of all the silly questions."

"I don't think it's so silly. I mean, I know you are a spirit, but I can literally feel the warmth of your hands. And earlier, when I was standing at the window, I could feel Gunter's weight as he pressed his body into my leg. Most spirits are whisps of air that take on the form of whatever they were, but with you and Gunter, I can almost forget you are..." Granny disappeared before he could finish his sentence. Gunter alerted, and Jerry turned to see April standing behind him.

She smiled and leaned in for a kiss. Pulling away, she plucked his coffee cup from the table and took it to the counter to refill. "You're a lucky man, Mr. McNeal."

Jerry looked her up and down, admiring how her thin robe skimmed her taut body. "No argument there."

The color rose in her cheeks. "I'm serious."

"As was I, but go on," Jerry said, taking the cup she offered.

She sat in the chair Granny had just vacated and sipped her coffee. "You're lucky I trust you enough not to think you're crazy when I walk into a room and hear you talking to someone that isn't here."

"That's a lot of trust," he said, lifting his cup.

"It helps that I have a daughter who is a psychic." April winked and tucked her chestnut hair behind her ear. "If not for Max, I'd have to send you packing."

Jerry leveled a look at her. "I didn't hear you objecting to my being here last night."

April's face turned a lovely shade of pink. "I haven't the slightest idea what you're talking about."

Jerry lowered his cup. "I'd be happy to remind you."

"Stay in that seat, Mister. Max will be up any

minute," April said, taking a sip from her cup. "So, who were you talking to?"

"Granny."

April glanced around the room. "Is she still here?"

Jerry smiled. "If she were, you'd be sitting in her lap."

April shifted in her seat. "I didn't mean to run her off."

Jerry shook his head. "You didn't, and couldn't if you wanted to."

"She didn't leave because I came into the room?"

"No, she left because she didn't want to hear what I had to say."

"Which was?"

"I reminded her she is dead."

"She doesn't know?"

"She knows. She just doesn't like to be reminded of it. It's like when a person discovers their own mortality. Until that moment, they think they're invincible and are suddenly reminded they are not. I've seen it often, both with the Marines and when I was a state trooper. A near miss or one of your brothers taking a hit – suddenly, it becomes real. Granny and Gunter both know they are spirits. Knowing is one thing. Being reminded of it is another."

"Even though I know you and Max can see them, it's still hard to fully wrap my head around it.

Can I ask you a question?"

Jerry lowered his cup. "Of course."

April ran a finger over the rim of her cup, then looked at him with solemn brown eyes. "You told me before that you were four years old the first time you saw a ghost. What was it like? I mean, did you know you were seeing a ghost?"

Jerry shook his head. "Spirit – that's what they prefer to be called. And no, I wasn't scared – not then. The spirit was my Aunt Edna – my dad's sister – who had always been nice to me. My parents told me she had died in a car accident and that we were going to her funeral. I'd never been to a funeral – at least none I could remember – so I didn't know what the word meant. We got there, and everyone was sad. Most were crying, and I didn't want any part of that. There were some other kids there, but we weren't allowed to play. I couldn't understand why anyone would want to go to a place that made everyone sad.

"My dad came and found me and took me to up to my Aunt Edna's casket. Nanna – Dad's mom – was standing there, crying and saying that mothers weren't supposed to bury their children. I looked at the woman in the box, who, at that moment, looked more like a statue outside the museum than my Aunt Edna. Then I looked up and saw Aunt Edna standing between my Nanna and Dad. I told them they didn't have to bury her because she wasn't really dead.

Then I pointed to where she was standing. Nanna began crying harder, and dad took me by the hand and led me away. When we got into the hallway, he told me I was bad for telling lies and how I'd hurt my Nanna's feelings. I tried to tell him I wasn't lying, but he told me I was never to talk about seeing her again."

"That must have been hard on you," April said softly.

"It was. Mostly because Aunt Edna knew I could see her and wanted me to tell my dad and Nanna that she was okay. I tried once, but Dad got mad all over again and forbade me to mention her name."

"He didn't know you had the gift?"

"He knew something was up because, when I was two, I'd warned my parents right before the house caught fire." He shrugged. "I woke in the middle of the night with my first vision and saw my room going up in a blaze. It hadn't happened yet, but my cries woke them, and it started just after they came into the room, so they were able to put it out before it got bad."

April frowned. "I can barely remember what I had for breakfast yesterday, much less anything from when I was two."

"Yeah, I don't know if I really remember it or if it's simply because I've heard the story so much that I feel as if I do."

April nodded her understanding. "Your dad

didn't believe you. What about your mom?"

"Mom knew. She'd grown up with my grandmother – who also saw spirits."

"But she couldn't see them?"

"No, Mom didn't have the gift."

"But she believed you, so why didn't she say anything?"

"She tried, but Dad didn't want to hear any of that voodoo stuff. Talking about it made Dad mad, so I stopped. No boy wants their dad mad at them."

April's frown deepened, and Jerry knew she was remembering the fact that she hadn't believed her own daughter when Max had known the relationship April was about to enter was doomed. April rubbed at her arms and continued. "Did it bother you that your mom didn't stand up for you?"

Jerry started to call her on her inner thoughts and decided against it. "It did for a while. I asked her about it later, and she just said it was causing too much friction between her and Dad, so she finally quit pushing the issue. Anyway, about a year after Aunt Edna's funeral, we were going to another funeral, and my dad pulled me aside and warned me not to say anything about seeing ghosts. I didn't plan on either seeing them or talking about it, but dang it if the woman didn't show herself to me."

"Where you scared?"

"Not of the spirit. But I was sure afraid of Dad finding out that I saw one. He was watching me pretty darn close, so I hid. That's when Granny found me, only instead of yelling at me, she told me she could see it too. Things changed for me then. Granny not only approved of me seeing spirits, but she also encouraged me to talk about them and other things I saw and felt. If I wasn't at school, I was hanging out with Granny."

"Sounds like she became your best friend."

Jerry smiled and glanced over at his grandmother's spirit, who had reappeared shortly after he started speaking. "In some ways, she still is."

April followed his gaze. "Do you think she will mind sharing you with me and Max?"

"I assure you that we have Granny's blessing. She has already started working with Max to help her fully understand her abilities." Jerry turned his attention to April. "Does that bother you?"

April sighed. "If you had asked me that same question a year ago, I would have thought you were crazy. I do not intend to let Max grow up thinking her gift is something to be ashamed of. I have no clue what to say to her when she tells me she can see spirits or talk to the dead. I trust you, Jerry. I know you love Max and won't let anything bad happen to her. I'm so glad I reached out to you and asked for help. Besides, look where it got us."

"I'm glad to be here. And even if I weren't, I would not let anything happen to Max. Neither would Gunter." Jerry smiled and nodded to where the ghostly K-9 lay on the floor between them. The sounds of galloping sounded overhead, letting them know Houdini was awake. "Or him."

They both looked to the stairs in time to see Max racing down with the German shepherd puppy hot on her heels. Max reached the bottom, and the pup sailed past her and ran straight through the closed door and into the backyard.

April sighed. "He keeps doing that, and people are going to start to talk."

Jerry ran a hand through his hair and nodded his agreement. Living with a ghost dog was easy. Living with a hybrid ghost puppy was proving to be a whole other story.

Chapter Two

With the exception of the womanly curves, Maxine Buchanan was the spitting image of her mother, right down to her chestnut hair and rich brown eyes. They even sounded similar – with the teen's voice being slightly higher than her mother's. Aside from the fact that Max – as she preferred to be called – was psychic, could see and speak with ghosts, and at thirteen years old, had a job as a forensic sketch artist with an unnamed agency and received a salary generally reserved for college-educated adults, she was a typical teen and currently being scolded for acting just like one.

"Maxine Buchanan, what have I told you about running down those stairs? It was dangerous before, but it's even worse now that we have Houdini. Remember what Jerry said about making him wait at the top of the stairs until you reach the bottom?"

Max sighed. "Sorry, Mom."

"'Sorry, Mom,' isn't good enough," April countered. "If Gunter is any indication, Houdini is going to be a big dog. It wouldn't do for him to race up and down the stairs while someone is on them. He knocks you down, and you could fall and break your neck. You may not be afraid of dying, but I'd rather Jerry not be the only one who can see you."

Max giggled. "I'd let you see me. Not all the time, but I know it's possible because Gunter lets people see him sometimes."

April looked at Jerry and gave him a look that said, *Are you going to help me out or just stand there?*

Jerry took the hint. "Max, we've talked about this. Houdini isn't like other dogs. We've got to get him trained fast so he doesn't draw unwanted attention to himself. Make him wait at the top of the stairs and only give the release after you've reached the bottom. Same thing with going up. Unless he is on a leash and walking at your side, he is not to be on the stairs when you are on them."

"Yes, sir," Max said, nodding.

Jerry pointed to the door. "While we're on the subject, Houdini needs to wait to go outside until we open the door. We can't have the neighbors see him walking through doors."

"Mrs. Gilbert believes in ghosts," Max countered.

Jerry stood his ground. "Houdini is only half

ghost. I've told you both how dangerous it could be for Houdini and all of us if people find out about him. Fred warned me that even the agency wouldn't be able to protect us from the nutjobs and paparazzi," Jerry said, speaking of the unnamed government agency boss that both he and Max worked for.

Jerry walked to the door when Houdini scratched to be let inside. He opened it and saw Granny leaning to the side, holding on to Houdini's collar while the pup squirmed to get away. She set her jaw and intertwined a leg around the pup to settle him. Jerry shook his head. *How is this my life?* He stepped aside to allow them both to enter. Granny released her hold, and the pup sprinted inside, jumping to get Jerry's attention. As he turned, he saw Max staring at him. "I didn't mean that the way it sounded."

Max shrugged a carefree shrug. "I know."

April looked at each of them in turn. "What did I miss?"

Max smiled. "Jerry was just thinking how lucky he is to be here with us."

Jerry jabbed a thumb toward Max. "What the kid said."

Max jutted her jaw. "I'm not a kid. I'm thirteen."

April looked at the clock. "A thirteen-year-old who's going to be late for school if you don't get a move on it."

Jerry glanced toward Max. "Want me to drive

you?"

"No. Chloe's mom is picking me up." As if on cue, a horn sounded near the front of the house. "There she is now." Max remained in place until Jerry took hold of the pup's collar before waving her goodbyes and heading to the door. Not wishing to be left behind, Houdini squirmed and barked his readiness to follow the girl he'd claimed as his own.

Jerry held on to Houdini's collar until the pup calmed, then shot a look at Gunter. "Don't let him follow her."

Gunter placed himself between the pup and the door, circling, weaving, and blocking until Houdini finally returned to the kitchen and looked to April for his breakfast.

April poured the kibble into the bowl, waited for Houdini to sit then placed his bowl on the ground. She stood, waited for him to make eye contact, then gave him the signal to take it. She saw Jerry watching and smiled a triumphant smile. "Someone has to take the training seriously."

"You're doing a great job," Jerry commended her. "He's getting better and hasn't eaten any shoes in nearly two weeks. Nor has he left the yard."

"Maybe that's because your grandmother is outside watching him." April winked as she took a seat at the table.

Jerry chuckled. "How did you know?"

"You and Max and Granny told me."

Jerry glanced at his grandmother, who shrugged her confusion. "What do you mean we told you?"

April smiled. "I may not have the gift, but I can see things. A few minutes ago, when you opened the door to let him in, Max didn't look down at the puppy. She looked up like she was seeing someone. You'd said earlier that your grandmother was here, so I deduced that it was she who Max was looking at and she who kept our little escape artist from leaving the yard."

Jerry walked over and kissed April on top of the head. "And that, my beautiful detective, is just one of the reasons I love you." April grinned up at him, and Jerry stole another kiss. He lifted her chin and stared into her eyes. "Earlier, when we were talking, I could tell you were worried that Max would hold it against you that you didn't always believe her. I want you to know she doesn't."

April sighed. "So, this is what it's going to be like living with a mind reader."

"I'm not a mind reader!"

April flinched.

Jerry instantly regretted his tone. *Way to go, McNeal. You want her to trust you, and you sound off like a buffoon.* Jerry caressed her cheek with his thumb, then blew out a sigh. "I'm sorry. I didn't mean to raise my voice."

April nodded to the chair on the other side of the table. "It's alright. I seem to have touched a nerve."

"It's nothing, really," Jerry lied.

April tilted her head. "It doesn't work that way – not anymore. If we're going to make this work, we are going to be a team. If something bothers you, I want to know about it. Now, won't you sit and tell me about it?"

Granny stepped up behind April and placed her hands on her shoulders. "Oh, I like her, Jerry. She's definitely a keeper. She and Max are just what you need to keep you grounded."

Gunter barked.

Granny laughed. "You too, Gunter."

Gunter smiled a K-9 smile. Not one to be left out, Houdini lifted his head from his food dish, barked once, then dipped his head back into the bowl.

Jerry nodded toward April, who was busy rubbing her arms against an invisible chill. "You felt that."

"The chill? Yes. What was it?"

"Granny. She's right behind you. She likes you."

"I wish I could have met you." April giggled a nervous giggle. "Did she hear me?"

Jerry nodded his head. "Every word."

"Wow, how is this my life." April sighed a contented sigh. "I have an amazing daughter, a hot boyfriend, and a house full of ghosts."

Jerry stared at her without blinking.

April frowned. "Okay, now you're really scaring me. You did know you were my boyfriend, right?"

Jerry shifted in his chair. "I kind of thought we were just sleeping together."

April's frown deepened. "Seriously?"

Jerry laughed. "Lighten up, Ladybug. I was kidding."

Houdini finished eating and headed toward the back door. Jerry jumped up to open it before he pushed his way outside.

"You two talk. I'll go out with him," Granny said, following the pup outside. She whistled to Gunter. "Come on, fellow, get out here and help an old lady out."

Thanks, Jerry said without speaking. He waited until the trio was outside before closing the back door, then turned his attention to April. "It surprised me that you said 'how is this my life.' I've said it so often that I thought I had coined the phrase. Then again, I'm not sure I've ever said it in the same context." Jerry held up a hand. "Before you ask, I am one hundred and ten percent happy to be here."

"Only a hundred and ten percent? I guess we'll have to work on that."

Jerry smiled. "I like the sound of that."

April waved him off. "Not with your grandmother so near."

Jerry waggled his eyebrows. "She's outside with the dogs."

April pointed to the chair he'd previously vacated. "Sit."

"Yes, ma'am," Jerry said, returning to his seat. She was staring at him, and he knew she was waiting for him to explain his earlier outburst. "My uncle was a mind reader. He and I didn't get along in the early years."

April knitted her brows. "What's the difference between a psychic and a mind reader?"

Good question. "A psychic can get a read on someone along with smidgins of information letting them know the truth."

"But Max can get inside your mind. From what she's told me, the two of you can speak to each other without words. Isn't that mind reading?"

Jerry ran a hand through his hair. It was hard trying to explain things when even he didn't know all the answers. "I guess. It's like that with Granny too, both when she was alive and now."

"So, how come you didn't know your uncle had the gift?"

While he wanted to be truthful, he didn't care to rehash everything from his childhood and recent years, so he decided to give her the condensed version. "Apparently, I did, but I didn't remember until he reminded me of it a few months ago. Until then, I thought he was… to be honest, up until that time, I couldn't stand the guy, as I thought him to be a chronic liar. He'd tell war stories about wars he never fought in and give details he shouldn't have known. I tended to avoid him as much as humanly possible because he really pissed me off. Have I mentioned that my family is a bit dysfunctional?"

April laughed, though her eyes showed no sign of amusement. "Sweetheart, I could write a book on dysfunctional families. My family coined the phrase."

Jerry started to ask her to elaborate, then decided against it. There was a difference between sharing family secrets and opening old wounds. While he'd had the chance to dust out his mental closet in recent months, April hadn't, and he wouldn't press her for her backstory until she was ready. "Uncle Marvin was Granny's brother. He had the gift until he was in an accident. After that, something changed. I don't know if the gift disappeared or morphed into something different. Either way, he was different afterwards. People thought the accident made him simple-minded. To be honest, I went through life thinking the same thing. But come to find out, he was a cunning old fox and used the head injury to his advantage."

April leaned forward. "How?"

Jerry debated how much to tell, and in the end, he kept talking. "Marvin used his new gift for capital gain. If something went wrong on a job, he would sue. The gift let him know who had cut corners, and because he could, he was able to give his attorney enough information to seal the deal. Most of his court cases were won out of court."

April sat up in her chair and brushed away the hair that had fallen across her eyes. "Your uncle sounds like a good man to have in your corner."

"I would have argued that point up until a few months ago." Jerry blew out a sigh. "I told you my brother died."

April's smile faded. "Yes."

"Joseph was working a job with Uncle Marvin. The driveway caved, and the truck Joseph was in rolled and killed him." Jerry pushed through the memory of blaming himself for his brother's death. "Anyway, long story short, Uncle Marvin was able to sue on Joseph's behalf, and I, being the beneficiary of my brother's estate, received not only Joseph's life insurance but the money from the settlement as well."

"Your parents are still alive. Your brother must have loved you very much to have made you his beneficiary," April said softly.

That she hadn't asked how much money was involved warmed his heart. Then again, between Max's salary and the reward money given to her by Mario Fabel for Max's part in helping find his sister's body, April didn't need his money. "Joseph said he felt as if he owed it to me."

"Did he say why?"

Jerry laughed and flexed his right hand. "Oh yes, we had quite the discussion about it."

April's eyes widened. "You spoke to him after

his death! That's why your hand was bandaged when you first came to Michigan to talk to Max about her dreams. She said you'd hit your brother. You corrected her, saying you'd hit the mirror."

Jerry sat back in his chair. "Not one of my better moments."

"We all have things we'd rather forget." April's words came out in a whisper. "I was young when I met Max's biological dad. I thought I was in love, but looking back, I think I saw him as a way to get out of my house. My family life was pretty crappy. I was out of the house long enough to get pregnant with Max, and then, when things didn't work out with Max's dad, I had no choice but to move back in with my family. If I thought it was bad before, it was worse then. My family treated me like a servant. I am not afraid of cooking or cleaning, but no one in the house ever lifted a finger to help. When they got done eating, they left their dishes wherever they were eating, and if I didn't clean up after them…

"Anyway, Max and I lived there until I met Randy. You'd think I would have learned my lesson, but apparently not. Max tried to warn me he wasn't nice, but I was already used to people not being nice to me. My mom told me if it didn't work out with him, don't bother coming back. I swore to myself I wouldn't ever go back home. That promise lasted until the first time he hit me. I called my mom and told her what had happened. She laughed and hung up the phone. So I stayed. Things got worse, but I had nowhere else to go. Max started acting out and getting in trouble in school. Everything was spiraling out of control, and I couldn't figure out how to stop it. I tried going to a shelter, but Randy found me and promised he would change." She shrugged. "Why do we believe that crap?"

"We went back to him. Once home, he told me if I ever did that again, he would find me. He said he would take Max, and I would never see her again. Then one day, Randy came home and said he'd been fired from his job, and we would have to move in with his family. His father was an alcoholic. Even without that, there was something about the way he looked at Max and me whenever he was around. I told Randy no. It was the catalyst that sent him over the edge. I won't go into detail, but he nearly killed me and then turned on Max. He probably would have killed us both if the police hadn't arrived so quickly." April looked up and saw Jerry staring at her. "Why do I get the feeling that none of this is coming as a surprise?"

Tell the truth, McNeal. "The agency leaves nothing to chance. Fred had you vetted before he even considered putting Max on the payroll. When he found out I was moving in, he asked me if I wanted to hear the 911 call."

April's face paled. "You said yes?"

Jerry shook his head. "Not at first. But Fred kept

insisting."

"Why?"

"He wanted me to be sure."

Tears brimmed her eyes. "I don't understand. What gave Fred the right?"

Fred Jefferies was a high-ranking official in an agency so secretive, there weren't any acronyms in the title. Fred joked about having a computer chip implanted in his head that allowed him to accomplish anything at any given time. The man was so convincing that Jerry was sure the man could make anyone on the planet disappear with a simple phone call. Jerry kept his voice calm. "To be honest, it wasn't about giving me leverage. The man was simply doing his job."

April narrowed her eyes. "How is invading my privacy doing his job?"

"It wasn't about you or me. It was about protecting Max. Fred knew your backstory. He knew what you and Max have been through and isn't taking any chances."

"It wasn't his place to tell you about my past. That is part of us getting to know each other."

"You're not seeing the big picture, April. Fred needed me to hear that tape because he needed me to hear what kind of monster your ex-husband is."

April blinked her confusion.

Jerry leveled a look at her. "Randy is out of prison."

"I know." Her voice trembled when she spoke. "He doesn't know where we are."

"And the agency plans to keep it that way. Fred has a man on him – all Randy has to do is screw up once, and he's back in prison. But on the outside chance he ever shows up at this door, Fred wanted to make sure I had the knowledge needed and enough hate for the man to do what needs to be done."

"What happens if you aren't here? My luck, he'll show up when you're out on assignment." The anger was gone, and April's voice now held a tinge of fear.

Gunter appeared at Jerry's side and growled a low growl.

Jerry leaned back in his chair. "Remember what happened the last time you were in trouble?"

April frowned as if searching her mind. Slowly, her lips curved upwards. "When the dog tried to attack me and Max…Gunter appeared out of nowhere and saved us."

Jerry nodded. "You are one lucky lady, April Buchanan. You are not only in with an agency that considers you part of the family, but you also have the spirit of a German shepherd who now considers you and your daughter one of his pack."

Houdini took that moment to stick his head through the back door.

Jerry nodded to the door. April's mood instantly transformed, her laughter filling the air as the pup pushed his way into the kitchen and jumped up, placing his paws on her lap.

Jerry chuckled. "My money's on the dogs."

Chapter Three

Jerry had just finished installing a new vent hood over the stove when his phone rang, displaying Fred's number. It had been weeks since he'd heard from the man. Jerry didn't know if it was because nothing abnormal was happening in the world or if his boss was just giving him time to settle into his new life. Since Jerry was enjoying the downtime, he hadn't felt the need to ask.

Gunter and Houdini were lying in the case opening, which separated the kitchen from the dining room, splitting the difference between Jerry and April. Both dogs looked up as April appeared in the doorway.

"Your phone's ringing," she said, stating the obvious.

Jerry glanced in her direction. "It's Fred."

April's smile faded, letting him know she was fully aware of the implications of the call. "Oh.

You're not going to answer it?"

Jerry sighed and looked at the phone. "I haven't decided."

"What happens if you don't?"

"He'll call back."

"So, you probably should go ahead and answer it."

"Probably." Jerry swiped to answer as April turned and returned to the dining room, where she'd been scraping wallpaper from the walls. "What's up, boss?"

"Just checking in to see how things are going."

Jerry hoped that was all this was, a simple check-in. "Better than I ever imagined."

"Good deal. The family's good?"

Family. It had a nice ring to it. "April and Max are doing great."

"And the dogs?"

"Gunter and Houdini are good."

"Any new developments?"

He's fishing. Jerry decided to call him on it. "What kind of new developments would that be?"

"I have no idea. I haven't heard from you in a couple of weeks. I thought maybe I would see how things were going. Is that a crime?"

"No. It's just not in your nature to beat around the bush."

"You want me to be more direct? Fine. When are you going to seal the deal and make your family official? You should marry the woman and adopt the kid."

Jerry laughed. "I think I liked it better when you were beating around the bush."

"So, no wedding plans?"

Jerry lowered his voice. "Not at the moment."

"Meaning there could be?"

"Meaning April and I are adults. We will figure this out and do things in our own time. But you didn't call to harp on me for living in sin. So what gives?"

"No, the harping on your personal life was just a bonus. I don't need you at the moment, but we have a situation brewing that could turn into something I will need you to look into. I wanted to give you a heads-up in case you need time to tie up any loose ends."

"I appreciate that. How long are we talking?"

"We have someone in the House of Representatives who is on the fast track for running for the Oval Office. Said party had some issues this past weekend while on vacation."

"What kind of issues?"

"That is still to be determined. Either someone is trying to set the person up for a fall, they are on the verge of a nervous breakdown, or maybe they had a visit from one of your friends."

Jerry chuckled. "So you're assuming all spirits are my friends?"

"Since you're my Lead Paranormal Investigator, yes."

Fred had a point: the government was paying him a hefty sum to do the job. "Where was the vacation?"

"Deadwood, South Dakota."

Jerry instantly thought of his friend Jonesy with whom he'd served in the Marines. Last he'd spoken with the guy, he was heading to Deadwood to spend some time. A pang of guilt flared, as it had been a while since he'd checked in to see how Jonesy was doing. It dawned on him he hadn't checked in with any of his friends since settling in Michigan. *Dang, McNeal, three months in, you're already acting like an old married dude.* Instantly, his thoughts went to April. Jerry smiled.

"You still there, McNeal?"

"I'm here. I have a friend in the area. I was just thinking going there would give me an excuse to check in on the man." *Liar. You were thinking of ...*

"Our person of interest is currently undergoing a series of medical tests. If everything checks out, then the next step is to send you. I don't have to tell you this will need to be kept under wraps. Something like this gets out, and it could be the end of this person's career."

That Fred hadn't already told him who the person was lent to the secrecy of the situation. "Understood."

"If this thing happens, do you want to fly or drive?" Fred asked.

Jerry laughed. "I thought you grounded me the last time I flew."

"I did. I was just checking to see if you remembered."

Jerry remembered, alright. He'd been traveling with Houdini and had nearly caused the plane to be redirected midflight. While Jerry knew he could request the Learjet to get him to his destination, he also knew it meant renting something to drive. His thoughts went to the souped-up jet-black Durango sitting out in the driveway. Bulletproof and carrying a hidden arsenal that could start or stop a small war, the SUV was loaded with enough bells and whistles to make him feel like James Bond while driving it. Okay, so it didn't float on water or produce oil slicks when being chased, nor could it talk to him, but that was Hollywood. This was real life, and the thought of driving a rental when he had the coolest ride he could dream of didn't make sense. Jerry looked at the shepherds, whose eyes were following his every move. "If I have to go, I'll drive."

"Okay, I'll be in touch one way or the other. Tell Max and April hello for me."

"Will do." Jerry watched as the screen lit up, showing Fred had ended the call. He stood, and both dogs scrambled to their feet. Jerry laughed an easy laugh. "Easy, boys. No one's going anywhere just yet."

***

Jerry spent the better part of the morning trying to decide how to approach April about the changes he thought to make to the house. While he'd been eager to show her the proposal, his chat with Granny had put a damper on his enthusiasm. Instead of sharing his drawings with her, he'd joined her in the dining room to help her scrape wallpaper off the walls.

"A penny for your thoughts," April said, breaking the silence.

Jerry smiled. "Granny used to say that."

April matched his smile. "Good, I don't feel so bad."

Jerry frowned. "I'm not following you."

"It lets me know I'm not the only one that's had to pry your thoughts from you."

Okay, she wants to talk, we'll talk. "I'm wondering where you see this going."

"This?"

"Us."

"You're not happy here?" April's words came out barely above a whisper.

Jerry climbed down from the ladder he was on and turned to face her. "Okay, I guess that didn't come across how I meant it."

"I guess it didn't. So how did you mean it?"

"For one thing, I've never been happier. You,

Max, the dogs, all of us living together like a real family. The past few months have been everything I never knew I wanted."

"But?"

"No 'but.' I love you and want this to continue forever. I just want to make sure you feel the same way."

Her smile returned. "Of course I do."

"Good. So that leads me to my next question. Do you want to stay in this house or move somewhere else?"

April wiped the back of her hand across her face and looked about the room.

Jerry knew she was thinking of all the work they'd already done to the place. "Staying here is fine. You and Max are comfortable here and have a support network when I'm away."

"But."

He smiled. "Does there always have to be a but?"

"Not always, but in this case, there is."

"I guess there is. Come, let's take a break." He reached for her hand and smiled when she intertwined her fingers in his. Gunter and Houdini scrambled to their feet and followed them into the kitchen. Jerry pulled the pad of paper from the drawer and showed it to her.

"What's this?"

"A crude drawing of the current floorplan." He flipped the page to show her his vision. "We could expand the whole back of the house to give you that room you fell in love with in Virginia."

Her eyes grew wide. "The glassed breakfast room?"

Jerry nodded. "Yes, there is more than enough room in the yard. We might have to take down a tree or two, but we can do all of this and still leave plenty of room for the dogs. Houdini, at least; we don't have to worry about Gunter."

She turned the paper and pointed. "What's this room?"

"A utility room. We could move the washer and dryer to that room and have a folding table." He remembered Granny's warning. "Unless you want to use the room for something else."

April shook her head. "No, I would love to have a dedicated laundry room instead of the laundry closet. But what to do with the laundry closet? A linen closet maybe or a computer nook for Max." Something was off. Jerry could feel it. April was nodding and saying the right things, but the energy around her showed her to be fighting, letting him know she was holding something back.

"We can do anything you want with it or keep it just as it is. The bottom line is if you want to keep the house, we can do whatever you want to it."

Her lips trembled. "I'm not sure."

Jerry's heart sank. "Not sure. About us?"

April shook her head. "No, I love us. I'm not sure

about keeping the house."

Granny was right. He shouldn't have assumed. "You want to move?"

She nodded.

Jerry sighed. "April, I'm not that guy. You don't have to be afraid to talk to me. We are a team. Tell me what's on your mind."

She nodded once more and sighed as if grasping for the right word.

He placed his hand on hers. "It's okay. Just tell me."

"Okay. When Max and I first moved here, we had nowhere else to go. If it wasn't for Carrie, we probably would have ended up in another shelter. She made me a great deal on this place, and I will always be grateful to her for that. Then we got the reward money, and now Max is earning more money than we could ever hope to spend. Anyway, I talked to Carrie, and she said she wouldn't get mad if we didn't stay in this house."

Jerry felt there was more to it. "This is what you were afraid to tell me?"

"It's just that you've done so much to the house since you've been here." She pointed to the paper. "And now you took the time to show me how it can be even more wonderful."

"We have done a lot to this place. You and I both. Any update we made or will make in the future will help with the resale if you decide to sell it."

"I wasn't really thinking of selling it. I was thinking of renting it out. You know, an investment property."

Jerry smiled. "That works too. I don't think we should worry about the addition, though. It would not bring enough of a return on the investment."

She frowned. "I don't know. Maybe we should stay. I've always wanted a sunroom."

"Then we will make sure whatever house we choose has one. Have you given any thought to where you want to move to?"

"Yes, but that was before. Now I feel it should be our decision, not just mine."

"Where?"

She laughed. "About a mile up the road."

"You already know the house? Let's go take a look."

"It's not a house. It is property – it's only five acres, but it's surrounded by farmland and feels like a lot more."

"Does the owner want to sell it?"

"No."

Jerry chuckled. "That might be a problem."

"Not really, considering I'm the owner. Carrie and her husband offered it to me before Fred offered Max the job. Once I saw Max's income, I knew I didn't have to worry about money, so I bought it. I thought maybe we would build a house someday, and Carrie and I would be neighbors."

"So the property is close to them."

"Yes, it was a section that hadn't been cleared for farming. I'm pretty sure it was Carrie's idea. It was right after Randy got out of prison. I was freaking out, and Carrie tried to get me and Max to come stay with her. I told her Randy didn't know where we live and that she was overreacting. The next day, she started mentioning the property. I think she wanted us closer so she could keep an eye on us."

The thought of anyone hurting Max or April made his blood boil. As if picking up on Jerry's anger, Gunter yawned a squeaky yawn. Jerry mentally thanked the dog for reining him in and forced a smile. "I'm glad you had someone looking out for you."

April smiled and nodded her head. "Carrie's the best."

Jerry liked Carrie. They'd only spoken a handful of times, but he knew the woman had April's best interests at heart. "What's changed?"

"What do you mean?"

"You said you'd thought about building there. What's changed?"

"You."

"Is there a reason we can't build there now?"

Her eyes lit up, but she kept her voice in check. "No. I wasn't sure you would want to live that far out in the country or that close to my friend."

"I think it would be the perfect solution. I

wouldn't have to worry about you when I'm away. Plus, it would be safer for Houdini. He gets out of the fence here, he would be wandering around town. He gets out there, he will probably go visit Carrie."

"So you would be okay with building?"

"Will it make you happy?"

"Yes, and you can pick the design."

"No, if we are going to be a team, this has to be a team effort. We will each make a list of things we want. Then you can scour the internet and find some house plans that you like. We can go over them together and decide. Don't worry if the plan isn't exactly perfect. That is what architects are for."

Jerry nodded toward the back door where Houdini stood with his head sticking out. "In the meantime, we should put in a doggy door and teach that pup how to use it before the neighbor gets wise."

"It's a good thing Mrs. Gilbert has poor vision." April pointed to the notepad. "Do you think we will be able to find a floor plan with a sunroom?"

"I promised you a sunroom, you'll get a sunroom. You'll be drinking your coffee out there before the end of the year."

April sighed. "Good luck with that. I couldn't even find someone to do the stuff you've been doing."

"Leave it to me, sweetheart. I've wanted to give you your own sunroom since the day I saw your eyes twinkling as you looked around the room at the safe house in Virginia." It was the truth; he'd just been too scared to tell her at the time.

April looked him in the eye. "You know, if you and I are going to be a team, we probably need to work on our communication skills. I like this house and feel safe here, and the thought of building a new house and living next door to Carrie sounds amazing, but the truth is I would feel safe anywhere you are. So, if you would prefer to move somewhere else, even if it is just to get closer to the airport, I'm okay with that."

That she was willing to make the sacrifice warmed his heart. He'd given it a lot of thought over the last few months, and the thought of living in the sleepy Michigan town of Port Hope rather appealed to him. "No, I like knowing you are in a safe area when I'm called away. The truth of the matter is I feel at home here too. I don't like crowds – they cloud my intuition. I like having a place where the energy feels calm. I think Port Hope is a good fit for us."

April sighed a contented sigh. "Us. I like the sound of that."

"So do I. Have you given any thought to whether you want brick or siding? Either way, you'll have lots of color options."

"Do you want a say in the colors?"

Yes. Jerry shook his head. "Not unless you choose something so hideous, I find I can't hold my tongue."

"So, ixnay on the purple siding?"

He studied her for a moment to see if she was serious.

April snickered. "I had you going for a moment."

"I can deal with a lot, but we may have to have a discussion about that."

"How are you with yellow?"

He considered that a moment. "I could live with yellow." April rewarded him with a brilliant smile, and Jerry ran his hand over the back of his head. "Honey, you keep looking at me like that, and I'll agree to purple with yellow polka dots."

"What about when I look at you like this?" April narrowed her eyes and pursed her lips together.

"Anything! You can have anything you want." Jerry laughed.

"Max won't be home for hours." A pink tinge settled on her cheeks. Both dogs scrambled to their feet as April rose from the table and headed toward the front of the house.

Jerry trailed after her. Gunter sat as Houdini started to push past him. Jerry held out his hand and gave the command. "Wait! Take a cue from your pop and wait until we are at the top. You know you're not supposed to be on the stairs with anyone."

Houdini whined but made no move to follow. Jerry took the steps slowly so as not to further entice the pup. Jerry had nearly reached the top when April came out into the hall. She stopped, waiting for him at the top of the stairs with a look he couldn't read. He hesitated. "Is there a problem?"

She turned and palmed a hand toward the bedroom. "You tell me."

Jerry stepped around her and walked the short distance to the master bedroom, blinking his surprise to see both dogs lying on the bed staring at him. Neither had followed him up the stairs, meaning both dogs had used unearthly means to find their way into the room. He turned and saw April had followed him. Jerry shrugged. "I don't think they cover this in the training manual."

April giggled a nervous giggle. "How is this our life?"

Jerry pulled her into his arms. "Because we're the luckiest two people on the planet."

Chapter Four

Four years ago...

Juanita Stim stared up at the ceiling, trying to calm her nerves. Why on earth had she made the phone call? *Do you really think you're going to just pack everything up and move to a town where you have no lifeboat? Sure, the town is quaint and romantically historic, but you won't know a soul. What if you get sick? Who's going to take care of Davie?* Juanita took a breath and then let it out in long, jerky motions. *Easy, Nita, you're going to wake the baby.* She drew in another breath. This one came out in a steadier stream. *I'm not afraid of going someplace new. I've done it many times... when David was alive.* The thought did little to settle her nerves. *It will be fine. I'll make friends.* The thought evoked a giggle. She'd moved into the one-bedroom apartment a few weeks after her husband died and had since only ventured out to get groceries or to take the baby to his doctor visits. "Okay, so I like being alone."

The baby whimpered. Juanita rolled onto her side and patted his bottom to settle him. *Only I'm not alone anymore. I need this.* She looked at her son. *No,* we *need this.*

***

Rain beat against the windshield as the wipers struggled to keep up. *Turn around, Nita. It's a sign. The universe is trying to tell you something.* "Stop it!" Juanita checked the rear-seat camera, happy to see she hadn't woken Davie. *Okay, take a deep breath and tell the voices in your head to knock it off. It's okay to hear the voices when you're writing. It's not okay to argue with them. Arguing takes you out of the eccentric department and settles you straight into crazy.*

Juanita turned the radio on low to settle her nerves. Her writing voices preferred the quiet, and she didn't need their input when it came to her current situation. *Okay, let's focus on the house. What are your deal breakers? Cracks in the foundation. Yep, that's a definite no. Roof leaks, also a no.* Juanita smiled. *Okay, I'm glad it is raining. I will know straight away if the roof leaks. I see any sign of water damage, and I'm out of there. This is good. Okay, what else? Mold. Maybe that can be fixed. No, remember that book you read with the person who got sick? Oh, yeah. Okay, mold is a firm no. You see mold, you leave.* She sighed. *Stop that. You don't even know if there is mold. Okay, stick to the list. What else? Water.* She remembered the house she and David had lived in after they were first married and wrinkled her nose. *Okay, no rotten egg smell in the water.* An image of David wearing his Air Force uniform flitted into her mind. Juanita pushed it away. *Shake it off, Nita. No time for feeling sorry for yourself today.*

The rain eased as Juanita took Exit 30 and continued west on US 14A. The drive up to Deadwood, with the pine tree-lined rocky cliffs, sheer rock walls, and thick pine forests, was just as lovely as she remembered. So beautiful, she had to keep reminding herself to keep her eyes on the road and not scan the mountains for big horn sheep. She'd seen one during her last visit. Of course, she hadn't been driving at the time. It was a few months after they'd gotten stationed at Ellsworth Air Force Base. Eager to see all the area had to offer, she and David had taken the short one-hour drive to Deadwood. After spending the weekend walking the streets of the historic town, they'd quickly fallen in love with the place and had spent the whole drive home making plans to one day make Deadwood home. That promise was one of the reasons Juanita had spent the last year poring over every listing that came onto the market within short proximity to the city. Only she hadn't seen any that called to her –

until now. The house had not only called to her, it had invaded her every thought over the past few days until she had no choice but to make the call.

Juanita rounded a curve, and the steep mountainous rock gave way to a more open landscape. While there were trees, they were tall pines with bare trunks, allowing the onlooker to see further into the forest. On occasion, she saw a house settled amongst the trees and pictured herself living there. *No, that is not suitable for a woman living alone with an infant. Toddler, s*he corrected. After all, Davie had just reached his first birthday. As the terrain continued to open, the rain ceased. *That's promising.* She looked at the blue-black clouds that hovered overhead – okay, ominous was probably a better word, but at least it had stopped raining. She rounded another curve, and the mountains receded. To her right lay open land with far fewer trees. To the left, houses were sprinkled close to the road.

A large bird soared in the distance. Juanita leaned forward to get a better look. *A bald eagle.* Her breath caught in her throat. She and David had seen a bald eagle shortly after declaring that Deadwood would one day be their home and had taken it as a sign they'd made the right decision. Juanita bit at her bottom lip. *Is that you, David? Did you send me a sign?*

A few miles later, the trees started inching their way toward the road. She saw the reason for the change a moment later when she passed the sign letting her know she'd reached the Black Hills National Forest. Traffic was nearly nonexistent. Now that the rain had stopped, Juanita found herself giddy once more.

The rock wall returned to her right, the base of the mountain littered with the occasional boulder that had let go and tumbled to a stop before reaching the road. *Stay over there.*

Juanita felt her ears pop and worked her jaw to relieve the pressure as she continued her trek up the mountain. A short time later, the mountains receded once more. Juanita sighed her frustration. "Come on already."

Davie mirrored her readiness to be out of the car with his own frustrated whine.

Juanita looked into the baby cam. "Was that baby for 'are we there yet'? Don't worry, Boogaboo, I'm just as ready to be there as you are. It's not much longer, I promise." As she started down the incline, she switched the radio to toddler tunes and sang along as she drove. This seemed to appease Davie, who cooed his own babyish tune from the confines of his car seat.

Juanita saw the yellow-gold sign sporting the name Deadwood. The sign was right at home among the hills, with two pearl-handled pistols and a gunslinger. The tag line in the lower left corner read "Where Western Legends Were Born."

Juanita giggled and blew out an excited breath as she slowed to a stop at the traffic light at the turnoff to Spearfish. *Oh my gosh, I'm really doing this. Easy, Nita, you're doing nothing except looking.* She giggled once more. *Looking to buy my first home!*

The light turned green. Juanita continued straight into Deadwood, stealing glances at the hotels and casinos that backed to the rock-walled mountains on the right. Juanita saw the arched sign signaling the entrance to Historic Main Street, her giddiness intensifying as she made a right on Volin Street. She followed the narrow street up a short distance and veered left onto Williams Street. Juanita didn't need her navigator to show her the way or a house number to tell her she'd found the right house. She'd taken the trip via Google maps at least a dozen times since finding the listing on Zillow.

Juanita knew the road was narrow, knew the houses on the cliff overlooked Historic Main Street, and knew there to be a steep set of industrial stairs nearby that would allow her access to the old section of town without her ever having to get into her car. It might be a pain doing so with a stroller, but she'd figure that out – if she bought the house.

Juanita parallel-parked her Subaru in the space in front of the house and took in a deep breath to calm herself. She exited, stood just outside the car, and stared at the large two-story stone Victorian. Painted a pale mint green with a brown Shaker-style roof, the house looked inviting despite the dark clouds hovering over the town.

Juanita turned her back to the car and looked out over the town. Okay, so the view was slightly marred by the roof of the concrete parking garage, but if she moved around a bit, she could see a building here and there. *I bet the view is even better from the upstairs window.* She sighed a contented sigh and circled the car to collect Davie from the car seat.

"Come on, young man, let's go see a lady about a house. Oh, and remember, if you see something, say something. You and I are in this thing together." Juanita walked up the stairs to the property, thinking to keep walking until she'd fully circled the house. She'd just reached the front corner of the house when she heard her name. She turned to see a plump woman in a dark pantsuit heading toward her.

"Mrs. Stim?" the woman asked once more.

Juanita smiled. "Yes. I thought I'd have a look around the outside before it starts raining again." Juanita left off telling her that if she found anything on the outside, she wouldn't even bother going inside.

The woman extended her hand. "I'm Nancy Wilde. It's a pleasure to finally meet you. And this must be David."

"Davie," Juanita corrected.

Nancy scribbled in the folder she was holding.

"Davie. Got it. How was the drive?"

It felt like it took forever. Juanita smiled. "Not bad. It only took an hour. I want to look at the foundation before I go inside."

Nancy took the lead, talking and pointing as she went. "I've walked around it myself multiple times. As I told you in my e-mail, the house is structurally sound. Looks like it's been freshly painted within the last year, and the roof is only three years old."

Juanita continued inspecting the house, her gaze searching each brick of the foundation and then traveling upwards to the roof. While admittedly she hadn't a clue what she was looking at, nothing jumped out, to warn her against further inspection. She turned toward Nancy and clutched Davie a little closer. "We would like to see inside the house now, if you don't mind."

Nancy smiled a triumphant smile and led the way up the steps to the front porch. She opened the oversized wooden door and stepped aside to allow Juanita to enter.

The second she stepped inside the house, Juanita knew she would not be leaving without making an offer. She did her best to keep her face neutral as she took in the unpainted woodwork and beveled glass transoms that sat above the doorways to each room. "It's nice to see they left the original woodwork."

"You'll see some of the original furniture as we walk through," Nancy replied. "One of the bedrooms even has the original bedroom suite."

Juanita scanned the doors that led off the living room. "Really? Which one?"

"We will save the bedrooms for last. Let's check out the rest of the house first," Nancy said, heading to the back of the house.

"Okay." Juanita wondered at the woman's abrupt departure but decided maybe she was keeping the best for last. The kitchen was spacious for a house of its age, with tall ceilings and plenty of cabinets that looked original to the house and in excellent condition. The stove, along with the rest of the appliances, was newer stainless steel. Juanita peeked inside the fridge. "I guess it doesn't hurt to have some modern touches."

"Trust me. You'll be happy with the utility bills with energy-efficient appliances. Want to see the upstairs?"

Juanita nodded and clutched Davie tight as she followed Nancy up a steep set of stairs. "They are steeper than I thought."

"Don't get discouraged. I have a plan," Nancy said over her shoulder. She turned to Juanita once they'd reached the top. "You said in one of your early e-mails that you were interested in someplace with a rental opportunity."

Juanita looked at Davie and frowned. "I was, but I was hoping to find a place with a room over a garage or something."

"Not likely. Not if you want something this close to town. Most of the houses on this street don't have driveways, much less garages. The ones that do are mostly just a structure carved out of the hillside. It's just you and the little one, yes?"

Juanita nodded.

"There are four bedrooms on the main floor. You won't even need the two up here. Hire yourself a contractor and open up the space. You do that, and it will be a huge studio. The house is well below your budget, so there will be room for renovations. They can add a bathroom and an outside entrance. You can close off the stairs completely if you want, or, lock them from the other side and only use them when you need to come up and clean."

Juanita surveyed the space. "I don't know."

"What is your hesitation?"

"Noise mainly. I don't want to rent to someone who will wake the baby. And I'm hoping to finish my book, so I need it to be quiet when I'm writing."

"Then only rent the room in the summertime. You'll be able to charge more as a vacation rental than if you are looking to find a year-round tenant. Most people who come to town on vacation don't come here to sit in their rooms. Write when they are away, or only rent it to singles, and list the rules of what you will and will not tolerate."

"Dang, you're good. You have an answer for everything."

Nancy winked. "It's my job. Think about it, and we'll check out the bedrooms." Nancy walked to the front window and motioned for Juanita to follow. "Just make sure you mention this amazing view in your write-up."

Nancy was right. The view was even better from this vantage point, as she was able to see the upper floors and rooftops of some of the older buildings. "Maybe we should take the top floor instead."

"I thought you didn't like the stairs."

"I don't, and I doubt I would want to deal with outside stairs in the wintertime." Juanita sighed and followed Nancy out of the room and to the steep stairway. She gripped the handrail and chose each step carefully. Davie must have picked up on her discomfort as he clung to her shirt, silently looking over her shoulder as they descended the stairs.

"At least they have a handrail," Nancy said, leading the way.

"If they didn't, I wouldn't be on them. I'm definitely up for closing that stairway," Juanita said once they'd reached the bottom of the stairs. So far, the steep stairway was the only thing she didn't like about the house.

"The bedrooms are set up a bit differently for a house such as this. We have two bedrooms off each side of the main living room. The one near the master could have been a sitting room, as split bedrooms weren't common when the house was built."

"The listing said the house is over a hundred years old."

"Yes. Is that problem?"

"No, I was just curious."

Nancy smiled. "Good. I thought you were going to ask if the house is haunted."

Juanita laughed. "I don't believe in ghosts."

Nancy mumbled something under her breath.

"I'm sorry, I didn't hear that."

"I said, let's have a look at the bedrooms."

Juanita wasn't sure what the woman had said, but it wasn't that. "Which one is the master?"

Nancy led her to the first two bedrooms. "All the bedrooms are about the same size, fourteen by fourteen, which, if you think of it, is rather large for a home of this age. The other two are over there."

"Are we not going to look at them?" Juanita asked when Nancy remained in place.

"They are mirror images of each other." Nancy made no indication of showing her.

Juanita shifted Davie to the other hip as she walked across the living room. She peeked in the first room, saw it was, in fact, a mirror of the rooms on the other side, then walked across the hall to the other room.

"Want me to hold the baby while you look?"

Juanita eyed Nancy. It was the first time she'd asked to hold Davie. "No, I'm good." She opened the door, noting the chill, then forgot about the temperature as she walked into the room, feeling like she'd stepped back in time. Juanita twirled, her eyes taking in every single detail. Dark wallpaper with bold-colored flowers floating within the print lined all four walls. An antique bedroom suite so well-preserved it looked as it if had just come off the showroom floor filled the space. She was drawn to the bed, whose headboard rose high against the far wall, and ran a hand along the wood, admiring the flowers carved within the wood. Davie reached out to touch the headboard as she bent to get a closer look. *Lilies.*

Juanita sucked in a breath. The first flowers David ever bought her were lilies. "It's a sign."

"What?" Nancy called from the hallway.

"The carvings in the headboard are lilies!" *Then again, you'd know that if you were to come into the room.* Juanita walked to the high dresser and armoire, once again running her hand along the carvings, then walked across the room to check out a smaller chest-style dresser. While the dresser itself was small, the mirror attached to it was rather elaborate – high and encased in a wooden frame that matched the wooden chest it was attached to. Juanita pulled out the under chair and sat looking in the mirror, which appeared slightly distorted compared to its modern counterparts. Still, it matched the bedroom suite, and it would be a shame to separate it from the group. "Do you think the owner wants to sell the bedroom suite?"

"It and the birdcage stay with the house!"

Juanita jumped as Davie twisted in her arms, trying to see over her shoulder. She looked in the mirror, expecting to see Nancy standing directly behind her. She wasn't there. *Wow, the house has some excellent acoustics.* "That's a good thing. It means I can put you in the bedroom across the way and will still be able to hear you." A smile touched her lips at the thought of them both getting a bit of privacy. She stood and adjusted Davie to a better position. "Come on, Boogaboo, let's go buy ourselves a house."

Nancy looked past her as she exited the room. "You should probably close that door."

"Yes, it is a bit cooler in that room than the rest of the house." Juanita reached around and pulled the door shut. "The owners have been here less than two years, and before that, it sold four times in eight years."

Nancy lifted an eyebrow. "You've done your homework."

What Juanita really wanted to ask was why they were selling it so cheap. She'd been watching the market for over a year, and never had a house been listed this far under market value. "What's wrong with the house?"

"The house is physically sound."

What kind of non-answer is that? "That's not what I asked."

Nancy looked at Davie and blew out a sigh. "Honestly, they think the house is haunted. I tried to tell them they probably won't find a house in Deadwood without some kind of history, but they wouldn't listen."

Juanita laughed. "You're telling me because the owners are afraid of ghosts, I get an incredible deal?"

Nancy's eyes grew wide. "You mean you're still interested?"

"I'm ready to make a full-price offer." Juanita looked at Davie and smiled. "You know my budget. I will go double that amount if we get into a bidding war."

Nancy blinked her surprise. "You're saying the temperature in the bedroom didn't bother you?"

Juanita raised an eyebrow. "If I didn't know better, I would say you are trying to talk me out of buying this house. Why did you even set up an appointment?"

Nancy shook her head. "It's not that I don't want to sell you the house. I just want you to be sure this is the right house for you and your son."

Juanita firmed her chin. "I like to think I'm a fair judge of what is best for us."

"Great. I'll draw up the offer."

Juanita smiled. "I'd like to take you up on the

offer to hold Davie for a moment. I want to make some notes while they are fresh in my mind." She handed Nancy the baby and jotted some notes. *Wide open spaces. The yard is small, but we are within walking distance to town. Large front porch.* She placed a heart beside that entry. *Updated laundry and bathroom* – another heart. Except for the one bedroom, most of the downstairs renovations were already done. That meant she could direct most of the money to renovations on the upstairs apartment. She peered at the huge wheeled antique birdcage as she shoved her paper into her purse. *Maybe I'll get a bird.* The thought struck her as odd. She'd never been a bird person. She reached for Davie, pulled him to her chest and smiled. *Today is a day of firsts.*

Chapter Five

As Juanita opened the door to her apartment, she was struck by the fact that the attic in the Deadwood house was larger than the small one-bedroom unit she shared with her son. She changed Davie, then sat him on his playmat and handed him several toys. Juanita sat near him at the kitchen table, which also served as a makeshift office. As she watched Davie play, her thoughts drifted to the house in Deadwood. In addition to the living area, kitchen, utility room, and bathroom, they would have four bedrooms – how incredible it would be to have that much space! She planned on claiming the one with the lilies as her own – after removing the hideous wallpaper. While she liked flowers, the dark wallpaper was slightly over the top. If she took that bedroom and used the one next to it as her office, it would be as if she and Davie had their own wings of the house. She would decorate one of the two remaining bedrooms for Davie and use the other as his playroom. She'd thought about putting a bed in her office in case she ever got a guest, but decided against it as the thought of having a dedicated office all to herself made her smile.

"A dedicated office." She looked over at Davie. "Do you hear that, Boogaboo? Mama is moving up in the world. I wouldn't need much. Heck, I could probably get by with a desk and chair in the beginning and then add some bookshelves later after I find out how much the renovations are going to cost. Most of the downstairs renovations are complete, so I can concentrate on converting the attic to a large studio apartment." Davie seemed content to hear her voice, so she continued. "The attic is wide open. Maybe I'll keep it like that and rent it as a studio. That way, it will be less appealing to anyone with children. Not that I have anything against children, mind you. I just don't want them running overhead. That wouldn't be good if you are trying to sleep or when I'm working. Perhaps I could do one of those Murphy wall beds. No, the room is too big. As soon as the bed goes into the wall, the space would feel like a barn. A king bed would fit nicely and still allow plenty of room for a living and eating area. I wonder if I should move the antique bedroom suite upstairs? It's not a king bed, but there is enough furniture to fill the room."

Davie puckered his bottom lip.

Juanita laughed at the coincidental reaction. She rooted around the table, found her notebook, and drew a rough outline of the attic. "Yeah, you're probably right. Not everyone appreciates antiques. Okay, so we go with something simple. Maybe one of those platform beds where you don't need a box spring. Yep, that would work. We need nightstands, so let me draw one of those on each side. Yes, that works. Keep it sleek. Same with the furniture – we will use leather. That way, it's easy to wipe clean after each stay. We'll stay to the same minimalist design in the kitchen area. Simple, sleek cabinets – color to be decided later, smudge-free stainless appliances, and I'll spring for matching granite countertops and tile in both the kitchen area and bath to class the place up so I can justify charging a bit more. Between the modern interior, the cool view of the historic downtown area, and quick access to restaurants and casinos, it will be one of the most sought-after vacation rentals in town. At least during the summer months. Isn't that right, Davie?"

Davie cooed at the sound of his name.

Juanita winked at him. "That's what I like about you, son. You agree with everything I say. What do you think about all that talk about ghosts? Does that worry you at all?"

Davie looked at her expectantly. "Dada."

Juanita wasn't surprised he'd said the word – it had been the first word he'd fully articulated – a simple word that had reduced her to tears at the time. Since that day, she'd come to terms with the fact that all babies learned to say it at some point in their life, whether they had a face to put with it or not. "No, Boogaboo, Dada isn't a ghost." *Not that I would mind if he were.*

Davie smiled and reached his arms to her. "Da da da da."

Juanita pushed from her chair and scooped him off the floor. Holding her son in the air with outstretched arms, she sang a different tune. "Momma, momma, momma."

Davie giggled his delight as she pulled him close and kissed his cheeks. She sank to the play mat and placed him on his back as she continued talking to him. "We aren't scared of no ghosts, are we, Boogaboo? That's right. We know the difference between real life and fiction. The only ghosts are the ones people make up to scare us. Well, they can try all they want. Daddy might not be here, but he made sure we have enough money to take care of us – at least until Mommy finishes her book. And it's not a scary book at all. Nope, it's a happy book where the lady finds the love of her life and lives happily ever after. I guess that makes it a fairy tale." Juanita sighed. "Oh, well, whether it's true or not, people seem to like that kind of thing. And it's going to be good. Good enough to get me a six-figure offer from one of the big publishing houses."

Davie answered by blowing spit bubbles.

Juanita dipped her head and brushed his face with her auburn hair. "Oh, ye of little faith. Momma is going to sell her book, just you wait and see! Ow! Let go of Momma's hair."

Davie pulled harder as his giggles filled the air.

Her cell phone rang. Juanita reached into her pocket and pulled out her phone as she worked to free her hair from Davie's fists. "Hello?!"

"Juanita, it's Nancy. Are you okay? You sound like you're in pain."

Nancy! Juanita's heart sank. It was too early for a call – the sellers must have taken another offer. "No, I'm fine. Hang on a minute. The baby has hold of my hair." While it was true, it would also give her time to compose herself so she didn't sound like a total wreck when Nancy gave her the news. She worked her hair free and handed Davie a set of toy keys to play with. "I'm here. I didn't expect your call so soon. I guess that means they've accepted another offer?"

"No, I'm calling to let you know they've agreed to take yours."

Juanita blew out a long breath. "Okay, how much is it going to cost me?"

"Asking price."

"Are you serious?" The words came out on a giggle. "What about the other offers?"

"There weren't any."

"Are you serious? Crap, I just asked that. My editor would red line that repeated line." *Well, they would if I actually had an editor*. She kept that last bit to herself.

"I had two showings after you. Both claimed they felt something in the house and begged off after I told them that the house is said to be haunted."

Juanita laughed. "Do you really believe in that stuff?"

"I've seen my share of weird happenings," Nancy assured her.

"Which can all be explained by non-otherworldly means," Juanita replied.

"Yeah, you remember that when you think about calling me at three a.m. to tell me you've been visited by a ghost and want to sell the house."

"The house is big enough for the two of us and a few ghosts." Juanita looked at Davie and winked. "So, when can we do this thing?"

"We should be able to get everything done and get you the keys within thirty days."

"I don't suppose they will let me have the keys early?" Juanita doubted the homeowners would go for it, but it was worth a chance.

"No way."

"I'm good for the money. I can have a cashier's check drawn up at the bank tomorrow."

"Sorry, sweety, no can do. It's not about the money or the paperwork. The homeowners are afraid you'll be scared out of the deal before it goes through."

"Scared out of the deal? Oh, you mean by the ghost that doesn't exist." Juanita pointed a finger at her head and swirled it around. *Crazy.* She smiled when Davie lifted his finger and tried to imitate her action. "Okay, fine, I will take possession of the house in thirty days."

"I see what you did there. And it's not funny. I've seen the movie *Poltergeist*."

"Exactly, it was a movie – you know, something writers write," Juanita said with a giggle. "Listen, I think we're going to have to agree to disagree on this."

"For now."

Davie pulled to his feet and attempted to stuff the toy keys into Juanita's mouth. "Deal. And don't let them take the bedroom suite."

"How'd you know it stays?"

Juanita frowned at the phone. "Um, you told me."

"No, I didn't."

"Yes, today. I asked if I could buy it. You said it and the birdcage stays with the house."

"I never said that."

Juanita nodded her head and made the crazy sign again. "Okay, I believe we've found another thing to disagree on. But the bedroom suite stays, right?"

"The homeowners said you can have all of the

furniture left in the house."

"Let me guess. They think the furniture is haunted too."

"Most likely. Do you want the stuff, or do you want me to call the thrift store to pick some of it up?"

"I'll take it all. I have some stuff in storage, but not enough to fill a whole house. That way, I can use my money for Davie's room and the renovations to the attic. Speaking of which, do you know any good contractors?"

"I'll give you a list, but be prepared to look outside of Deadwood."

"Let me guess, the contractors are afraid of ghosts."

Nancy's laugh floated through the phone. "No, it's a small town. The ones to be had probably already have work. I assume you will want the renovations done sooner rather than later."

"I do. I won't kid myself into thinking I will get any income this year, but that's okay. We'll manage as long as I can start bringing in some money next year. Maybe a little longer, depending on how much the renovations eat into my budget."

"I admire your courage," Nancy said softly. "I know this can't be easy on you."

"David and I pretty much had things planned before he got sick. I'm just following the course of what he and I already discussed."

"I understand that. But I think most women in

your place would have returned to their comfort zone. For me, that would have meant moving back in with my parents."

Juanita felt a chill race the length of her arms. "My parents are not my comfort zone. They made it their mission to tell me how I should live my life. They weren't happy when I married David. If I were to go back home, it would be a constant barrage of 'I told you so.' Davie and I have gotten along just fine thus far. I intend to see that continues. He will have a yard to play in and a room to call his own."

"I really hope it works out for you both, Juanita."

"Things are already looking up. I'm buying a house. I'M BUYING A HOUSE!" Juanita squealed.

Nancy laughed. "You sure are. I'll get the paperwork started and be in touch when it's time to sign everything. Talk to you soon."

Juanita sat there for several moments, revisiting the call. Finally, she looked to the ceiling as her eyes brimmed with tears. "Thank you."

***

Juanita stood in the doorway, watching as Gary from the moving company wheeled the last of the boxes up the stone steps. She moved aside to allow the man access, her eyes tracing the room full of boxes.

Gary eased the stack beside the pile of boxes already in place. "That's the last of them. Are you sure you don't want some help moving them into the rooms?"

Juanita shook her head. "No, I've done enough military moves that I have a system." What she didn't tell him was some of the items would be going right back out. She hadn't been in any frame of mind to go through her husband's belongings when he died. She'd just had the movers pack everything up and had it placed directly into storage when the military moved her out of Air Force housing.

Gary gathered his clipboard from the top box and flipped through the stack of papers. He handed her an ink pen. "Okay, I need your initials here, here, and here, and a full signature here."

She signed where he'd told her and handed him back the pen.

Gary slid the pen behind his ear and looked up when Davie's giggles rang out from his playroom. "That's one happy little man. Most kids would be screaming for their mother and not content to play on their own."

"He just started walking a couple of weeks ago. The apartment we lived in was quite small. I think he's happy to have enough room to toddle around in."

Gary surveyed the room. "Do you want me to set up the crib? I don't mind."

Juanita started to say no. It was one of the few things she and her husband had purchased for the baby the day they'd found out she was pregnant. Her husband had put it together that very night. After he died, she was no longer eligible to live in base housing and had moved into the first apartment she'd found. At the time, she'd been so distraught, she hadn't taken into consideration how much space a baby would need. There'd been no room for the crib, so she stored it with everything else. Davie slept in an oversized drawer for the first few months. When he outgrew that, he slept in a Pack 'n Play, folding it out of the way when not in use. The thought of putting the crib together by herself made her heart ache, but it had to be done, as they would be spending their first night in the house tonight.

"I don't mind," Gary said, pulling her out of her musings. He winked. "My wife is pregnant, and I could use the practice."

"Congratulations. Is this your first?"

"The first of many, hopefully. That's why I need the practice."

"What about your partner?" she asked, speaking of Juan, the man who'd helped him unload the truck.

Gary smiled. "He walked downtown to have a quick look around. I'm going to meet him for a beer after I'm done. I'll call and tell him to take his time. He won't mind."

Juanita smiled her gratitude and pointed to the bedroom next to the playroom. "If you're sure you don't mind. It will be one less thing I have to do before Davie goes to bed."

Gary pulled the crib from behind the boxes and carried it into Davie's room.

Juanita paused at the playroom door and stared over the gate. She'd been working on both his bedroom and this playroom for the past week, keeping Davie in the main living area in a playpen in front of the television as she painted both rooms yellow. She'd then added colorful hot-air balloon appliques to the playroom walls and added an oversized rug that was pricey but much too cute to pass up, as it, too, had hot-air balloons. She tried to tell herself her son wouldn't be any the wiser if she had gone with a less expensive option, but in the end, cute and matchy won out. Her gaze trailed to Davie sitting on the rug in the middle of the floor with his back to her, babbling and playing with his toys. She smiled. The rug wasn't so expensive that they would miss a meal, and he looked so cute sitting there amongst the hot-air balloons.

She sighed her contentment as she walked through the sea of boxes looking for the one marked "linens," intending to place sheets on the bed in the lily room. She opened the door and was immediately hit with a blast of ice-cold air. "What's with this room? It's freezing."

Juanita pulled the boxcutter from her back pocket, slid it through the tape, and pulled out the bag with the sheets. She opened the bag, which began expanding before her eyes. *At least I had the presence of mind back then to vacuum seal them to help keep them clean.* Her teeth chattered as she walked around the bed, wrapping the mattress with the fitted sheet. Then she shook the flat sheet, placing it on top and tucking it in. *They didn't sell the house because of ghosts. They sold it so they wouldn't freeze to death.*

"All done. Sorry, ma'am, I didn't mean to scare you. I just wanted to let you know I am done," Gary said when Juanita jumped. He frowned. "Why is it so cold in here?"

"I haven't the slightest clue. The room was cold the day I toured the house, but nothing like this."

"Have you checked to make sure the vents are open?"

Juanita shook her head. "No. I never even thought of it."

"Mind if I check?"

Juanita casually reached to her back pocket to ensure the cutter blade was where she had left it. It wasn't that she didn't trust the man, but she'd read enough books to know people weren't always as they appeared. She waved him into the room. "Be my guest."

Gary walked around the room looking for the air vents. Finding one, he sank to his knees to check the vent. "This one is open." He stood and continued walking the perimeter, stepping around the furniture. Not finding a second vent, he went to the dresser, lifted the end, and pulled it away from the wall. "There it is."

"Is it open?"

"Can't tell from this angle. I'll have to pull it out a bit more. Want to grab the other end so I don't scratch the floor?" Juanita took hold of the other end, and they eased it away from the wall. She watched as Gary bent and fiddled with the floor register. He stood and grabbed the end of the dresser. She helped him slide it back into place. He shook his head. "They're both open. I think you're going to have to call a professional."

Juanita sighed. "I'll add it to the list."

Gary wrinkled his brow. "Anything I can help with?"

Juanita smiled and shook her head, following him from the room. "No, thank you. You've done more than enough. I appreciate you putting the crib together for me. At least the baby's room is warm and mostly put together."

Davie's babble sang out from the playroom. Gary walked across the hall and stopped at the gate. "I could stand here and listen to him all day."

Juanita stepped up beside Gary. Davie sat in the middle of the room, facing the opposite direction and carrying on a conversation with himself. The baby leaned forward, reached for the plastic keys, and held them up as she'd seen him do so many times before when he was trying to place them in her mouth. He giggled, dropped the toy to the floor, and stretched his hands up as if he expected to be lifted into the air.

Gary laughed a nervous laugh. "Almost sounds as if he's talking to someone."

Juanita swallowed. And for the first time since making an offer, questioned her decision to buy the house.

Chapter Six

Juanita paced the living room with her phone plastered to her ear as she waited for her call to be transferred to the manager.

"This is Bob Rawls."

"Mr. Rawls, my name is Juanita Stim. Are you the manager?"

"I am. How can I help you?"

"I've been transferred three times and been on hold for twenty-two minutes waiting for someone to agree to come look at my furnace. Let me be clear. It's not like anyone is saying you have a waitlist. They are refusing to come."

"That's the house on Williams Street in Deadwood, correct?"

"It is," Juanita said and gave the full address.

"Mrs. Stim. It's not that we don't want your business."

"Then why won't you agree to come?"

"Because we've already been there."

"No, you haven't. This is the first time I've called. I just moved in a week ago."

"You're right. We haven't been there in the last week. However, we've sent a crew to that address twenty-three times in the last five years and never found an issue with the original furnace, which was replaced two years ago against our recommendation."

Juanita blew out a sigh. "Maybe the issue is with the ductwork."

"We've used cameras. All the ductwork is in proper working order."

Juanita continued to pace the room. "What am I supposed to do? I can't sleep in my bedroom." It was true. She'd remained in bed for two hours the first night in the house before finally giving up and taking her comforter to the couch. Since then, she'd done multiple experiments, including leaving the bedroom door open to see if doing so affected the temperature in the rest of the house. It did not. It was like there was some invisible barrier at the entrance to the bedroom, keeping the cold air inside. "If your company won't help me, I'll have no choice but to call someone else."

"You're welcome to get another opinion. You might even find a company that would be happy to replace the furnace or ductwork, but I'll stake my reputation that neither of those options will fix the issue."

"So, you're saying I just have to deal with it? I'm having some renovations done to the attic and will need an independent unit installed upstairs. Does that mean your company will refuse to help with that as well?"

"Of course not. We would be happy to get your business."

"Just not with the bedroom."

"Mrs. Stim, are you aware of the history of your house?"

"You're asking if I know the house is supposed to be haunted?"

"Yes, ma'am."

"I've heard." She'd wanted to tell him she didn't believe him, but the truth of the matter was, in addition to a bedroom that felt like a morgue, Davie seemed to be conversing with someone who wasn't there. She'd been trying to convince herself that he was just opening up now that he had a colorful room to develop his imagination further. "I'm a writer. I specialize in the make-believe."

"Have you written anything I might have read?"

"I'm still working on it. But I know the lengths a writer will go to tell a good story. Every story begins in someone's imagination. I don't believe in ghosts, Mr. Rawls."

"Give it time."

"What's that supposed to mean?"

"My sister and her fiancé used to own the house a few years back. If you think it's cold now, wait until you start doing the renovations."

"Are you saying the room gets worse with renovations?"

"Not the room, Mrs. Stim. The whole house. I think each family that has lived there has done a few updates, but so far, no one has been able to tackle the bedroom with the wallpaper. Whoever or whatever is causing the chill ramps it into deep freeze whenever anyone tries."

"That sounds like a bunch of hogwash."

Rawls laughed. "Then it shouldn't bother you to learn that your neighbors have a poll on how long you will remain in the house."

"And just how would you know that?"

"Did I fail to mention that I'm one of your neighbors?"

"Let me guess, you created the poll."

"No. I just placed a bet. Come to think of it, I may need to stop by and have a look."

"You said there's nothing to fix."

"There isn't. I just need you to hang around for a few more months so I have a better chance at winning. Listen, all kidding aside, my sister said the main issue seemed to concentrate around that bedroom. If it were my house, I would close off the bedroom and use another."

"If it were that easy, why did your sister sell the

house?"

Rawls's voice grew serious. "I could lie and tell you she bought it with the intention of living in it long enough to flip it, but I'd be lying. The truth of the matter is, unlike you, my sister does believe in ghosts. The happenings in the house freaked her out, and she sold it."

"What kind of happenings?"

"She saw things and heard things. I believe the final straw was when her daughter started playing with an imaginary friend."

Juanita hurried to the playroom to check on Davie. She'd removed the gate, only keeping it in place when she needed to do something that would prevent her from fully watching him. Thus far, Davie seemed content to play in the room even when she wasn't in there with him. Juanita relaxed at seeing him sitting on the rug playing with toys without jabbering at someone she couldn't see. "This imaginary friend, did it try to hurt the child?"

"No, not that I'm aware of."

"That's good."

"Not that you believe." There was humor in his words.

"Of course not. Hey, what's the longest bet on the poll?"

"Three years."

"How much to play?"

"Twenty."

"And the winner gets the pot?"

"Yep."

"Okay, put me down for twenty dollars on my staying fifty years."

Rawls chuckled into the phone. "You sure?"

"I am."

"Okay, it's your money."

"Yes, and I intend to keep it. Goodbye, Mr. Rawls."

"Have an uneventful day, Mrs. Stim."

The screen lit up, showing the call had ended. Juanita pocketed the phone and joined Davie on the rug. "Hey, little man. You don't have any ghosts hanging out in here with you, do you?"

Davie looked past her and smiled.

***

Six months later…

As the season warmed and construction to remodel the attic began, the front porch of the house quickly became Juanita's favorite place to spend the day. Mainly because Rawls's predictions proved to be true.

Each day, the moment the contractors showed up, the temperatures inside the house plummeted. Thankfully, the temperature would rise again once the workers left for the day. While she'd initially thought the porch a nice thing to have, it had become the house's saving grace over the last few months. She'd asked the contractor for a gate to block off the steps so that Davie could move about within the railing without worry, which left her free to get a few words written during the day. Few, because it was somewhat challenging to write with all the distractions.

She could handle the construction noise. Hearing the power saws and air compressors let her know things were getting done. What she found most distracting was that a few of the men within the crew were practically drool-worthy. Not good when she wasn't mentally prepared for a relationship. Still, having the men near did help with writing pivotal scenes during her own personal dry spell.

A worker came up the walk carrying a stack of 2x4s over his shoulder.

"Hello, handsome. Here for a good time?"

Juanita looked toward the birdcage, which now housed a large talking parrot named Charlie, and sighed.

The guy – a man named Dewey – veered off the path and walked to the porch. He lowered the boards he was carrying and whistled.

Davie hurried to her side and crawled into her lap, giggling as Charlie returned the tune.

Juanita laughed. "I'll sell him to you for a dollar."

Dewey shook his head. "No can do." He waved at Davie, who buried his head between his mother's breasts.

"Why not? He seems to like you well enough." The truth of the matter was the bird seemed to like all men. Then again, he could like women too, but she'd yet to have any women visitors since moving into the home.

"Because I rent out rooms to dudes who come to town for work during the summer months. The last thing I need is for one of them to get the wrong impression."

As if on cue, Charlie repeated his favorite greeting. "Hello, handsome. Here for a good time?"

Juanita nodded her understanding. "I can see where that might cause some conflict. So, how are things coming along?"

"We're right on schedule. The air ducts are in place. Rawls and his team will be here any minute to do their thing, and the kitchen cabinets will be delivered by the end of the week. I expect everything to be finished by the end of the month."

"As long as everything's completed before it gets too cold out, I'll be happy. Then again, it will probably still be warmer out here than in the house. How is the temperature upstairs?"

"Not bad, for the middle of April."

That was the problem. It wasn't April, it was late July, yet no matter what she tried, when the workers were on site, she couldn't get the temperature inside the house above sixty degrees. She started to apologize for the hundredth time.

Dewey read her mind and waved her off. "We've told you we don't mind the chill. Normally, we get an attic job in the summer, and it zaps our strength. I'll take the chill over the heat in an attic any day." Dewey picked up the 2x4s and nodded to a diesel pickup idling in the street in front of the house. "Looks like Rawls and his crew are here. I guess I'd better let the rest of the guys know."

Juanita had spent so much time on the porch over the past couple of months, she recognized the pickup. Then again, she knew most of the vehicles that frequented the street. Dewey took his leave. Davie started to get down, and she pointed to the truck and handed him his sippy cup. "You may as well stay up here. It looks as if we have company." Two men went to the back of the truck and began unloading the AC unit while another started up the hill to the house. Davie leaned against her and drank as the tall, dark-haired man approached the house. He saw her and headed for the front stairs, stopping at the gate.

Juanita narrowed her eyes at him. "What's the poll up to?"

He smiled. "Five hundred eighty dollars. You cost me twenty bucks."

Juanita jutted her chin. "You and everyone else. I told you I'm not leaving."

"Hello, handsome. Here for a good time?"

"Hello, Charlie," Rawls said without looking at

the bird. He was staring straight at her, obviously trying to gauge her reaction to him knowing the bird's name.

"I guess it is safe to assume one of the neighbors heard the bird and told you about him," she said coolly.

"No. But it doesn't come as a surprise that he is here."

"Why is that?"

Rawls leaned against the rail. "Because this is his home."

She glanced at the bird. "I'm not following you."

"The bird is a legend. Everyone that has owned this house has purchased him. When they leave, they take him back to the same shop. That owner has made a small fortune selling that bird."

"You're telling me the bird is haunted?"

"No, I'm saying whoever is haunting the house likes that bird."

Juanita stared at the antique birdcage. Maybe the house truly was haunted, as that was the only explanation she had for such an irrational purchase. She'd never wanted a bird. She liked things nice and quiet, and yet every time she'd seen the empty cage, she had an overwhelming desire to fill it. *Well, crap.*

"Are you alright? You look a bit pale."

"Just trying to process things." She watched as the two men who had arrived with Rawls came up the incline carrying a new outside air conditioning unit and almost told them to take it back, as it wasn't needed. Then again, she held out hope that once the renovations were finished, the house would return to normal. If that happened, her guests would welcome the relief.

"Other than the bird, have there been any weird happenings?" Rawls asked, drawing her attention.

"You mean other than my son playing with someone I can't see and the house feeling like an icebox?"

"No issues with the playmate?"

While the thought of her son playing with a ghost freaked her out initially, she hadn't seen any behavior from either to cause her alarm. She'd gotten so comfortable that she had been able to unpack everything and even managed to get some writing done. Although, to be safe, she had set up a camera system in the playroom so she could monitor her son even when she wasn't in the room. "To be honest, it's been rather nice."

Rawls raised an eyebrow. "How so?"

"It's like having a built-in babysitter. Don't look at me like that. It's not like I leave them alone in the house together. Davie is developing well, and I haven't seen his head spin around once. Believe me, that happens, and I might consider moving."

Rawls chuckled. Then eyed the front door. "The whole house is cold?"

"Ever since the renovations started."

"And yet you never called me."

She narrowed her eyes at him. "You said there was nothing you could do." She shook off the look. "Besides, it's only when the workers are here. Soon as they leave, the temperature is fine. We're talking instantly back to normal."

"Is that why the two of you are outside?"

"Three." She smiled. "Don't forget about the bird."

"It's pretty warm out. Have you tried opening the windows?"

Juanita thought about covering Davie's ears and blasting the man with obscenities. "Of course I have. I'm not stupid." She blew out a sigh. "The windows won't open until after the workers leave for the day. After that, they glide open as if greased with butter. When I wake in the morning, they are closed again and will not budge. It is as if they are nailed shut."

"Anything on the cameras?"

"Nothing. One second, the windows are open; the next, they are closed."

"Fascinating."

"Truly. I've thought about selling tickets."

He laughed. "Want me to give them a try?"

Men and their egos. She smiled. "Be my guest. But if you break a window, you'll pay to fix it."

"Fair enough." He nodded to the gate. "May I enter?"

Juanita waved him in.

"Hello, handsome. Here for a good time?"

Davie giggled at the bird and jabbered something she couldn't make out. She stood, sat her son on the chair, and pulled on the sweatshirt she had draped over the back. She wrapped the blanket around Davie and followed Rawls into the house.

Rawls wasted no time moving from window to window, attempting to open each one. That he knew his way around the house was apparent. He made his way to the utility room. "This room was added on when my sister owned the house. Up until then, there weren't any washer and dryer hookups."

"Interesting. I'm grateful she added it. Not having one may have been a deal breaker."

"Don't like laundromats?"

She wrinkled her nose. "I can't imagine having to carry both the laundry and baby up and down that hill every couple of days."

Davie struggled to get down. She tried repositioning him and finally let him go when he started crying. Happy to have gotten his way, he waddled off toward the playroom. "I guess he'll come back if he gets too cold."

Rawls smiled. "Have you found any of the secret hiding places yet?"

"No, and I've looked."

His smile turned into a grin as he led the way back into the kitchen. He pointed to an upper cabinet.

Juanita frowned. "I've been all through the cabinets. I cleaned everything before I put things away."

"Do you have a stool?"

She nodded. "Yes, a folding one tucked in between the refrigerator and cabinet."

He pulled it out and placed it in front of the cabinet in question. Moving out of the way, he motioned her up. Juanita stepped up and opened the cabinet door. Seeing nothing out of the ordinary, she frowned. "It's just a cabinet."

"Take those bowls out."

She removed them, lowered them to the counter, and looked at Rawls for direction.

He pointed. "Look at the depth of the lower opening compared to the one above it."

"It's not as deep! I can't believe I didn't notice it before."

"Push on the left corner."

Juanita did as he said, gasping as it moved inward. She pulled at the right side, and it teetered to show a narrow opening. "What do you think it was used for?"

"A money can."

Juanita raised an eyebrow. "You seem pretty sure of your answer."

"That's because it was still there when we found the hiding place. Had seventy-two dollars in it."

"Probably all the money in the world back then."

"Depending on when it was placed there, you could be right."

"And yet no one ever found it."

"Probably because the cabinets are in such good shape. No one ever felt the need to redo the kitchen."

"True, but there were other owners."

"You didn't find it, and you said yourself you'd cleaned them. The only reason I discovered it is because I found it odd the measurements were off. Want me to show you the others?"

"Yes." She turned away from the cabinet. As she started to step down from the stool, it felt like someone shoved her from behind, sending her forward and straight into Rawls's arms.

He wasn't expecting her, and they both landed in a heap in the middle of the kitchen floor with her on top of him. She'd not been this close to a man in over two years, and her breath caught as she looked into his deep blue eyes. She felt the burn in her cheeks as she scrambled to her feet. "That wasn't an accident."

He smiled. "If you're saying you meant to jump into my arms, you might want to give me a little warning next time so I can catch you with a bit more dignity."

"No, I'm saying it felt as if someone pushed me. Davie!" He had been there only moments before. What if they had landed on him? She ran from the room in search of her son and found him staring up at her from the safety of his crib. He reached for her. She pulled him into her arms and was still shaking when Rawls entered the room. She stared at the man, willing him to understand her words. "He was inside the crib."

Rawls smiled.

Juanita narrowed her eyes. "I don't know what you find so amusing."

"Donna – the woman who lived here before my sister – met her fiancé in the house. He was remodeling the bathroom and had taken a break when she fixed him lunch. The way he tells it, she fell into his arms, but according to her, she was pushed. Either way, it makes for a pretty cool story. It's not everyone that can say they have a ghost playing matchmaker."

"We could have fallen on my son."

He winked. "You mean the one that was somehow whisked out of harm's way before it happened?"

"I'm afraid to disappoint you, but I'm not interested in a relationship."

"That's good, because I'm not available." He rubbed his ring finger with his thumb. "Going on a year. I don't wear my wedding ring when I'm working. Too many horror stories of fingers getting amputated."

Bummer. Knock it off, Nita. You're not even remotely interested. Liar. She smiled to hide her inner thoughts. "Good. At least we know we're on the same page."

He nodded. "I'll show you the rest of the hiding places."

"No, I think I'm good."

Rawls frowned. "You don't want to know?"

"Oh, I want to know, but I think finding them will be part of the fun." Davie arched his back in an effort to get down. "We'd best be going back out. I wouldn't want to start any rumors."

Rawls's frown deepened. "I'm sorry. I didn't consider your reputation. You must think me a real jerk."

She smiled at Rawls. "Actually, I get the feeling you're a man of honor."

He started toward the door. "How's that?"

"Maybe I'm overthinking things, Mr. Rawls, but the fact that you didn't think to consider my reputation means you did not lead me into the house under false pretenses. That means you, sir, are a true gentleman."

His frown became a beaming smile as he splayed his hand toward the door. "After you, madam."

Juanita waited until Rawls was off the porch and disappeared around the side of the house to remove her sweatshirt. She settled Davie with a snack and picked up her laptop. Recalling how she felt when she first stared into his eyes, she began to type.

Chapter Seven

Three years ago…

Juanita sat at her desk typing. Davie coughed, and she looked at the baby monitor. He'd been miserable for days, with the doctor assuring her it was just a summer cold. The fact that he'd not fought his nap told her he wasn't feeling well. Her phone buzzed – a notification that her tenant had just keyed in the code, unlocking the upstairs apartment.

Juanita looked to the ceiling, picturing the space as the person renting the upper apartment entered the room. She listened as the footsteps went toward the front of the house and knew her house guest was taking in the view from the picture window. Her smile broadened when the footsteps led to the bathroom. A few seconds later, the sound of water rushing through the pipes within the walls let her know he was done. In the year since she'd started renting out the space, she'd become accustomed to the path her visitors took when entering the apartment overhead. First, they would take in the view. Second, they would relieve themselves. Occasionally, the events would be reversed, but overall stopping to take in the view won out. Of course, that could be because that was what she played up most when creating the ad for her vacation rental. She'd even managed to downplay the fact that the view was marred by the concrete roof of the parking garage by letting them know the steps that edged the garage would lead them straight to the heart of historic Deadwood.

Juanita checked the time on her phone. If nothing failed to go haywire within the next two minutes, that meant the man currently leasing the room was unattractive – something she'd quickly discovered after the first couple times of leasing out the space overhead. Though she'd yet to see the entity that haunted her home, she thought it was a woman. Mostly because the said woman seemed to want nothing more than to find Juanita a man.

It bothered her at first, as Juanita was not looking for a relationship. She still wasn't, but she'd come to grips with the fact that while slightly annoying, the matching attempts were harmless. Juanita checked her phone once more. The window had closed, leading her to believe Mr. Turner was less than desirable. Good. That meant he would be able to enjoy his stay without any minor inconveniences. At least she hoped that to be the case, as she planned on working on her personal manuscript this weekend, something she hadn't been able to do as often as she wished, as she'd become something of a hot commodity in the ghost-writing world.

While she loved seeing her books in print, the nondisclosures she had to sign while working on each one kept her name out of the spotlight – meaning that even though she had a half dozen books in print, when it came time to publish her own manuscript, no one would know her name. The difference was that, unlike most unknown authors, she was getting paid. Not only that, but since she didn't have to pay for book covers or editing, everything coming in was pure profit.

Juanita reached her arms overhead and shook off her pity party. "Shake it off, Nita. It doesn't matter if anyone knows your name. At least you're doing what you love."

Davie's cries drew her attention.

Juanita looked at the monitor and saw him sitting up in bed. She pushed from her desk, hurried to his bedroom, and found him crying. She sat next to him and pulled him into her arms, feeling the heat of his skin against hers. "It's okay, Boogaboo. Mommy's here."

She took him to the kitchen and gave him medicine to ease the fever, then moved to the freezer, removed a popsicle, and took them both to the front porch. He was still whimpering as she sat on the swing and handed him the treat, which he eagerly accepted. At seeing them, Charlie hopped to the side of the cage and squawked his hello.

Juanita looked at the bird, who enjoyed being outside on the covered porch during the day. "Use your words, Charlie. No one likes a loudmouth."

"Teething?"

Juanita jumped. While she wanted him to use his words, that wasn't one she'd heard him use before.

Charlie took hold of his perch with his beak and pulled himself onto the swing. "Hello, handsome, here for a good time?"

Juanita sighed and looked over the rail to see a man whom she presumed to be her current tenant. While no heartthrob, the man was easy on the eyes, which surprised her since she hadn't been summoned to the apartment to attend to whatever clever inconvenience her unearthly house guest had drummed up. "Mr. Turner, you gave me a scare. I thought the bird had learned something new."

He looked past her, focusing on the bird. "He's rather loud. Does he stay out all night?"

It wasn't the first time a tenant had taken issue with Charlie. She shook her head. "No, I bring him inside when the temps cool."

"I closed the windows to block out the noise," Turner replied. He turned his attention to Davie. "Your kid sick? I heard him crying."

Juanita nodded. "Just a little cold."

"I hope it doesn't keep him up all night."

Juanita knew it to be a veiled translation for *I don't want my visit marred by a sick kid.* While she totally understood, her momma bear instincts took over. "Children get sick, Mr. Turner. If you are worried about your stay, feel free to find another place. I won't hold it against you and will refund your cleaning deposit if you leave within the hour."

Turner gave her a long look. "That won't be necessary. I plan on going down to the casino and drinking enough that I won't hear a thing this evening."

Well, at least he's honest. Still, Juanita felt the need to remind him about the stairs. "Just remember to stay clear-headed enough to find your way back to your room tonight. People don't realize how many stairs there are until it is time to climb them."

He laughed. "You could charge a premium by offering rides up from town."

She matched his laughter. "Now that would just spoil the whole Deadwood experience for you. Climbing those stairs is a must."

He raised an eyebrow. "Meaning if I'm going to throw up, you'd rather I do it before I get back to my room."

She smiled and looked at Davie, who was now covered in orange syrup from the popsicle. "Mr. Turner is a smart man."

Turner rocked back on his heels. "Smart enough to know noise works both ways, and if I can hear you, then you can probably hear me. I will keep the little guy in mind when I come in from my boozing and gambling."

"Thank you, Mr. Turner."

"Hello, handsome. Here for a good time?" Charlie called out, then rang the bell inside his cage.

"That's a rather interesting vocabulary your friend has," Turner noted.

Juanita nodded her agreement. "One I wasn't aware of until after I brought him home."

"Does he say anything else?"

Juanita glanced at the bird. "Yes, but he seems particularly fond of that particular phrase, which tends to come at the most inopportune times."

"Maybe he's just trying to play matchmaker."

The last thing she wanted was to give Turner the wrong idea. "I'm sure my husband would take exception to that." The second the words came out of her mouth, she felt a pain in her calf. She rubbed at her leg. "Ow."

Turner looked over the side of the rail. "Something wrong?"

Juanita plastered on a fake smile. "Charley horse."

"Eat a banana. They help."

"Good to know, thank you." Actually, she already did know and further knew a banana would do nothing in this particular case as she was pretty certain she'd just been kicked.

***

It was late into the evening before she was finally able to put Davie to bed. She tried to get him to sleep with her, but he'd sobbed uncontrollably while insisting on sleeping in his bed. She knew it was her fault, as she'd always treated him like a mini adult. With the exception of calling him Boogaboo on occasion, she'd never given in to the temptation of speaking baby talk to him or over-coddling him. While they both enjoyed their cuddle time, Juanita had reinforced independent play. It wasn't that she withheld affection. Her son knew good and well that he was loved. But there was a difference between showing love and allowing your own insecurities to reflect on your child. Having worked in a childcare setting for a number of years in her late teens, she'd witnessed children who fell apart if their mother wasn't at their side every minute of the day.

The moment she learned her husband was terminally ill, she promised him she would do her best to see that his child grew up capable of thinking and acting independently. It was working too. Davie was bright, able to play alone for long periods of time, and his vocabulary was rather advanced for his age. At just over two, he knew most of his shapes and colors and was quickly learning his numbers. The only flaw in the perfect little being that she and her late husband had created was Davie's vision. Something she'd discovered only recently. At first, she was worried about his needing glasses, but Davie had adapted to wearing them as seemingly unaffected as he faced most of life's distractions.

She checked on her son for at least the tenth time since putting him to bed, then turned up the volume on the video monitor that faced his twin bed and double-checked the books she kept underneath the base to allow her to see over the safety rail attached to the side of the bed. She moved to the doorway and stood watching him sleep, all the while debating grabbing the bedding from her bed and sleeping on the floor beside him. She knew she was being overprotective. She was always on edge anytime her son got sick. How could she not, when she knew all too well how quickly someone she loved could be removed from her life?

Removed from your life. Give it a rest, Nita. Your husband wasn't a character in a book you decided to erase. He died. She sucked in her breath. *Stop working yourself up. Davie doesn't have cancer. You took him to the doctor yourself. He is a kid – kids get colds. You've done all you can do. Now go to bed so you can be awake enough to tend to him in the morning.*

Listening to her own advice, she headed across to her room and climbed into bed. Sleep was slow to come as she lay staring into the monitor, watching her son sleep. As she lay there, she recalled the day she'd surprised her husband with the news and showed him the double lines on the home pregnancy test she'd taken. They'd lived with the joyful news precisely five days before another test robbed them of their joy. David, Juanita's husband of seven years, was diagnosed with High-Grade Neuroendocrine Carcinoma – cancer so rare, those affected by it were called zebras. Unfortunately, it hadn't been caught in time, and David was dead before she'd even started to show her pregnancy.

Juanita drifted off to sleep and woke sometime later to the sounds of footsteps overhead. She heard the familiar sound of the water rushing through the pipes, more footsteps, and then all was quiet once more.

***

"Wake up."

Juanita opened her eyes but saw no one.

"You must come."

Though she couldn't see anyone, the woman's voice was loud and clear. "Who…who are you?"

"Come."

Juanita worked to calm herself. "Come where? Who are you?"

"Get up. The child is burning with fever."

Child? Her child? "Davie!" Juanita was on her feet in an instant, pulling on her robe and tying it as she hurried to the other side of the house and into

Davie's room. She lowered the safety rail and sank to the bed, placing her hand against his cheek. She gasped. *He's burning up.* She took the thermometer from the top of the dresser and ran it against his skin. *104.2* Panic threatened as her head swarmed with all the things that could be wrong. "I've got to get him to the doctor."

"In due time. You must put that boy in the bath to cool the fever first."

Juanita scooped him into her arms, undressing him as she went. To her surprise, the tub was already filled with water, tepid to the touch. "How?"

"There is no time for questions."

Davie moaned as she lowered him into the tub and kept hold of him with one arm while using the palm of her other hand to scoop water over him. "He needs a doctor."

"Keep him in that water until the fever comes down."

"Who are you?" Juanita waited for an answer that never came. After some time, Davie's skin cooled. He whimpered as she lifted him from the tub and wrapped him in a towel. Not knowing what else to do, she dressed him in his pajamas and hurried out the door.

***

It was just before dawn when they returned. As Juanita carried Davie up the hill to the house, she saw Mr. Turner standing in the picture window. He moved from the window and appeared on the steps at the side entrance a moment later. "I don't mean to be nosey, but I heard the kid crying and then heard you leave a few hours ago. Is everything okay?"

Great. So much for him leaving a good review. "I'm sorry if we disturbed you. My son developed a dangerously high fever, and I had to put him in the tub to cool him off. After I got the fever down, I took him to the ER."

Turner had made his way down the stairs and met her near the porch. "Couldn't have been too serious if they sent him home."

She shook her head. "Double ear infection. I had him checked by the doctor just the other day. At that time, it was only a cold."

"Yes, those ear infections are nasty things. They come on pretty quickly." He shrugged. "My sister has two kids."

"I'd better get him back inside. If I'm lucky, he will go back to sleep for a while."

Turner stepped to the porch and unlocked the gate for her. "Your husband didn't go with you?"

"My husband is out of town for the weekend," Juanita lied. "Thank you for checking on us, Mr. Turner. Now, if you'll excuse me, I really need to get my son inside."

Juanita hurried inside without waiting for his reply. Once inside, she locked the door and watched through the window as her weekend tenant turned and headed back to his apartment.

"Why must you push all the eligible men away?"

Juanita turned toward the voice, her heart rate increasing at seeing a dark, shadowy figure. It took everything she had not to scream.

"Go ahead and scream. I'm sure that nice young man would be happy to come to your rescue."

"I don't feel the need to scream, nor do I need to be rescued." At least she hoped that was true, but something had changed. Not only could Juanita hear the spirit, but she could also sense its presence. She felt the spirit follow her as she walked to Davie's room. A part of her wanted to tell the entity to leave her and her son alone, but the other part knew if not for the ghost, she wouldn't have known her son had taken a turn for the worse. Even the ER doctor had commended her for getting Davie's fever under control before leaving the house – something she would not have done if not for being instructed to do so. She felt the weight of her son in her arms and lowered him onto his bed. He rolled onto his left side and mumbled something she didn't quite understand as she tucked his blanket around him. She raised the safety bar and checked the camera angle before leaving the room.

Once out of the room, Juanita walked to the birdcage and checked Charlie's food and water. "You know, I never pictured myself owning a bird."

"Technically, I own him. You just paid to get

him sprung from jail."

"By jail, you mean the pet store?"

"All I know is that every time my house guests leave, they take my bird away."

Guests? Is that what we are? "How is it the same bird keeps coming back, and how did you get me to buy him? Did you take over my mind or something?"

The spirit laughed a haunting laugh. "Darling, if I could take over your mind, you'd be lying with that man upstairs right about now."

Juanita stilled at the thought. She lifted an eyebrow. "But you can make me buy a bird."

"I can make you look at an empty cage and know it needs to be filled."

Why does that not bring me comfort? "You're a woman, right?"

Another laugh. "Have you ever seen a man with breasts?"

Juanita finished filling the bird's dishes and turned. She twisted her leg to show the bruise. "I suppose you're the one responsible for this."

"What'd you expect? Whenever I find you a man, you do something to screw it up."

"I don't need your help finding a man."

"The heck you don't. You barely leave the house on your own. I wasn't happy with the changes, but I can't say I mind having a man in the house every now and again. Good-looking too. And what do you do? Lie to them. You have men crawling out of the woodwork to see you, and you're doing nothing to let them know you're available."

Juanita started to tell her she was the only one crawling out of the woodwork and decided against it. "They aren't coming to see me. They're coming to the apartment I have for rent. I'm renting out rooms, not running a brothel. I don't make my living on my back."

The apparition grew bright, flickered several times, then appeared so vivid, Juanita would have sworn her to be real. "I'll not have you judge me in my own house."

Juanita resisted the urge to take a step back. "Judge you? It was a jo…" She took in the spirit's floor-length gown. Rich black and cut so low it nearly pushed her breasts out of the lace-trimmed dress, it spoke of a woman who was exceedingly comfortable with her body. While Juanita wasn't an expert, it also spoke to someone who had money. "You were a prostitute?" *That explains the bird's vocabulary.*

The apparition walked the floor as if considering her words. "I was many things in my life. It's what I had to do to survive. At the end, I was a madam, and the girls under my care respected me. Everyone wanted to work for Madam Lillian. I had the reputation of being fair and not laying a hand on any of my girls."

"So what? Your plan is to use me to continue your profession?"

"I know loneliness when I see it. And I am selective in my choosing. I would not suggest you sleep with a varmint. The gentleman of my choosing must be of good stock. I would not have just any man putting his boots under my bed. Nor would I expect you to go to bed with a heathen."

This was all getting to be a bit much. "I am not one of your girls."

"No, you are older than I would have chosen. Then again, you are easy on the eyes, and the men seem to be attracted to the vulnerability you project."

Juanita firmed her chin and stopped short of stomping her foot. "I do not project vulnerability."

"Oh, but you do. Alone in the world with no man to look after you or your child."

"I do not need a man."

"You wouldn't know that by the words I've seen you put into that machine of yours."

"It's called a computer. I am a writer. Putting words into that machine is my job."

"Yes, well, I didn't have a machine to make my words for me. Though if I did, I'm sure I could think of more creative things to say and do under the sheets."

How arrogant. Then again, considering her profession, she's probably right. The thought intrigued her. She'd often given credit to her muse. And she was working as a professional ghostwriter, but what if the ghostwriter's muse was actually a ghost? *Cool.* She smiled at Lillian. "How long have you been dead?"

The temperature in the room chilled.

"Hello?" *Nothing.* A chill raced the length of Juanita's spine as the reality of the situation struck her. *She doesn't know she's dead.*

Chapter Eight

Three years ago…

Tyler took hold of the canvas tarp and slowly pulled it from the Harley, watching as each curve of the black and chrome hog came into view.

"You going to ride it or make love to it?"

"I haven't decided," Tyler answered without looking away from the bike.

"I vote ride. What I wouldn't do to be able to go with you."

Tyler looked to see his buddy, Josh, leaning heavily on his crutches, looking at the bike with such a yearning that Tyler had to look away. They'd been in the same unit until a little over a year ago when the accident happened. Their unit was out on routine maneuvers when Josh stepped on a land mine that destroyed his lower right leg. It was only by blind luck of a buddy calling out to Tyler, drawing his attention long enough to keep him from moving forward, that he wasn't next to Josh when the mine exploded.

Tyler felt the jab of the cane and turned back toward Josh.

Josh narrowed his brows. "Stop!"

"Stop what?"

"Feeling sorry for yourself."

Tyler wasn't sure what the guy meant. "I'm not following you."

"The heck you ain't. I can't tell you how many times I've given that same look. We all have. You see a Marine missing a limb or with half of his face blown off, and the first thing you feel is pity. Then you have this snake that courses through your skin, wiggling straight up into your brain that says, 'Why him and not me? What makes me so special?'"

"Okay, so what does make me special?"

"You're not."

Tyler smiled. "That's a little light."

Josh shrugged. "It's all I've got. I never said I was a philosopher. I just said I recognize the look." Josh used one of the crutches to point to the other side of the garage. "Listen, Jonesy, if you hear of anyone looking for a ride, have them hit me up. I'll make them a legit deal."

"You sure?"

"We both know I won't be riding it…the wife gets emotional every time she sees it. Kind of reminds her of the man I used to be."

Tyler knew it also reminded Josh of the same thing. He nodded his understanding as he shoved his gear into the saddle bags. "I'll keep an ear out. Hey, man, I appreciate you letting me keep my bike here while I was away."

Josh nodded. "Anytime, brother."

While Tyler didn't doubt the man's sincerity, he knew he needed to find someplace else to store his bike during his next deployment. He had plenty of time to work out the details, as he'd just come home from tour. For now, he just wanted to go for a ride. He took hold of the handlebars and righted the bike. He lifted his left leg over the seat, straddling the hog, then shifted it into neutral and walked the Street Glide outside.

Josh hobbled out after him. "You going back to the barracks?"

"No, checked out on leave an hour ago. Going to Indy to see my sister and her kid."

"Indianapolis? That'll be a nice ride. Think of me when you're winding through the mountains."

"I sure will, brother," Tyler promised. He held out his fist, and Josh did the same, touching knuckles. "You take care, my brother."

Josh eyed the helmet. "Not planning on wearing that?"

Tyler shrugged. "Only when I have to."

Josh tapped a crutch to his leg. "I thought I was invincible once." Josh leaned into the crutches as he turned and walked into the garage. "Tyler."

Tyler craned his neck. "Yeah?"

Josh tilted his left hand, holding out his index and middle finger in a sideways peace sign. "Stay safe, my friend."

Tyler nodded.

Josh took hold of the crutch and went inside without another word.

Tyler pushed start, and the big Harley rumbled to life beneath him. The smile on his face was instantaneous, making him glad he'd waited until Josh was inside. Easing the throttle forward with his right hand, as the bike started down the driveway, he lifted his feet to the touring pegs, made a right onto the street, and roared off.

***

Tyler made it to Charleston, West Virginia, before calling it a night. If he were in a car, he would've pulled off somewhere and gotten himself a bit of shuteye in the front seat, but since he wasn't, he couldn't. Instead, he picked the first hotel he found that looked decent enough and paid fifty-four dollars for the room. It wasn't the Ritz, but the rooms all opened into the parking lot, which was precisely what he was looking for. He idled his way through the lot, pulled into the space in front of his room, and lowered the kickstand as he turned off the bike. The curtains separated ever so slightly in the room next to his, then came together once more.

Tyler opened the door, surveyed the space, and sighed. The room wasn't anything to write home about – then again, he'd slept in far worse places in his lifetime. The bedspread was threadbare, with what looked like cigarette burns, and appeared as if it had seen better days.

He walked in without laying anything down, pulled a pillow away from the headboard to check for bugs and breathed a sigh at seeing none. A television on the other side of the wall did nothing to drown out the person in the room next door. He only heard one side of the conversation, so he guessed the person must be talking on the phone. He listened to the person – a male with a deep voice – mention the words "bike" and "Harley" in the same sentence. *Good thing I'm not a light sleeper.*

Tyler tossed his shaving kit on the bed, removed his leathers then left the room. He walked across the street to the convenience store to forage for his dinner. Not finding anything else that looked appealing, he purchased a couple of hotdogs, a bag of chips, a large fountain drink and a Budweiser. As Tyler exited the convenience store, he saw a man wearing a ballcap checking out his bike. He moved everything to his left hand, leaving his right hand free to reach his pistol if needed. The man looked up, saw him coming, and hurried inside the room next to his.

Tyler stopped at the bike and made a show of

turning his back to the building and reaching over the seat of the bike. As he did, he pulled his shirt enough so that if anyone was watching, they would see the pistol in his waistband. Sometimes it was enough just to let the other guy know the nature of the person they were dealing with. He placed his meal on the table inside and opened the window half an inch. He went outside and moved the bike to the sidewalk directly in front of his window. He opened the saddlebag and removed a spool of fishing line. Cutting a long piece, he tied the line to the handlebar closest the building and threaded the rest through the opening in the window. He pulled out a change of clothes and then shut and locked the saddlebag before returning to his room. Once inside, he tied the other end of the string to the helmet he'd placed on the table. Of course, the helmet would not stop anyone from stealing the bike, but if anyone attempted to roll the bike away, the line was strong enough to pull the helmet from the table, thus alerting him to the attempted theft. He'd performed this same ritual before, which was why he preferred the end room, as there was less chance of someone complaining about the bike on the sidewalk.

Satisfied with his handiwork, he sat in one chair, propped his feet on the other, and pulled the tab on his beer can. Just as he finished the first hotdog, his cell rang. Tyler looked at the screen, saw it was his sister, then swiped to answer the call.

"Oh, good. You answered. Does that mean you stopped for the night?"

"Yep."

"Good. It's late. You don't need to be falling asleep on your bike. Trenton's excited about you coming. I'd hate to have to tell him you have to be scraped off the road first."

Tyler took a drink of beer. "Is this about my not wearing a helmet?"

"It's not called a brain bucket for nothing."

"You're just jealous you decided to put out instead of buying a bike."

"Cheap shot, little brother. I wouldn't trade Trenton for all the Harleys in the world. Neither would you."

"All of them, like in more than one Harley in exchange for a snotty-nosed kid?"

"Yeah, all of them, and Trenton's grown out of the snotty-nose phase."

"Good to know. He's still a kid, though, right?"

She laughed. "Meaning, does he still worship his Uncle Tyler? You're all he ever talks about."

"No."

"No, what?"

"No, I wouldn't trade the kid for all the Harleys in the world. I need someone to remind me how awesome I am."

"Don't forget good-looking. Gorgeous chestnut hair, sleek facial features and stunning brown eyes covered in lush lashes."

Tyler laughed a hearty laugh. "Are you looking in the mirror?"

"Maybe. That's the best part of looking so much alike. Every time I want to see your face, I can."

"Unless you're taking hormones to let you grow a beard, you're missing the whole picture."

"You have a beard?"

"No, just stubble, but enough to know we don't currently mirror each other. Not that they ever truly did."

"Good, you probably fit right in at that seedy motel."

"How do you know I didn't spring for a nice room?"

"Because you can't keep an eye on that baby of yours at a nice motel. Let me guess, the fishing line through the window routine."

"It works." At least in theory; he'd never actually witnessed the plan in action.

"So does springing for a nice hotel in a safe part of town and parking under a streetlight in the parking lot."

Tyler laughed. "You don't think bikes get stolen from under streetlights?"

"Not as much. Besides, that's what insurance is for. Admit it. You're paranoid when it comes to that bike."

"You didn't tell Mom I was coming in, did you?"

Tyler asked, changing the subject.

"Of course not. I know you want to surprise her. I figure you can come by here first, and we'll go over there together so I can record the reunion."

"Which you will then shamelessly post on social media."

Tera laughed. "Of course. Those homecoming videos get all the feels."

"Fine, I'll shave before heading out in the morning. Listen, I'm going to finish my beer and get some shuteye."

"Okay, I'll see you tomorrow. And think about wearing the helmet. At least when Trenton is around."

"Fine."

"Fine, you'll think about it, or fine, you'll wear it?"

"I'll think about wearing it." Tyler blew out a sigh. "Fine, if it is that important, I'll stop and put it on before I get there so the kid can see me wearing it."

"Thank you."

"Tell Little Man I said hey."

"Love you, bro."

"Love you too, sis." Tyler swiped to end the call and pulled the last hotdog from the bag. He'd no sooner done so when his cell rang once more. *Jonesy, you're one popular dude.* He used his thumb to answer. "Yello'."

"Jonesy?"

Tyler smiled. "McNeal? You sound disappointed. Who'd you expect to answer?"

A sigh drifted through the phone. "I knew it was your number. I just wasn't sure if you were back stateside yet. To tell you the truth, I was hoping you weren't."

Tyler eyed his beer. "Dude, I've only had one beer. Either I've become a lightweight overnight, or you're not making a lick of sense."

"Yeah, I guess there's no easy way of saying this, but I called to tell you to stay off your bike for a while."

Tyler glanced at the helmet sitting next to him. "No can do, dude. I'm heading to my sister's in the morning."

"Rent a car."

Tyler laughed. "I'm sitting in a motel in the middle of West Virginia. I'm not leaving my bike. So, what, is this one of those feelings you get?"

"Something like that."

"Just tell me what to look out for, and I'll keep my eyes open."

"You know it doesn't work like that."

"This thing. Is it going to happen soon?"

"I don't know. I just know it's going to be bad."

Tyler could picture the man running his hand over his head, something McNeal did when he was nervous or trying to concentrate. He himself rubbed his fingers together as if rolling a piece of paper into a ball. Both were coping mechanisms given to them by Doc to help them stay calm. "Okay, I'll tell you what. When I get to Indy in the morning, I'll have my sister take me to rent a car – something boring like my grandmother would drive. I'll travel on four wheels until you tell me your feeling is gone. How does that work for you?"

"I don't know."

"You never know until it happens. I'll be extra careful. But that's all you're going to get right now. I appreciate the call, but I'm not leaving my bike."

"Roger that, brother. You stay safe out there."

Tyler ended the call and sat staring at the helmet. McNeal had a pretty remarkable track record of knowing when something was going to happen. Still, the man had been known to be off on the timing. All he needed to do was get the bike to Indi, and he could store it in his sister's garage until McNeal gave the okay. Tyler leaned across the table and pulled the helmet a little closer, stopping when the fishing line grew taut. He stared at his shadowed reflection in the lacquer, replaying the conversation in his head, then pushed back in his chair and spoke out loud. "Okay, I don't know who is listening, but I can't imagine you'd have me survive what I did and then take me now. So, I'll make you a deal. If I'm not supposed to ride my bike tomorrow, then don't let it be here when I wake." He reached into his pocket and withdrew his pocketknife. Opening the blade, he cut the fishing line, leaving his destiny in the hands of fate and lying on the bed without bothering to remove his clothes.

He woke in the same position in which he'd started, looked toward the table, saw the helmet, and smiled. The expression waned when he remembered cutting the line. He rose from the bed, walked to the window, and looked out. The smile returned. "Okay, McNeal, the gods have spoken. It's not my day to die." The words had no sooner escaped his lips than his hand instinctively went to the window frame in search of a piece of wood to knock on.

He took his time showering and shaving before finally double-checking the room and heading outside. He was glad the sun was out. Had it been raining, he would have opted to stay another night. He loaded his saddlebags and then took his time hovering over the bike, checking for anything that looked amiss, even going so far as moving it into the parking lot and checking the tires for stones. The only thing he found amiss were bug guts on the windshield, something he would rectify when he stopped for gas. He strapped the helmet to the back and threw his leg over the Harley, and started the bike. As the motorcycle rumbled beneath him, he reconsidered his decision. It was hard to feel invincible with McNeal's words still hovering in the back of his mind.

Tyler reached behind him. Unlashing the helmet, he brought it in front of him and kissed the top. "Here's to you, McNeal." He strapped the helmet to his head, took out his phone, and typed a message to his sister. > *Heading out now. See you later today.* Hitting the button to bring up the camera, he clicked the icon to turn it around. He pointed to the head bucket, took a selfie, and hit send.

***

The drive from West Virginia to Indianapolis was anything but enjoyable, as Tyler found himself analyzing every decision. *Do I ride to the left, to the right, or stay in the middle? Will passing this semi prove to be fatal?* Even simple tasks, such as stopping to relieve himself, ended with an inner debate. What if getting off at this exit is where the accident occurs? He often considered saying the heck with it and having his bike trailered the rest of the way to Indi. Ultimately, he remained on the bike by the pure stubbornness that had led him through life thus far.

As he exited the interstate heading toward his sister's workplace, he found himself wishing that McNeal had never called. At least he would have enjoyed an otherwise uneventful ride. He rode down Emerson Avenue and got caught by a light at Luan Street. He eased to a stop and stretched his back. *Almost there and still in one piece. Thanks for nothing, McNeal.*

The light turned green, and he continued on his way. Traffic was thin and moving easily a few miles over the speed limit. He checked the mirror and slipped into the right lane, watching the red light in the distance. Just as he'd hoped, it turned green just before he approached Edgewood Ave. He saw the oncoming cars slowing and increased his speed. Too late, he saw a beige minivan cut around a car and continue through the intersection. He turned his head and made eye contact with the woman driving. He saw the look of terror, could tell she was screaming, and increased his speed to avoid the brunt of the impact. He felt the crush and tightened his grip as the Harley wobbled beneath him.

***

"Mr. Jones?"

Tyler opened his eyes and then shut them once more, listening to the video game.

"Mr. Jones?"

He lifted his eyelids and blinked until his vision cleared. He saw a woman wearing blue scrubs standing over him. He turned his head toward the beeping. *Not a video game – a heart monitor.* He looked at the woman.

She smiled. "Welcome back."

Okay, that must have been some coming home party because I don't remember a thing.

"Mr. Jones, do you know when your birthday is?"

"Yes."

"Can you tell me when it is?"

"January 27, 1992."

"Good."

"Do you know where you are?"

"You're wearing scrubs, and I'm hooked up to that thing. So, I presume I'm in a hospital. I need to call my sister."

"She's already here. We'll allow her in after we get you settled into your room."

"My room? What's wrong with me?"

Her brow creased. "Don't you remember?"

"No... wait, I was riding my bike. There was a minivan. McNeal was right."

"McNeal?"

"Doesn't matter. How's my bike?"

"I'll have to ask. Are you in any pain?"

"Nope." Hopefully, that was a good sign. He tried to lift his hand and was met with resistance. He looked and saw his hands were fastened to the sides of the bed. He tried to jerk them free. "Why am I handcuffed?"

"You're not. They are soft restraints. We didn't want you waking up and pulling your IV out or touching your face."

"What's wrong with my face?"

"You've sustained significant injuries to your face as well as the rest of your body."

Tyler stared at the woman. "How significant?"

"You have a large laceration on your right cheek, along with various cuts, scrapes, and abrasions on your body. I'm afraid your left leg took the brunt of the impact and couldn't be saved."

My leg is gone? I won't be able to ride my hog. He instantly thought of Josh and the sadness in his eyes as he stared longingly at the bike and the words that had haunted him at the time. *My wife can't stand looking at it because it reminds her of the man I used to be.* At least Josh had a wife. He didn't even have a girlfriend and wouldn't get one now. "You're telling me you amputated my leg?"

"Yes. Below the knee. After the wound heals, you can be fitted with a prosthesis."

"Who gave you permission to remove it?"

"Your sister, but it was just semantics. The leg was mostly severed at the scene. I assure you there was not even a remote chance of saving it."

Tyle moved to scratch his head and was met with resistance. "Take these off."

The doctor nodded. A nurse he hadn't seen until that point began removing them.

"Why don't I remember the accident? I can remember seeing the woman's face, but I don't remember anything else."

"Your brain blocked out the trauma. There's a medical term for it, but basically, it is a form of amnesia. Oh, and you are a very smart man. I can tell you for certain that if not for the fact you were

124

wearing a helmet, we wouldn't be having this conversation."

The nurse finished untying the restraints and then moved the tray table closer. Tyler lifted the lid to raise the mirror. He ignored the nurse's warning and peeled the bandage away. Angry, raised, and jagged, the scar that ran from just outside his eye curved onto his cheek and traveled to the top of his jawline. For the first time in his life, it was hard to imagine his sister staring back at him.

Chapter Nine

Tyler leaned into the curve, feeling at one with the bike. He'd removed his helmet at his last stop and welcomed both wind and sun as he weaved his way down the mountain. He would stop to put it on before seeing Trenton, but for now, he was one with the bike. Safe and free.

He came upon a semi, checked his mirror, and moved to the left lane to pass. He saw the carcass of a deer just to the edge of the road and held his breath. Too late, the rot stung his nostrils long after he passed the bloated animal. He increased the throttle, hoping to outrun the smell. It worked – the stench was replaced by the delicate scent of wildflowers. He scanned his surroundings, looking for the flowers, but all he saw was the rock mountain that bordered the interstate. Strange, as the smell was so strong, as if the flowers were blooming all around him.

"They've got to be here."

"What has to be here?"

Tyler opened his eyes and realized it had all been a wonderful dream. The events of the day slammed into him. He recalled the conversation with the doctor and knew the only time he would ever return to his bike would be in his dreams. He heard a noise and turned his head toward the sound. Tera stood beside the bed, staring at him with tear-filled eyes. The noise he'd heard had been her crying.

She sniffed and smiled a weak smile. "Hey."

"Hey, yourself. And I should be the one crying. You pulled me out of a perfectly good dream."

"Sorry." While her words rang true, her eyes held pity. He knew the look all too well, as it was the same way he'd looked at his buddy the day before when picking up his bike.

Tyler shook off the memory. "No worries. It was just a dream. I thought I smelled wildflowers. Must have been your perfume."

She sniffed once more. "I forgot I was wearing any. How are you feeling?"

Pissed off at the world. "You want me to tell you the truth or lie to you?"

"We've always been able to tell each other the truth. I hope we still can."

"Then I'm angry. Seeing your face makes me even more so." He shrugged. "It's just that you remind me of someone I used to know."

"I'm not going to stand here and pretend to know what you're feeling. But I know that, inside, you are still you. It's understandable to be angry or scared or whatever else you might be feeling." She trailed her hand lightly against the bandage. "The doctor said it took over three hundred stitches to close the wound on your face. She said it was a good thing you were wearing your helmet, or you would have died. I know you sent me a text telling me you were going to. But God help me, it was the first thing I asked when I got the call. To be honest, I am not sure I could have stood here without being angry with you if you hadn't been wearing it. Thank you for listening to me."

Tyler didn't have the heart to tell her it was his buddy that convinced him to wear it, so he said nothing.

Tera placed her hand on his. "Are you in any pain?"

He groped the bed and found the clicker device used to deliver his meds and held it up for her to see. "Nope. Flying high as a kite. Probably a good thing because, at the moment, I don't even care that you gave the doctor permission to cut off my leg."

Tera's eyes grew wide, then recovered as she blinked back fresh tears. "You know good and well I didn't make that decision lightly. I begged her to find another way and made her get a second opinion. Both doctors assured me there was no chance of saving it."

Tera started to pull her hand away. Tyler grabbed hold of it and stared her in the eye. "It should have been my choice." He knew he was being unfair, but at the moment, she was the only one he had to blame. That was part of the problem. He and his twin sister had always been close; the last thing he wanted was to spend the rest of his life blaming her for what he'd lost.

"If you were in any shape to have made the decision, they would have asked you. As it was, I thought maybe you'd rather lose your leg than bleed to death."

"You thought wrong!" He let go of her hand and thumbed toward the door. "You should leave."

She stood her ground. "Do you remember anything about the accident?"

"No." He shook his head. "Not the accident itself, but everything leading up to it. I remember seeing the light turn green and checking to make sure the oncoming cars were going to stop. Then a minivan appeared out of nowhere, and I saw it cut over into the other lane. I saw the woman driving and nothing else until I woke up in this room. The doctors say it's some kind of amnesia and that I may never get that block of time back. I guess it's the body's way of protecting me from reliving the trauma. I was going to ask the doctor if the woman that hit me was okay, but it slipped my mind. How about you? Have you heard anything about her? Is she okay? Were there any kids in the van?"

His sister narrowed her eyes. "The woman's fine. She was the only one in the van."

He frowned. His sister could come across as having a hard edge, but in reality, she was a compassionate person. "You don't sound happy about that."

Tera proceeded to pace the room, the heels of her shoes clicking against the floor, each tap a further reminder that she and he no longer looked alike. "According to witnesses at the scene, the woman who hit you didn't even try to slow down. One guy went so far as to say he thought she did it on purpose. Said it looked like she was gunning for you."

"She wasn't gunning for me. She was distracted. She was talking on her cell phone."

Tera stopped pacing and turned to face him. "I thought you said you didn't remember."

"I said I don't remember the accident. I saw the woman with the phone in her hand. She dropped it when she saw me, and I saw her scream. She wouldn't have screamed if hitting me was intentional."

Tera crossed her arms. "Yeah, well, she probably wouldn't have hit you if she hadn't been on the phone."

Tyler chuckled. "Spoken like a true attorney."

"I'm not an attorney. I'm a paralegal, but I will

take that as a compliment. We'll subpoena her phone records. If the woman was on the phone, we will know it."

"Why do we care?"

"What do you mean, why do we care?"

"Just what I said. Why do we care?"

"Because you're going to sue her."

"Don't I get a say in this? Maybe I should take some time and think it over."

"Listen, there's not really a lot to think about. I'm not saying you can't live a productive life, but this can set you up so that you don't have to worry about anything. The woman was in the wrong, and we have witnesses to prove it." Tera made her way back to the side of his bed. "Trust me, little brother, you'll thank me for this later." She'd used the little brother card, something she did on occasion when she wanted to remind him that even though they were twins, she – having been born first – was older and should be listened to.

"Fine."

"Fine, you'll listen to me, or fine, you'll think about it?"

"Fine. Whatever you say."

Tera smiled a triumphant smile.

Tyler closed his eyes.

She frowned. "What's wrong? I thought you said you weren't in any pain."

He opened his eyes. "I was just looking at your

beautiful face."

She placed her hand alongside the coverings on his cheek, then moved it to his chest and mirrored the gesture using her other hand. "We are still the same in here."

He closed his eyes, afraid of the words that crossed his mind. It wasn't that he was being vain, it was that with the exception of hair length, they had looked identical for the last twenty-eight years.

"I love you, Tyler. You're going to get through this, and if you need help along the way, I will be right here for you."

Tyler recognized the speech. It was the same one he'd given her when she'd come to him in a panic after finding herself pregnant. He opened his eyes and smiled the best he could without pulling at the stitches. "I love you too, sis."

***

Tera waltzed into the room, waving a folder. "We've got her."

"Her?"

"The woman who hit you. You were right. She was on the phone." Tera laughed. "Get this. She was on the phone giving her kid's coach an earful about following the rules."

Tyler sighed. "That'll be a good story for the support group. Right after one of the others tell their story about having stepped on a land mine. It'll be the perfect segue. I can say, 'Oh yeah, well, I lost my

132

leg to a soccer mom who was pissed off her son didn't get more field time.' I'm sure that will be good for a laugh."

"No one's going to laugh at you. How was physical therapy today?"

"It's not physical therapy. I'm learning how to walk on crutches."

"I hear there is a whole art to it so that you don't get chafed under your pits."

"So they say." Tyler shrugged. "I must be doing okay. I was told they are kicking me out soon."

"How soon?"

"The day after tomorrow."

"Cool. You're staying with me."

"What do you mean I'm staying with you?"

"Just until you get back on your feet." She winced. "Sorry, poor choice of words. Unless you want to stay with Mom, but I have to warn you, she's added another cat."

He felt his nose wrinkle. "The woman already has five."

"Wow, you are behind on things; she had six. Beethoven makes seven."

He lifted a brow. "In that one-bedroom apartment?"

"Yep."

"The neighbors don't say anything?"

"Not that I've heard."

"Then why haven't you said anything?"

Tera shrugged. "She's happy, and I want to keep her that way."

"Because if she's unhappy, she will want to move in with you."

"Bingo."

"So why me?"

"Why you what?"

"You don't want Mom moving in, but you're okay with my moving in?"

"Yep."

He recognized that smug smile. He'd seen it on his own face too many times. At least, he used to. "What's the catch?"

"That you get to spend more time with Trenton."

"In other words, you need a babysitter."

"Maybe. To be honest, I've been seeing someone, and it's hard to build a relationship when I bring Trenton on all our dates."

"Why haven't you gotten a babysitter before?"

"Because Trenton's not a baby. Any man I date has to know that Trenton and I are a package deal. Still, it would be nice having some alone time every now and again. Listen, that's not the only reason I want you to move in, but it would be an added bonus on my end. You know he adores you and would never give you any trouble."

While Tyler knew his sister was telling the truth about needing someone to help look after Trenton, he also could see her using her skills to manipulate him into thinking it was his idea. She knew he'd been feeling down about losing his leg and not continuing his enlistment with the Marines. This was her way of pulling him out of his funk without adding to his pity party. Besides, the last thing he wanted was to be left alone with his thoughts. "I guess it won't hurt to hang out with you and the kid for a few months. But I'm not a freeloader. I'll pay my share of the rent."

"Of course, you will. You're going to pay your share of the food bill too."

"And I will charge you for keeping an eye on Trenton. What's the going charge for a babysitter?"

"You're not going to be babysitting. You're going to be on uncle duty."

"Okay, what's the uncle rate?"

"You mean besides having a five-year-old idolizing you?" Tera eased her way onto the side of his bed. She waved her arm, encompassing his body. "This sucks majorly. I'd give anything if you could walk out of this rehab center on your own two feet, but God help me, I am glad you will be able to spend some quality time with your nephew. I think it will do you both some good. There's one catch."

"I should have known. What's the catch?"

"Your bedroom is on the second floor."

It was all he could do not to say no, but that would let her know he was terrified to navigate a single flight of stairs.

"Take it easy, little brother. We will let rehab know you will be sleeping on the second floor so they can work with you to make sure you can make it up to your room. Until then, you are welcome to sleep on the couch."

That was the thing about sharing a womb with a sibling – sometimes they knew you better than you knew yourself.

Chapter Ten

Thirteen months ago…

Unable to sleep, Tyler woke and debated attaching his leg. Though his amputation site was long healed, he'd never fully made peace with the prosthetic. He'd seen others in his support group stride around the room as if their prosthetic were a natural appendage, but not him. It didn't help that his hip was still wonky from the accident. Even with months of therapy, he still hobbled around using crutches to aid his step and often used a wheelchair when he needed to walk great distances. The only reason he continued to use it was he'd promised his sister he would continue trying.

He strapped on the leg and finished dressing, then sat in the chair in his room, mindlessly surfing social media on his phone, biding his time until he needed to wake Trenton. He'd been sitting there for over an hour when the sound of glass breaking had him moving, and thankful he'd chosen to strap on his leg.

He placed his pistol in the back of his pants and picked his way downstairs as quietly as he could, hoping to surprise the intruder before whoever it was decided to check out the upper floor where Trenton was still sleeping.

Once downstairs, he left one of the crutches leaning against the wall and kept the other to help steady himself. He pulled his pistol, drew in a calming breath, and walked through the lower level, silently clearing each room until the only room left was the kitchen. He stepped into the room, relaxing when the would-be intruder turned out to be his sister.

Dressed in a pencil skirt and heels, Tera stood in front of the coffee maker, frowning as if she'd lost her best friend. She jumped and pulled a knife out of the holder. "Holy cow, Tyler, you scared the crap out of me. What are you doing sneaking around with a gun?"

"It works best if criminals don't know you're coming. Great reflexes with the knife, by the way." Tyler lowered the pistol, sliding it back into the waistband of his pants. "You're supposed to be at work."

Tera returned the knife to the holder, filled a cup with coffee and handed it to him. "I took the morning off."

"Give me a heads-up next time. I've been awake for over an hour keeping quiet so I didn't wake little man." He took his cup to the table and sat with his back to the wall.

Tera brought her coffee and a doughnut box and sat at the table facing him. Her dark brown hair fell in front of eyes that matched his. And, for a moment, it was like looking in a mirror – only the image before him was not marred with either scars or tattoos. Tera pushed the strands over her shoulder and looked him in the eye. "We're moving."

Tyler took a sip of his coffee. "Cool. Where are we going?"

"Not we, as in you and me. We, as in me and Trenton. Robert asked me to marry him and I said yes." Robert was his sister's boyfriend. A professor, he'd taken an administration position at a college in Singapore a year earlier. Tyler knew he was the reason Tera hadn't joined Robert at the time and also knew, by his sister's increasing moodiness, that it was only a matter of time before love won out over sibling obligation. Still, knowing didn't cushion the blow of actually hearing it.

"You're taking Trenton to Singapore?" *Stupid question. Of course she's taking the kid.*

Tera raised an eyebrow. "You'd have me leave my son?"

He drummed a finger on the coffee mug. "I'd have you both stay, but it's not up to me, is it?"

Tera shook her head. "No, it is not. He's good to us, Tyler. Both of us. Trenton adores him and Robert treats him like his own son."

"I don't have a problem with Robert. I just don't like him taking the two of you away from me. I guess that means I'll have to find a new place to stay."

Tera blew out a sigh. "You knew this wasn't a permanent arrangement. Besides, it isn't good for you to lie around the house all day. I think maybe it's time you find a job."

"I don't need a job." He plucked a chocolate doughnut from the box and took a bite.

She took a sip of coffee as if debating her next words. Finally, she lowered her cup and firmed her shoulders. "You can't just sit around the house and play the stock market all day."

"I've never heard you complain about how I make my money when I hand you my share of the rent."

"I'm not complaining about your playing the stock market. I'm worried about you shutting down. You barely leave the house except to go to therapy or get a tattoo. You're young and have a lot going for you."

Tyler looked at her over the rim of his coffee cup. "You forgot good-looking."

Tera stopped midbite. "What?"

"You used to follow that up with 'good-looking.' You'd say, 'Of course my friend will like you;

you're young and good-looking.' Guess we can cross that one off the list."

She brushed her hair behind her shoulder once more. "Of course you're good-looking. We're nearly identical."

"We used to be."

"Not my fault you covered yourself with all those tattoos."

"The tats give people something to look at besides my scars."

"You could have had plastic surgery to have made them less noticeable."

"The last time I had surgery, they hacked off my leg." Tyler waited for her to reply, but instead, she reached for a second doughnut, letting him know he'd touched on a nerve. He softened his tone. "Listen, I'm glad Robert asked you to marry him. He's a good guy. I just don't like the idea of him taking you and Trenton halfway across the world. There are plenty of jobs to be had in the States. And what about your job?"

"I'll find something to keep me busy. It's always been my and Robert's dream to travel. He just got a bit of a head start. You're doing better, so it's time for me to join him. The change will be good for Trenton as well. You may not believe it at the moment, but I think it is the best thing for you too, as it will get you out of your comfort zone. You don't want a job, don't get one. God knows you don't need the money. You've always loved adventure; maybe you should travel."

He felt a glimmer of hope. "To Singapore?"

"For a visit someday, maybe, but not to live. You need to find yourself again, Tyler."

That person is long gone. He shrugged off the thought. "I'm not sure I'm the traveling sort. There was a time, but not anymore."

"Oh, poor Tyler, feeling sorry for yourself. Let's have a pity party."

Her words, though true, felt like a slap to the face.

"You have to snap out of your funk. You're hurting, I get that, but you can't let this destroy the rest of you. I haven't said anything because it's been nice having you around. And Trenton thinks you're the greatest, but that's why I think this move will be good for him. I don't want my son to grow up thinking life stops when something goes wrong." She curbed her tone. "I used to envy you, Tyler. If you wanted something, you went for it. When you said you were going to join the Marines, Mom was terrified."

Tyler smiled. "She made me watch the movie *Black Hawk Down.*"

"I remember. She thought it would scare you into changing your mind. I think it made you want it that much more."

"It did."

"What happened to that guy? What happened to that sense of adventure?"

"I think we both know the answer to that question."

Tera stood and moved around the table to where he was sitting. She wrapped her arms around his shoulders. "I think you're wrong. I think that guy is still here. He's just hiding behind a scared little boy."

"Trenton will be fine."

She kissed him on top of his head. "I wasn't talking about Trenton. I was talking about you. Promise me you won't stay here."

"I can't. The lease is in your name."

She released him and reached in to collect his coffee cup. "I meant here in Indianapolis."

The thought of leaving the area caused his heart to flutter. "Where would you have me go?"

"Travel. There's nothing keeping you here."

"Not anymore," he snapped.

She ignored his comment. "If I were in your position, I'd pick a spot on the map and just go. If I liked it, I'd stay. If not, I'd keep going until I found the one place or person that lets me know this is the time to stop."

Tera had a point. With her and Trenton gone, and their mom having died of a heart attack last year, there was nothing holding him here. "Will you help me pick a place?"

She shook her head. "Nope."

"That's harsh."

"This is the year for new beginnings, Tyler. We've walked in each other's footsteps ever since we were kids. If I hadn't been pregnant with Trenton, I would have followed you into the Marines. We will always be connected here." She placed her right hand on her heart. "But it's time to see what we can do on our own."

"I remember that speech."

She smiled. "You should. It's the same one you gave me the day you left for bootcamp."

"Singapore, huh?"

She winked and did her Forest Gump imitation. "It's like a whole other country."

"Yeah, well, just you wait until you find out where I'm going. It's way cooler than Singapore."

"Any ideas?"

He chuckled. "Not even an inkling of a clue."

She smiled. "You'll know it when you find it."

"I wish I was as confident with that as you are."

"You were once. You will be again. Just do me one favor."

"What's that?"

"Get out of your comfort zone."

Tyler blew out a sigh. "This whole conversation is out of my comfort zone."

"I get that, but I have faith in you to figure it out." She returned to the table and placed an atlas in front of him. "Here's something to get you started. I'm going to wake Trenton for school."

He waited for her to leave the room and pulled out his phone. It had been a while since he'd reached out to Doc, but at the moment, he felt the need for a lifeline. He found the number and pressed send.

Doc answered on the second ring. "Jonesy, what's up, my brother?"

"Feeling a bit on edge, Doc."

"That hip of yours still giving you problems?"

"Every minute of the day, but that's not it. My sister is leaving the country and taking the kid with her."

"Dang, Jonesy, what'd you do to piss them off?" He laughed. "Sorry, brother, I couldn't help myself. I know how close you are to her and the kid. You alright?"

"No, but I will be. The thing is, I can't stay here, and Tera thinks I should go off and explore the world."

"I don't see anything wrong with that."

"That's because you have two good legs."

Doc's voice grew serious. "You're an amputee, not a cripple."

"Is there a difference?"

"Come on over to see me. I'll take you to meet some of the amputees we have here at Walter Reed. Wounded warriors that are missing multiple limbs and have half of their face blown off to boot. I'm not belittling what happened to you, Jonesy. That really sucks, but it isn't the end of the world. Your sister is right. If I was in your place, I'd go out and do things and see what the world has to offer."

"Oh yeah? Where would you go?"

"I'd go to Florida to see the bikinis. When I was tired of that, I'd go to Colorado to hike the mountains. Then I'd go to Deadwood."

"Deadwood?"

"South Dakota."

"I know where it is. I'm asking why you'd go there."

"Because it is someplace I've always wanted to go. It has mountains, casinos, and an abundance of history. I don't know, something about walking the same streets as Wild Bill Hickok just does it for me. Listen, brother, I have to go, but keep me up to speed with where you decide to go."

"Will do, Doc."

"You good, Jonesy?"

"Golden, Doc."

"Be cool, brother." The phone lit up, letting him know the call had ended. Tyler thought about what Doc had said. There'd been a time he would have jumped at the thought of chasing bikinis, but not anymore. Nor did he see himself hiking mountains anytime soon. Deadwood, hmmm. *I like history.* He flipped through the atlas until he found South Dakota. As he looked at the map, he discovered himself actually getting excited at the possibility.

***

Tyler spent days reading up on Deadwood and scouring the Internet, looking through possible vacation rentals before finding one that caught his eye. The listing was for a short-term rental just steps from the heart of Deadwood. He'd never been there before, but after talking to Doc and researching the area, the thought of spending the summer in the former gun town appealed to him. He skimmed through the photos and stopped on the one showing the stairs that gave access to the street above the historic district. *That's a lot of stairs, Jonesy. Yeah, well, Tera wants me to get out of my comfort zone, and it doesn't get much further out than this.*

The thing was, he really didn't want to travel from town to town like a vagabond. He wanted to immerse himself in whatever town he chose. A weekend here and there wouldn't tell him if he was home, but after a six-month commitment, he'd know. While he didn't want short-term, he didn't want to chance being stuck in a place he hated for an entire year. He decided to find a place that would agree to a six-month lease. To help pave the way, he'd created an account and reached out to a few friends who'd claimed to have rented to him, all of which gave him glowing recommendations. He'd even uploaded a photo of him in his dress blues. By the time he was finished with his profile, the only things that were real were the fact that he'd been in the Marines and his name: Tyler Randal Jones.

He didn't like to mislead people, but he knew better than to put a current photo on his profile. One look at his face and he'd get rejected outright. It wasn't his fault he looked like a pirate. Okay, he might have helped the look along by growing his hair out and covering his body in fierce tattoos, but since his nephew insisted on calling him a pirate, he figured he might as well look the part. Okay, so he had a titanium leg instead of a peg leg, but to a five-year-old, a missing leg was a missing leg – it didn't matter what the substitute was made of. At first, the tattoos were a way to cover the scars, but then he realized when he stared in the mirror, he looked as menacing as he felt. He liked that his new look kept people from asking too many questions about his scars and missing leg. Still, while dark and brooding might be good for keeping people at bay, the new look didn't say, *Come to my home and stay for as long as you like.* Even his own sister had gotten tired of his brooding. *Crikey, Jonesy, give it a rest. Tera isn't leaving because of you, and you know it. Yeah, well, she's not staying because of me either.*

Tyler rolled his shoulders and finished filling out the form. He added a note to the owner requesting special consideration for a six-month accommodation, offering to double the nonrefundable deposit and pay for the entire stay in advance. He hovered his finger over the keyboard for several moments before finally hitting send, then stared at the screen for several moments, wondering if he'd suddenly taken leave of his senses. If his reservation were accepted, he'd spend half a year in a small town he'd never even visited, living in a studio apartment above strangers he might not get along with and walking up stairs – lots of them. Tyler extended his fingers and clamped his hand on his head, wondering if he should have them rescan his brain at his next appointment.

The door opened. Trenton – a mini version of the boy Tyler used to be – raced to where he was sitting, holding out a picture he'd drawn in school of a woman, a child and a man. Tyler's heart swelled at seeing that Trenton had drawn him in the picture with him and Tera. "That's great, Little Man. Did you do this all by yourself?"

"Yep. That's Mommy, me and Robert!"

Robert. Of course it was Robert. The stick figure in the picture had short hair and two matching twig legs. Tyler struggled to hide his disappointment. "It's a great picture."

"Mommy said we're going to be a family." His smile waned. "I want you to be our family too, Uncle Tyler."

Tyler smiled. "I may not be moving to Singapore with you, but I will always be part of your family."

"Really?"

"Yes, really. I'm your uncle and always will be."

Trenton's smile returned. "Can you say it, Uncle Tyler?"

Tyler scowled, stamped his prosthetic leg, then gathered the boy in his arms. "Arrr, shiver me timbers!"

Squirming to get away, Trenton giggled with childish delight.

"Okay, young man. That's enough. Take your picture and put it on the fridge so that Robert can see it when he comes," Tera said, coming into the room.

Tyler released Trenton, who grabbed the paper and ran from the room.

Tera cocked her head, looking at the computer screen, which still had the screen showing he'd submitted his application. "You found a place?"

He shrugged. "Maybe. I won't know until I'm approved."

"Of course you'll be approved. Why wouldn't you be?"

"Because I asked for a six-month lease."

Her eyes widened. "What happened to traveling the country?"

"I'll be traveling. I've just decided to slow the pace a bit."

"Okay, I'm dying to know. Where are you going?"

"Deadwood, South Dakota." He closed out of the screen and showed her the photos. "Well, what do you think?"

"I think that is a lot of stairs."

Tell me about it. "You told me to get out of my comfort zone."

She laughed and rubbed his shoulders. "Oh, you did that alright. What happens if you can't manage that many stairs?"

"I'll stay in my room and call Uber Eats."

"Do they even have that in Deadwood?"

He closed his laptop. "The heck if I know. I've never been there."

Chapter Eleven

Thirteen months ago ...

Juanita lay in bed, looking up at the ceiling and mulling over her latest dilemma. Just before turning in, she'd gotten an e-mail request asking to rent her apartment for six months. Not only would that tie up her apartment for the entire summer, but it would take her well into fall. While she wouldn't mind the added income, she'd set the November first cut-off for a reason. November through May was supposed to be her time. Months she could dedicate to writing. Besides, she liked the revolving circle of guests who stayed a night here or a week there—short-term visits with no expectations from either party other than clean rooms and quiet tenants. The system had worked well enough since its inception. Why change the rules now? Because doing so would provide a guaranteed income and the added months would provide a buffer to boot.

Juanita pulled on her robe and walked to her desk. Her plan for a designated office had been curbed when her ghostly housemate refused to give up her bedroom. Juanita had resigned herself to the fact that she'd purchased a three-bedroom home since Lillian's ghostly abode was permanently off-limits. The space wasn't the room she'd initially imagined, but it was functional, and for that, she was grateful.

Juanita waited for the computer to come up and logged into her account. Once there, she pulled up the request and skimmed his email. *The whole summer – why couldn't you have made this easy on us? You could have asked for a few days or even a month. Why be greedy? Because it's Deadwood; who wouldn't want to stay? Then do what normal people do and rent an apartment.*

Juanita chewed at her bottom lip. While she wouldn't mind a break from deep-cleaning the space between tenants, she'd been warned not to rent to anyone for more than thirty days. The last thing she wanted was for someone to move in and refuse to leave.

There were other considerations, especially since the room in question was the entire second floor of her home. What if the guy was a creep? What if he didn't clean up after himself? *He could bring in bugs. I'd never know it until it was too late. I can't have my whole house infested with bugs.*

What if he liked to party? Partying she didn't mind as long as he did it off-premises – this was Deadwood after all – many tourists came to town to gamble and enjoy the nightlife. She was selective in who she rented to and carefully vetted the renters, ensuring that each had previous vacation rental history with a gold-star rating. She'd never had trouble renting the place, primarily because of her write-up enticing the renters with the size of their accommodations and the fact that it was easy walking distance down nearby steps, straight to the heart of Deadwood's shopping, casinos, restaurants, and nightlife. Steps that might not be as friendly if one overindulged. To drive home that point, she'd made sure to take photos of the stairs from the street looking up and added those to the listing. Still, even with the perfect write-up and sought-after location, she'd never had anyone ask to stay longer than a few weeks, which was precisely what made her so uncomfortable. She could deal with an unpleasant situation for a couple of months. But this was six months. If she'd wanted a permanent resident, she would have advertised as such.

Juanita stared at the screen, studying the rental history of Mr. Tyler Randal Jones, which listed him as a Marine veteran and touted him as a perfect renter. The reviews didn't get much better: Great renter, never knew he was here. Left the place like he found it, welcome to come back anytime. Rented to Mr. Jones for the entire summer. *Okay, that one's encouraging.* Quiet and clean, Mr. Jones even did a few repairs while here. *That could come in handy.* Not that she had anything that needed fixing at the moment.

Juanita clicked on his profile photo. Her heart clenched and she almost pressed decline. Handsome and staring out at her with mischievous brown eyes, the man reminded her of her late husband – mostly because of the military haircut.

"Hello, handsome. Here for a good time?" Charlie called from the top tier of his birdcage.

"That's enough, Charlie – this is not a brothel and there'll be no good times in this house." *Or anyplace else, not since David died.*

Charlie grumbled something unintelligible and rang the bell.

Juanita looked at the image once again. The last thing she needed was a six-month reminder of all she'd lost. Her finger hovered over the screen for several seconds, debating. *I'm not going to do it. I can't. Not for six months.* She lifted her hand, about to hit the button to decline the reservation, when the button lit up, showing the reservation had been accepted. She blew out a sigh. "Dangit, Lillian, I don't want him here."

"You're not getting any younger, you know. It won't be long before the perkiness is gone. Take it from me – one minute you're pointing like a teenager; the next, everything heads south. When that happens, the only man you'll be able to get won't be worth his salt in bed. If you won't think of yourself, think about that little boy in the other room. You're doing a disservice to him not letting him grow up with both a mommy and daddy."

"He had a dad – he died." Juanita sighed. "Why am I even arguing with you?"

"In my day, you would've been remarried by now, and little David in there would have a brother or sister to play with."

"His name is Davie, and I've told you before to stop trying to play matchmaker. I'm not interested in getting remarried. How did we go from renting a room to getting married?"

"Okay, so skip marriage. You don't have to be married to have a good time," Lillian purred.

Charlie whistled and banged at the bell inside his cage. "Here for a good time?"

Great, even the bird was ganging up on her. Juanita turned to Lillian. "Stop trying to pimp me out."

"I'm not a pimp. I'm a madam. From what I've seen on that picture box of yours, pimps are seedy-eyed bullies that don't know the first thing about how to treat a woman. If one of those buggers were to come in here, I'd pull the derringer from my garter and shoot the heathen." Lillian smoothed her skirt with her hands. "I've told you before; I never laid a hand on any of my girls."

Lillian was right; they had had this discussion before – nearly every time a single man rented the room. To her credit, the woman was selective in her matchmaking and didn't press the issue unless the man in question was good-looking enough to – in her words – place his boots under her bed. Juanita softened her tone. "I didn't mean to upset you, Lillian. But you do this every single time."

"It's not like I have anything better to do."

"You could take a walk downtown."

Lillian went to the window and heaved a heavy sigh as she looked out. "I don't like to go downtown when it's so busy."

Juanita felt a pang of guilt for having suggested it. She knew it wasn't the crowds that bothered Lillian. As near as she could tell, Lillian's spirit was confined to the house. Probably a good thing, as she doubted the woman would enjoy seeing the building she used to own being used as a place to hawk t-shirts and trinkets to the tourists, knowing she was powerless to do anything about it. "Why do you stay here, Lillian?"

Lillian laughed a haunting laugh. "This is my home. Where else would you have me go?"

Juanita started to remind the woman she was dead but decided against it. She'd tried many times, and it only ended up making matters worse. Lillian would get depressed and give her the cold shoulder

– only a cold shoulder took on a whole new meaning when living with a ghost.

Once Juanita got the courage to speak to her, the woman answered and the two had become unlikely friends. When Davie was three, he started mentioning the lady that watched over him, Juanita knew she had to set some ground rules – no swearing or other off-color language, and the woman had to cover her voluptuous bosom, at least when Davie was near.

At first, Lillian balked at being told what to do in her own house, but she'd finally agreed as long as Juanita allowed Davie to call her Grandma Lilly. Since Lillian was already watching over her son, and never having had a grandmotherly figure of her own, Juanita readily agreed.

Charlie squawked a hello as Davie plodded into the room, rubbing the sleep from his eyes. Lillian turned from the window, smiling, and stretched out her arms, welcoming the tow-haired boy who bypassed Juanita and ran straight to the ghostly woman.

Juanita shook her head. "I'm not sure what bothers me more: that I'm invisible or that he's not wearing his glasses."

Lillian bent, scooped Davie into her arms, and kissed his cheek. When she spoke, her sadness was forgotten. "You don't get to be invisible; that's my job. Besides, when Grandma is in the room, you must wait your turn."

Charlie rang the bell on his cage. "Here for a good time?"

Davie giggled. "Here for a good time?"

Juanita closed her eyes and pressed her head into the back of the chair. The moment Davie had begun to mimic the bird, she had googled parrots to find out their life expectancy. Getting rid of the bird wasn't an option, but she'd thought maybe if the bird was nearing the end of his life, she would be rid of him, a thought she'd quickly set aside after realizing the bird would probably return as a ghost. Now she included the bird in her nightly prayers, praying for a long, healthy life because at least she could put a live bird in the other room or cover him with a sheet when she wanted to quiet him. After a moment, she opened her eyes. "That bird is going to get him kicked out of pre-school."

Lillian brushed the hair out of Davie's eyes. "What did Grandma say about repeating Charlie?"

"You told me Mommy's a prude."

"Lillian!" Juanita scolded.

"What?"

"What kind of language is that for a four-year-old?"

"You're making my point. Besides, I didn't ask you to buy my house. Nor did I give you permission to bring this little bugger into my home." Lillian's voice softened as she brushed Davie's face with the palm of her hand. "But I'm mighty glad you did."

***

Tyler hoisted his seabag over his shoulder and made his way to the staircase. He inhaled and blew the air out several times before taking the first step. He could manage stairs on his own as long as he took his time. Traversing them while carrying things proved a bit more difficult, as it threw his balance off. He was halfway down the stairs when Tera appeared at the bottom, saw he was struggling, and started in his direction. He waved her off. "I've got this."

She hesitated then took another step. "Don't be ridiculous."

"I'm not a cripple. Let me do it."

"I know you're not a cripple. I also know how much trouble you have with stairs."

"Then you'll know why I need to learn to do this on my own. You saw the pictures of the house in Deadwood. Do you think I'm going to have help getting everything up the stairs and into the apartment?"

"Wouldn't it have been easier to find something on the first floor?"

He took another step and winced at the pain in his hip. "What would have been the fun in that?"

Tera laughed a nervous laugh. "Great, so now every time you go up or down the steps, you'll curse my name."

"Only for taking Trenton away from me."

Tera heaved a heavy sigh. "I showed you how to use the video chat. You can talk to him anytime you want."

Tyler took another step. "How about you leave him here with me, and you video chat him whenever you want?"

"I don't think so, little brother."

He firmed his grip on the seabag and took the remaining stairs one after another. "It was worth a try."

She cast a glance over his shoulder. "How much more do you have?"

"My computer bag and a couple of small boxes."

"Can I at least help with the boxes?"

Tyler relented. "Just the boxes. I'll go back up for the computer bag."

Tera smiled a triumphant smile. "Deal."

He listened as she raced up the steps – what he'd give to have that luxury just one more time. "Suck it up, Marine. Life could be worse."

"Who are you talking to, Uncle Tyler?"

Tyler lowered his seabag to the floor and turned to his nephew. "Myself. I was going through my mind to make sure I'm not forgetting anything."

"Can't you just look and see?"

Tyler feigned surprise. "Arrr, shiver me timbers, why didn't I think of that?"

Trenton grinned. "I'll do it."

"Okay, off with you then, before I make you walk the plank."

Trenton took off toward the stairs, passing Tera as she reached the bottom. Tera set the boxes next to the seabag. "Where's he off to?"

"He's making sure I didn't forget anything."

"The only thing left is your computer bag. You sure you want him carrying it down the stairs?"

"Safer with him than me."

Tera frowned. "Your hip giving you trouble?"

"A little. The physical therapist said it will take a while for my body to get used to the new prosthetic."

Tera wrung her hands, her newly placed wedding ring sparkling as she did. "Maybe I was wrong to tell you to leave the city since all of your doctors are here."

"They have doctors in South Dakota. I've already scheduled my first physical therapy appointment for next Monday. Stop worrying about me. You have enough on your plate."

"I can't believe we're actually doing this. I'm moving my kid to Singapore. What on earth was I thinking?"

"That eloping with your professor and moving across the ocean was the only way you were going to get rid of me."

She slugged him in the shoulder. "Brat. Only you

could make our love story sound cheap."

Tyler winked. "Just calling it as I see it. I offered to pay for a decent wedding, but no, you had to go before the judge."

"We had to work around Robert's schedule. As it was, I had a month to get ready for this move. There was no way I was going to throw wedding planning into the mix. Besides, I've had the big wedding. Those are highly overrated."

Only because the jerk you married left you for your maid of honor six weeks after the wedding. Tyler decided to leave that remark unspoken. The only thing Tera's jerk of a husband had done right was leave her pregnant and later agree to give up all rights to the child.

Trenton arrived at the bottom of the steps, holding the computer bag with both hands. "Uncle Tyler, you almost forgot your computer. You need it to talk to me when we get to our new home."

Tyler took the bag from him. "By golly, you're right. Good job finding it for me."

Trenton beamed under the praise.

Tera's phone chimed. She glanced at the screen and a frown tugged at her lips. "The driver is on his way."

Tyler reached for his seabag and hefted it onto his shoulder. "I'd better get the car loaded."

Tera scooped up the boxes. Trenton took hold of the computer bag as they walked out and loaded everything into the trunk, along with Tyler's crutches and wheelchair.

Trenton screwed up his face. "If Uncle Tyler is taking our car, what will we drive?"

"Uncle Tyler is taking our car because we won't need one. Wherever we go, we can travel by train. If we need a car, we will take a cab or call a driver like we're doing today."

"Did you hear that, Uncle Tyler? We get to ride the train." Trenton's smile faded and his bottom lip began to quiver as he looked at Tyler. "I want you to come too."

Tyler swallowed. "I wish I could, Little Man. But this is your adventure."

Trenton sniffed. "But I'll miss you!"

It was all Tyler could do to keep his emotions in check. "You're going to have so much fun riding the train and exploring the city, you won't have time to miss me. But I need you to do something for me, okay?"

"What?"

"I need you to really pay attention to everywhere you go so you can tell me all about it. I've never been to Singapore before, and so you'll need to be my eyes. Can you do that?"

Trenton sniffed and shook his head. "Uh-huh."

A black sedan pulled up to the curb. The driver got out.

Tera turned to him. "I only have a few suitcases.

They're just inside the door."

"I'll get my backpack." Sadness forgotten, Trenton ran after the man.

Tera stepped forward. Tyler wrapped his arms around her. "Thanks for pulling me out of the wasteland, sis. If not for you, I'm not sure I would have survived."

She placed her hand on his cheek then trailed her fingers along his scar. "You would have found yourself sooner or later."

Tyler wasn't so sure, but this wasn't the time to argue the point. "You or Trenton need anything, just say the word."

"That works both ways, you know."

No, it doesn't. If it did, you wouldn't be leaving. "Call me to let me know you made it."

"You be safe, little brother. I hope you find something to make you smile."

Trenton ran up. Tyler lifted him into a hug then let him down again without a word. He couldn't speak, because if he did, the boy would know his heart was breaking.

Chapter Twelve

Juanita stood looking out the living room window, watching for her new tenant. She'd spent the better part of the day refreshing the living space in the second-floor apartment and adding extra toiletries and paper products in preparation for the man's arrival. Even though she had misgivings about the reservation, she wanted to make a good impression on her guest, who was currently three hours past his arrival time. Not that she was worried. He'd paid handsomely for the room – monies that both parties agreed were nonrefundable – since renting to him meant forgoing other bookings for the next six months. She took comfort in the fact that if Mr. Jones failed to show, she had half a year's worth of rental income to sustain her. Even with that knowledge, she knew she would do everything she could to rent out the space and return any monies for days that she was able to fill. She was a smart businesswoman, but she wasn't a crook.

As time ticked on, she went from wondering what was keeping him to worrying something had happened to him along the way. She was also anxious to meet the man whose photo had reminded her slightly of her late husband – mainly to get the awkwardness out of the way early, so she was not caught off guard when she saw him. The last thing she needed was for him to sneak up on her unaware and for her to think he was a ghost. She shook off the thought. One ghost in the house was enough for a lifetime. The rustling of Lillian's skirts drew her attention from the window.

"Mr. Jones is late," Juanita informed her.

Lillian waved her to the sofa. "You're acting like a worried mother hen."

"He's coming from Indiana. What if something happened along the way? It could have, you know."

Lillian nodded her agreement. "Of course, I know. Why, I'll never forget my trip over from Cheyenne on the wagon train. Oh, what a trip that was. The wagon I was riding in lost a wheel and nearly went off the side of the mountain."

Juanita blinked her surprise. "You came over on the wagon train?"

"I most certainly did. How did you think I got here?"

"I guess it never crossed my mind that you weren't born here. How old were you when you arrived?"

"The ripe old age of sixteen. I came in on the wagon train with over a hundred others, some of them quite famous at the time."

Juanita was intrigued. "Really? Like who?"

"Wild Bill and Calamity Jane. I'd heard of them and was eager to meet them, but they were just like regular folks. Some folk found luck in Deadwood, others did not. Bill Hickok was one of the unlucky ones – he was shot in the back less than a month after we arrived. Such a shame he was killed. Bill was such a nice man."

"You knew him?" Juanita gasped. "That's amazing!"

"All us girls knew him." Lillian smiled a knowing smile, then returned to her story. "Wagon trains were the way of it back then. It isn't as if there were train rails or automobiles at the time. We couldn't very well walk all that way."

Juanita hung on every word. "What year did you come to Deadwood?"

"1876, the summer of my sixteenth year."

"What brought you here?"

Lillian's face turned a lovely shade of pink as she pressed the wrinkles from her skirt with her hands. "I came over with Madam Mustache and Dirty Em."

While she knew Lillian had been a madam, she didn't know the details. "You were a prostitute?"

"Don't act so surprised. There weren't many

other things for a girl of that age to do. And I prefer the term 'working girl.' Madam Mustache recruited me just before we left on the wagon train. My father wasn't the nicest man and my mother had long passed. I had no prospect of marriage at the time, so it was either stay and continue to be my father's...let's just say I chose to leave. The only time I regretted my decision was when the town caught fire. I'd never been so scared in my life. People running around screaming and everyone grabbing buckets of water and throwing it anywhere we saw a blaze, which was pretty much everywhere you looked." Lillian splayed a hand across her chest. "There was so much smoke, I could barely catch my breath. And ash floating through the air so thick, it looked like black snow. The fire destroyed pert near the whole town. I'll tell you one thing – that was a cold winter. I didn't complain – not that it would've done any good if I did. We had a tent. That was a good deal more than some had. A lot of people left after that, but not us girls. The men who stayed to rebuild the town took comfort in what we had to give."

"You've seen a lot in your lifetime." Juanita realized what she'd said and blushed.

"I know what you meant, and it's true. I've witnessed fires and floods and more fires. I was here when the first train came to town, watched as they buried Wild Bill on the hill, then later when they laid

Calamity Jane in the grave next to him." There was a melancholy in her voice as she spoke.

Juanita sighed. "Very romantic."

"She asked to be buried there. Some thought it was because she loved him, but that wasn't the case. They were friends, but Jane had a way about her that could get under the skin. She did it to torture him, knowing he couldn't get away from her." Lillian smiled a sly smile. "I wonder if she's still following him around."

Juanita started to ask if she had any ghostly insight but decided against it, knowing the woman didn't take kindly to being reminded she was dead. She opted for a more discreet approach. "What was your first impression of Deadwood?"

"I thought it utterly dreadful and delightfully invigorating all at the same time," Lillian replied.

Juanita laughed. "Care to explain?"

"It had rained in the days prior to our arrival. The streets greeted us with rivers of mud. Oh, they put down planks, but a bit of timber only goes so far when you have that many people walking across them. The town was nothing more than a handful of buildings located at the base of the mountain. The bathhouse could only accommodate so many, so we girls went to the creek. We boiled water and strung sheets on the trees to give us privacy while we cleaned. Just because we came here for work didn't mean we weren't modest about such things." Lillian grinned. "Our wagon train brought over a hundred people into town that day, but it was us girls the miners were most happy about – they were mighty grateful for our company."

Juanita was intrigued. In all the years she'd lived in the house, Lillian had never opened up so deeply about her past. Normally, Lillian would disappear when asked, and the house would grow cold for days. Still, she couldn't resist pressing for more information about the woman who shared her home. "You never fell in love and married?"

Lillian pushed from the couch and paced the floor, her dress swishing with each movement. "A miner fell in love with me. He'd found a nice bit of gold in the creek and asked me to marry him. When I said yes, he bought out my contract."

Something about the way she'd said it bothered Juanita. "You said he fell in love with you. You didn't love him back?"

The room grew cold. Lillian shook her head. "I loved him for how kind he was to me. But I wasn't in love– not the way most people who cherish each other are. My father did things to me that made falling in love impossible."

Juanita bit her bottom lip. "I'm sorry."

Lillian waved her off. "Don't you go fretting about things you can't change. I've had plenty of time to leave those memories behind."

Lillian seemed inclined to talk, so Juanita

pressed for more information. "Did you marry the man?"

"His name was Henry, and I did. Only we didn't get married in the church on account of what I was and all. It didn't matter much to me, but I could tell it bothered Henry a good bit. He was kind to me, and lucky that man was, let me tell you that. Why, by the end of our first year together, he'd found enough gold to build this house. Henry chose this spot because it overlooked Main Street. He liked standing in front of that big window as much as you do."

"If you were married, how did you become a madam?"

Lillian's eyes clouded over. "Henry was a lucky man, but he was as greedy as he was lucky. He was shot for jumping a claim. The man who shot him was brought to trial, but it's like stealing a horse. That sort of thing just wasn't tolerated. I wasn't about to go back to my old life, nor did I have any mind to leave this house Henry built for me. So I used some of the money he'd set aside and rented some rooms downtown. I took the stagecoach to Rapid City – it wasn't much to look at back then, but I recruited me some girls and became Madam Lillian. I kept it simple, as I only had a handful of girls, but they were a different caliber than the rest in both the way they looked and the way I made them dress. My establishment was high-class and the menfolk in town knew it. They also knew I wouldn't stand for no shenanigans. Why, if a man were to lay a hand on one of my girls other than to caress her the way a woman should be caressed, my girls knew to call out to me, knowing I'd shoot his…"

Juanita coughed and nodded to Davie, who was sitting in the recliner watching television. "I get the picture."

Lillian continued. "There were no contracts – my girls were free to come and go as they pleased. If a girl wanted out, they would come to me and give me enough time to fill their bed. That wasn't difficult to do; the word was out how I treated my gals, and I didn't have to go far to find a replacement."

Footsteps sounded from the floor above and they both looked to the ceiling. Juanita realized she'd missed her tenant's arrival and was okay with that. Listening to the hardships Lillian had to overcome seemed to put things in perspective. Suddenly, being in control didn't seem as important at the moment. Juanita had overcome adversities of her own, and she, too, had shown her ability to survive. So what if the man upstairs bore a slight resemblance to her late husband. She'd seen David a hundred times since his death when her son said or did something that reminded her of him. That was why she chose to keep the boy's hair a bit longer, so it wasn't a constant reminder.

Juanita glanced at Davie, saw he was still

enthralled with his television program, and turned her attention back to Lillian. "I'd love to hear more if you're of a mind to share."

***

Tyler plastered himself against the wall, waiting for the shooting to stop. Bullets zinged past, ricocheting off the far wall. If they didn't get that sniper soon, someone was going to die. Another shot zoomed past, someone called out and screams filled the air.

Tyler tried to go to the man and realized he was tangled in the curtains. He tore at the coverings, took a step and fell flat on his face. Seconds later, a child's cries filled the air. Tyler was instantly awake. *Trenton!*

Tyler wrestled his way to the bed, pulled himself up and turned on the lamp. Nothing looked familiar. The bed was turned at the wrong angle, the color of the walls was not right. Even the bedding seemed foreign. *This isn't my bedroom. Where am I?* He was just beginning to panic when he saw his seabag sitting next to the boxes and remembered where he was. *Not Afghanistan. Only a nightmare.* He hadn't had one of those in a while. The gunfire seemed so real. As real as Trenton's screams. No, he'd been awake when he'd heard the child.

Tyler sat on the edge of the bed, trying to make sense of things, but heard nothing except the pounding of his heart. Okay, he couldn't actually hear it, but he could certainly feel it beating within his chest.

He stood, thinking to hop his way to the bathroom. Still feeling a bit off-balance, he decided to use his crutches instead. The bathroom was spacious, which was one of the things that drew him to the unit in the first place. It was the first listing he'd come across where all the rooms looked large enough to easily move around without bumping into things. He liked to let his leg breathe when he was alone and knew it would be easier to move around if he didn't have to worry about crutch placement within a small space. If not for it being on the second floor, it would be the perfect space for a wheelchair. He had one in the trunk but didn't want to attempt wrestling it up and down the stairs. If the crutches proved to be inadequate, maybe he'd look at getting a lightweight chair for indoor use.

Tyler turned on the water and splashed it across his face, then used the hand towel to dry off. He looked up and saw his reflection. "Tyler, you're one ugly son of a…" He turned, wondering if he'd really heard a knock on the door. The knock came again, much louder this time. *Someone's not happy.* Suddenly glad he'd decided to wear shorts to bed, he tossed the towel aside and made his way to the door with the help of the crutches.

He looked through the peephole and saw an auburn-haired woman with rich brown eyes – cute –

or could be, if not for the fact that she looked madder than a caged badger. Given this was a rental property, he wondered if maybe the visitor was looking for the previous tenant. *Awfully early in the morning for visitors.* He'd just decided against answering when he heard a key enter the lock. All chivalry aside, whatever this woman had on her mind was more than he was willing to deal with respectfully at three in the morning. He slid the chain into the slide, berating himself for not having already done it. The door opened and jerked to a stop. He was glad the person on the other side of the door was a woman of small stature, as he wasn't sure he'd be able to brace the door well enough to stop someone from breaking through the flimsy chain.

"Mr. Jones?"

Okay, not so random after all. "Yes."

"My name is Juanita Stim. I own this property." Though she'd made an attempt to sound polite, her tone showed this wasn't a social call.

Tyler leaned heavily on his crutch, bracing in case he needed to use the other to block her entry. "I would say it's nice to meet you. However, since you're currently trying to enter the premises unlawfully, I'll refrain."

"It's my house." She sucked in a breath of air. "I heard you fall and got worried. You didn't answer the door when I knocked, so I thought maybe you were injured or perhaps too drunk to get off the floor."

So that was it. "No, ma'am, I'm not drunk."

"I should hope not because I have strict rules about that. You should've received them in the e-mail that accompanied your acceptance."

Tyler suddenly regretted his decision to agree to a six-month nonrefundable agreement. *Maybe a good lawyer can help me out of this. Surely unlawful entry would be grounds for breaking the agreement.* "I did. And as I already stated, I am not drunk."

She softened her tone. "If I could just step inside to see for myself."

Before he could answer, Tera's ringtone sang out, alerting him to her call. "Thank you for your concern. I need to take a call."

"It's a bit late for a phone call, don't you think?"

Tyler shut the door without responding and hurried to retrieve his cell phone. "Hey, sis."

"Tyler, are you alright? You sound out of breath. You haven't been overdoing it on those stairs, have you?"

"It's three in the morning."

"Sorry. I'm so jet-lagged, I don't even know what day it is. If it's three a.m., why are you out of breath?"

He was going to tell her about the nightmare and the encounter with the landlady but didn't want to worry her. "Did you know Deadwood has badgers?"

"Doesn't surprise me. They probably have bears

too. Don't go out at night and make sure to keep your doors locked."

He stifled a laugh then remembered hearing the child crying. "How is Little Man doing?"

"Trenton's great – babbling a mile a minute about the flight, the train ride and all the lights in the city. Listen, I'm going to let you go for now. I just wanted to let you know we made it safe. We still have so much to do to settle in, and we both need to get some sleep."

Tyler looked at the door. *Depends on if Miss Crazy returns.* "Okay, sis. Take care and give Little Man a hug for me."

He held on to the phone long after his sister ended the call then set the device on the nightstand. He placed the crutches within easy reach and turned off the light. As he lowered himself to his pillow, he made a mental note to begin his next rental search in the morning. If this evening was a preview of coming attractions, he'd be leaving this place sooner than expected.

Chapter Thirteen

Juanita stared at the door as anger boiled inside. How dare he shut the door in her face. She had half a mind to go to the shed, grab the bolt cutters and cut the chain. That or call the police and have them force their way inside. That would show that self-righteous Mr. Jones who was boss. *Who gets phone calls at three in the morning anyway? Drug dealers! Great, I've rented my home to a criminal.* She pulled out her phone, intending to call the police, when she stopped. If he did have drugs, they might seize the whole house. *Then where would I be? I'll kick him out. Yes, that's what I'll do. I'll refund his money and kick him out first thing in the morning. There's still time to get summer bookings, so it won't be a total loss.*

Lillian was waiting for her the moment she entered the main house. "You sure left quite the impression on that young man."

"You were listening? I thought you were down here keeping an eye on Davie."

"You were madder than a man who didn't get what he paid for. Someone needed to keep an eye on you. Besides, Davie was asleep before you reached the side stairs."

"I'm still mad. But I've got a plan. I'm giving Mr. Jones his money back and sending him packing first thing in the morning."

"The man apologized. You're being a bit hard on him, don't you think?"

"Hard on him? I don't care what he says. If he read the contract, then he knows the rules, one of which is to be quiet. Instead, he's banging around up there and scaring my son."

Lillian looked toward the ceiling. "He fell out of bed."

Juanita crossed her arms. "Grown men don't fall out of bed unless they're drunk or on drugs and so high they can't walk straight. The jerk wouldn't let me in, so I couldn't check his eyes to see if they were dilated."

"Have you thought that's why you're so upset – because he wouldn't let you in?"

"You're darn right I'm upset about that. It's my house," Juanita assured her.

"Which he rented and paid good money for in advance. I'm sure he thinks that affords him a bit of privacy."

"Mr. Jones can have all the privacy he wants as long as he gets it somewhere else. I have my son to think of."

Lillian smiled. "Yes, you most certainly do. You're not going to be any good to him if you don't get some sleep. Give your ire a bit of time to settle. If you're still angry in the morning, you can send Mr. Jones packing."

"I will. Just you wait and see." Juanita went into her bedroom, climbed into bed and stared at the ceiling. It was bad enough she had a drug dealer staying in her house. But his bed was directly above hers. Oh, what she wouldn't give to grab the broom and keep him up the rest of the night by poking it at the ceiling. The only thing that stopped her was her fear of waking Davie. He'd already been traumatized once tonight; she would not add to his misery.

***

The sun was pouring in through multiple windows when Tyler woke. Tera's townhouse in Indianapolis was a shared unit in which his room only had one window that did not afford much light. He liked the way the upper floor of this rental had been renovated into an open-concept, sun-filled space. If not for the craziness of the evening, it would have made him happy he'd chosen this place for his first foray into his newly sought independence. As it was, he was currently wrestling with how to tell Ms. Stim he wanted out of their agreement and further insist for her to return the monies he'd paid. The latter could prove difficult, since it was he who'd suggested she add the nonrefundable clause when she'd balked at agreeing to a six-month lease. That was before he'd known she was crazy. He decided to try to reason with the woman first. If that didn't work, he would threaten to leave an unfavorable review, telling how she attempted to enter his room at three a.m. If that still didn't work, he'd resort to legal means. He wasn't sure where to go from here, but decided he'd figure that out after she agreed to his request.

He attached his leg, then dressed before packing his seabag and moving it along with his crutches near the door. He gave thanks for the fact that he was too tired to bring everything in last night. He thought about taking the seabag with him but decided to leave it where it was until he spoke with the woman. He placed his pistol on the table. The last thing he wanted was to be tempted to shoot the woman if she came unhinged when he told her he wanted his money back.

The crispness of the morning air surprised him, as it had been stifling hot in Indianapolis in the weeks prior to his leaving. Too bad he'd rented from a psycho; he could get used to mornings like this.

Between the long drive and the fall, his hip wasn't happy with the stairs. He picked his way down, chiding himself for not bringing his crutches to help him navigate once he reached the bottom. He gave thought to going back for them then decided against it, as the physical therapist had warned him against becoming dependent on them.

Tyler stepped onto the front porch, noted the mound of blankets on the porch swing, and wondered if they were for sitting outside drinking a cup of coffee on cool mornings such as this. The thought pulled at him, making him wish he hadn't gotten off to a wrong start with the owner. He took a moment to collect himself then knocked on the door. As he waited, he appreciated his surroundings. The house overlooked historic Deadwood, which seemed to be coming to life for the day. He recalled some of the things he'd read while researching the town and the famous people who'd once walked the streets below, and made the decision to try to find a room and explore the area for a couple of days. Present situation aside, he liked the energy of the place, plus it would be good to give his hip a chance to settle down before driving any distance.

Tyler was about to knock again when he heard a sob. He walked to the side of the porch, listening. He heard the sound again and realized it was coming from beneath the pile of blankets.

He pulled them back to reveal a boy who looked to be slightly younger than Trenton. The child had a mop of long blonde hair and tear-stained cheeks.

"Yo, Little Dude. What seems to be the problem?"

The boy squinted, then pulled a hand out from under the blanket. He opened a pair of plastic-rimmed glasses with lenses that looked much too thick for a child of his size. The boy held them to his face without putting them on and looked him up and down.

Tyler half expected him to run screaming when he saw him, but he only blinked. Taking that as a good sign, Tyler sat in the chair next to the swing. "You seem pretty upset. Anything I can help with?"

The boy shook his head.

"You got a name?"

"Davie."

"I'm pretty good at fixing things. I could help if you tell me what's wrong."

Davie sniffed and held out the glasses. "Mom said I have to wear them, but I don't want to."

"So that means you can see just fine without them?"

Another sniff. "No."

"You know, if I had a fine pair of glasses that could make me see whatever I wanted to see, I would wear them all the time."

Davie's eyes grew wide behind the lenses. "You would?"

"Sure I would."

"My friends laugh at me because I look different."

184

"So do mine."

Davie crossed his arms. "No they don't. You're bigger and look mean. Nobody's going to make fun of you."

Tyler didn't like that the boy thought he looked mean. "Arrr, but they do, matey!"

Davie smiled. "You sound just like a pirate."

"You know what else?"

"What?"

"I've got me a pirate leg." Tyler pulled up his pant leg to show him. Davie's eyes grew wide. Tyler lifted his leg so the boy could feel it. "You have glasses to help you see, and I have a titanium leg to help me walk. I couldn't walk across this porch if not for the help of this leg, no more than you can see me without those glasses of yours. I don't really like wearing the leg, but I'm not going to take it off just because someone makes fun of me. Why, that would be just silly."

Davie cocked his head. "It would?"

"Sure it would. Then they would be making fun of me because I couldn't walk. I don't worry what people say or think. I just worry about doing what makes me happy."

"I get happy when I can see," the boy agreed.

"Then it doesn't make sense to hold those glasses in your hand when they could make you happy, now does it?"

Davie shook his head then looked to the door.

"Grandma Lilly said I should bring you inside."

Tyler looked over his shoulder and saw nothing.

Davie maneuvered the glasses onto his face, threw the covers aside and pushed off the swing. "Come on."

Tyler followed him inside, expecting to see the boy's grandmother.

"Hello, handsome. Here for a good time?"

Tyler looked to see a large green parrot sitting on a play structure on top of a large cage. He almost laughed. Trenton had always wanted him to get a parrot for his shoulder. Too bad the situation wasn't different; he'd love to take a photo with the bird on his shoulder to send to his nephew. He returned his attention to Davie. "Is your momma home?"

"She's in the shower. Grandma Lilly's in the kitchen. She'll be out in a minute." Davie stepped around him and locked the door. "I'm supposed to keep it locked when Momma's in the shower."

Tyler thought to ask if he was supposed to be outside on the porch when his momma was in the shower but decided against it. Obviously, the boy's grandmother knew he was there. Tyler wasn't sure if he was comforted that the boy knew to keep the door locked or freaked out at being inside the room alone with the boy whose mother had already shown herself to be slightly unhinged.

Davie scratched his head. When he did, Tyler saw a bruise on the child's forehead that had been hidden under the kid's mop of hair. Instantly, he pictured the woman with the dark eyes and wondered if she'd used that anger on her son. He thought of Trenton, and his jaw clenched at the thought of anyone hurting the child.

Tyler pointed to the bruise. "That's a mighty nasty bump you've got there."

Davie touched the bruise and his face screwed up. "I ran into the wall."

Sure you did. "Seems to me if you ran into the wall, you would've broken your glasses."

"Not if said glasses weren't on his head at the time. I'm Lillian – Grandma Lilly," she corrected.

Tyler looked to see a woman of considerable age standing in the doorway. She wore a long black gown that would have shown a great deal of cleavage if not for the lace that covered her bosom. Her hair was pulled up on the sides and hung in long, loose curls across her shoulders. Even at her age, it was easy to see she'd been rather striking in her prime. Given the style of her gown and the way she wore her hair, Tyler figured she was dressed for some kind of reenactment. He shrugged his apologies. "I'm sorry, ma'am. I didn't mean to imply…"

"Yes you did." She turned her attention to the boy. "Davie, tell Mr. Jones how you got hurt."

Davie stuck out his bottom lip. "I already told him."

"You told him you ran into the wall. You didn't tell him why."

Davie looked to the ceiling then lowered his eyes. "Cause I was sleeping when I heard the noise. I jumped out of bed and forgot to put on my glasses so I could see."

The noise the boy had heard was him falling out of bed. Davie was the child he'd heard crying. Tyler's mouth went dry. *His mother didn't hurt him. The bruise is my fault.* That explained why Juanita had been so angry. She hadn't been acting like a caged badger. She'd been acting like a momma bear. And for good reason.

Lillian placed her hands on Davie's shoulders. "As you can see, Mr. Jones, things are not always as they seem."

Juanita came into the room, took one look at him, and her eyes grew wide. She must have realized who he was, as they instantly narrowed.

Lillian nodded in his direction. "Davie was just telling Mr. Jones what happened to his head. I was further explaining that things are not always as they seem."

Juanita looked him up and down, her eyes narrowing further. "That's putting it mildly. You, sir, look nothing like the photo you use in your profile."

"The picture is me." Tyler shrugged. "At least, it used to be. I didn't think you'd rent to me if you saw a current one."

"This is Deadwood, Mr. Jones. I assure you your looks are not all that unique here. All the same, I would like you to leave."

Even though it was what he'd wanted, her telling him to leave bothered him. "We have an agreement."

"One you broke. My rental policy is stringent for many reasons." She glanced at Davie. "I will not put my son in harm's way."

Lillian cleared her throat. "Juanita here thinks you were drunk or possibly on drugs last evening and that that was the reason for your fall. Would you care to shed some light on the matter?"

Tyler hesitated.

Lillian smiled a reassuring smile. "I assure you that you are among friends."

He wasn't sure how the woman knew, but something told him she did. As for being among friends, the woman standing beside her looked to be one of the most unfriendly people he'd ever met. Still, he'd rather see her anger than her pity, which would happen if he told her the truth. Tyler shook his head. "I'm afraid your daughter has already made up her mind about me."

Juanita firmed her shoulders. "She's not my mother. As far as what you've paid, if I can fill the rooms, I will issue you a refund, less last night's stay and the cleaning deposit."

He started to argue the point but thought of the

boy and nodded his agreement. "Do you by chance have a directory of local hotels? I would like to stay in town a few days to check the place out."

Juanita started to answer, and Lillian cut her off. "You can stay here until you're ready to check out."

"Yay, you get to stay!" Davie ran to him and clutched his hand. The gesture tugged at his heart, as it reminded him of Trenton.

Juanita's face turned red. She started forward and Lillian blocked her way. "Davie's wearing his glasses."

Juanita's face softened. "You didn't tell him to put them on?"

Lillian shook her head. "No, he and Mr. Jones had quite the conversation. Davie now sees the importance of wearing his glasses."

"You do?" Juanita smiled. It was the first time Tyler had seen her do so. The transformation was most becoming.

Davie shook his head. "Mr. Jones is a pirate."

Juanita's smile vanished. "Davie, be nice. Just because the man has a few scars…"

"No, Momma, he's a real pirate." Davie dropped to the floor and pulled up Tyler's pant leg. "See!"

Lillian looked at Juanita, whose face remained unreadable. "Mr. Jones wasn't under the influence last night. He had a nightmare and fell out of bed."

Tyler felt his mouth fall open and hurried to close it again. He hadn't told anyone about the nightmare, not even Davie. *There must be cameras in the house.* Anger bubbled at the thought of someone witnessing his vulnerability. "There's no way you could know that unless you have hidden cameras in my room."

Juanita started laughing.

Tyler was used to people staring, but for the woman in front of him to blatantly laugh at him infuriated him. "You won't find it so funny when I call the police."

Davie scratched his head. "What's so funny, Momma?"

Juanita tried unsuccessfully to curb her laughter. "Mr. Jones is angry about Grandma Lilly watching him."

Davie peered up at him through distorted lenses. "Don't be mad at Grandma Lilly; she's special like us."

What was that supposed to mean? Tyler looked to Juanita, who was now laughing so hard, she snorted. He turned to Lillian. "Would you care to explain what she finds so amusing?"

"I was watching you, Mr. Jones, but not in the way you think."

"Grandma Lilly's a ghost." Davie beamed. "She watches everyone."

Tyler's anger vanished as he looked the woman up and down. Sure, he'd questioned her attire. It hadn't dawned on him that she might be a spirit. He wanted to speak, but his mouth wouldn't cooperate.

While he'd seen ghosts before, this was the first time he'd spoken to one.

Lillian smiled and faded in and out several times before returning to full form. "As I told you before, Mr. Jones. Things aren't always as they seem."

Juanita regained control and smiled what appeared to be a genuine smile. "I'm afraid we've gotten off on the wrong foot, Mr. Jones." The smile faded as she instantly realized what she'd said. Her cheeks turned a vivid shade of crimson. "I'm so sorry… I didn't mean."

Tyler waved her off. "You didn't say anything wrong. I use that expression all the time."

At the mention of the word, Charlie squawked. "Hello, handsome. Here for a good time?"

Tyler raised an eyebrow as he looked at the antique birdcage. "Is the bird real?"

"The bird is very much alive, Mr. Jones." Juanita nodded to the womanly spirit. "We can thank Grandma Lilly for his vocabulary. She and the bird have a history that goes back many years."

"It's an interesting home you have here, Mrs. Stim." Tyler winked.

She looked at him as if debating her words, then slid a glance at the spirit before speaking. "I couldn't agree more. Welcome to our home, Mr. Jones. I hope you will enjoy your stay."

When he first chose the apartment in Deadwood, it was to needle his sister, who had forced him from his comfort zone. Never in his wildest dreams could he have imagined just how far out he was stepping. He'd only been in Deadwood for a few hours, and already he felt more alive than he'd felt since the day that had taken away his sense of adventure. He locked eyes with Juanita. "Thank you. I look forward to exploring all that Deadwood has to offer." Tyler grinned as the blush returned to Juanita's cheeks.

Chapter Fourteen

April rooted in the fridge and brought out several containers. She placed them on the counter and pointed to them in turn. "You have egg salad, tuna salad, sliced ham and smoked turkey. I've added chips and made you some chocolate chip cookies."

At the mention of cookies, Gunter yawned a squeaky yawn. While his earthly counterparts weren't supposed to eat chocolate, the ghostly K-9 didn't have to worry about the ill effects of eating it. In fact, since attaching himself to Jerry, the dog had proven to have a rather robust sweet tooth.

Jerry chuckled and scratched the dog on the head. "Don't worry, boy. I'll share."

April opened the plastic container and handed Gunter a cookie. "There are plenty for both of you."

Houdini licked his lips and barked an eager yip.

April closed the container and opened the canister that held the homemade peanut butter dog treats she'd made especially for the pup. She held it for the pup to see, then waited until Houdini sat before handing him one. "Good, sit."

Jerry smiled. "I was going to ask if you wanted me to take Houdini with me, but it looks like you two are doing just fine."

"I think we will be okay. Houdini is doing better with the doggy door, and so far, he hasn't seen fit to push through the fence. Besides, Max would miss him."

Jerry raised an eyebrow. "Just Max?"

April sighed. "No, not just Max. I like having the dogs here."

"What about me?" Jerry pulled April into his arms. "Are you going to miss me?"

April's phone rang before she could answer. "It's Max."

The doorbell rang. Both Gunter and Houdini raced to the front of the house, each barking their own alarm. While Jerry was the only one who could hear Gunter's ghostly barks, Houdini's yips would be heard even through the closed door.

Jerry released her. "Answer your phone. I'll see who it is." As he neared the door, the back of his neck began to tingle. Jerry motioned to Gunter to be on alert. The dog planted himself and tilted his ears forward. Houdini took more of a straightforward approach, doing his best to push his way past Jerry.

Jerry turned his hand over, extended his fingers

and gave the command to sit. Houdini instantly lowered his bottom to the floor. Jerry was just opening the door when April called out to him.

"Max said to be careful opening the door."

With Max's warning, the tingle on the back of his neck intensified. Jerry hesitated, then decided to open the door. The last thing he wanted was to go out of town and leave April to deal with whatever was pinging both his and Max's psychic radar. He braced himself for trouble then opened the door, surprised to see Mr. Mills standing on the porch wearing a plaid shirt and baseball cap that half covered his face but did nothing to hide his scowl.

Jerry knew the man had to have heard the dog, but he hadn't actually seen him. While he wanted to think the visit had nothing to do with Houdini, his instincts and the sour look on Mills' face told him otherwise. Jerry looked over his shoulder and whispered to April, "It's Mr. Mills. Call Houdini in the other room and keep him there unless I call for you."

April called Houdini. Eager to be released from the sit, he jumped up and ran out of the room.

Paying no attention to Houdini's departure, Gunter remained plastered to Jerry's side.

Jerry took his time opening the door, keeping his body positioned so the man couldn't see inside. He kept his voice even. "Mr. Mills, how can I help you?"

The man leveled a look at him. "That you're not inviting me in tells me you already know why I'm here. I'm missing a puppy. Furthermore, it has come to my attention that you have one that looks just like the one that went missing. What I don't understand is why. I already agreed to sell it to Ms. Buchanan. To have her come and steal the dog from under my nose just doesn't make sense. And then she had to go and lie about it. She's a good actress, that one. Nearly had me fooled with all that concern when I told her the pup was missing. Next thing I hear, she has a puppy the same color and size as the one that went missing. I don't know why, but my wife told me I have to give her the benefit of the doubt. So here I am to find out the why of it so I can decide if I am going to call the police."

That Mills hadn't already called the police spoke volumes in letting Jerry know he might be able to convince him not to. Jerry reached and unlocked the screen door, then stepped aside to allow the man entry. Mills sniffed the air as he entered and scanned the room, obviously looking for signs of the dog. While Jerry knew Mills had not heard Gunter's ghostly barks, he had no doubt he had heard the barks of Gunter's pup, who was looking and sounding more and more like his phantom father each day.

Mills started for the kitchen, then curved his path and continued to the living room, where he plopped into a chair with a heavy sigh. Once in the chair, he looked over his shoulder. "April's in there with the pup, right?"

Jerry nodded.

"Might as well come on out! Bring the pup so as I can see he's okay," Mills yelled from the comfort of the chair.

Jerry looked to the kitchen where April was squatting, petting Houdini, and nodded for her to come.

April released the pup's collar. Instead of bolting into the room, he waited and walked by April's side.

Mills removed his hat and leaned forward in the chair, eyeing the pup. "Yep, that's him alright. Come here, boy." Mills slapped his leg, encouraging the dog.

Houdini leaned forward but didn't move from April's side. As if to ensure he wouldn't reconsider, Gunter stepped in front of the pup, blocking the way.

Mills' face remained unreadable as he leaned back in the chair. Finally, he looked up and locked eyes with Jerry. "I liked you from the moment I met you. When you asked me to have your back when that gangster-looking chap came to town, it was invigorating. Until then, I'd spent the better part of the year as my wife's caregiver. But not that day. No sir, that day, as I sat holding that pistol under that newspaper, I felt like a real man again. That's why when Ms. Buchannan here asked me to sell her one of the pups, I agreed." Mills looked over at April. "If money was a problem, we could have worked something out, but to have you take him from me, that's just wrong."

"My fiancée is not a thief," Jerry said, holding Mills' gaze. "She didn't know anything about the pup's whereabouts until I brought him here. Before you jump to conclusions, I didn't steal him, and you were paid a nice sum for him." Jerry glanced at April and saw a pink tinge covering her cheeks. She blushed deeper and turned away. *She has to be mortified that the town thinks she's a thief.*

"What do you mean you brought him? My memory isn't the greatest, but I don't recall you ever coming to my house and handing me a check," Mills fumed.

Jerry took a seat on the sofa across from Mills. "Did you not recently come into a nice little inheritance from an uncle you never knew existed?"

Mills blinked his surprise. "I did, but I didn't tell anyone about it, not even my wife."

"Why not?" Jerry asked firmly.

"It was just like you said. The uncle never existed. I have my family traced back to Ellis Island, and that guy isn't anywhere on that list."

Jerry smiled for the first time since Mills entered the house. "I'm guessing that didn't stop you from cashing the check."

Mills shook his head. "It did not. I didn't spend

it, though. I put it into a separate savings account to let it grow interest until the rightful owner comes to collect it."

"You are the rightful owner, Mr. Mills. That money was given to you in payment for the puppy."

Mills looked at Jerry and scratched his head. "I know you are mixed up with some bad people. Did they steal the dog? Is that the reason for the cloak and dagger?"

Jerry so wanted to tell him "yes," as it would make for an easy out, but he couldn't bring himself to lie to the man. Instead, he drummed his fingers on the arm of the couch, trying to get a read on the man. Everything in his gut told him Mills could be trusted. "Mr. Mills, before I answer your questions, would you mind if I ask you a couple of my own?"

Mills looked from Jerry to April and shrugged. "I guess that would be okay."

April slid onto the couch beside Jerry and motioned Houdini into a down position. Jerry glanced at her, saw that her color had returned to normal, and relaxed. He leaned back and placed his hand on her knee as he spoke. "How did Lady get pregnant?"

Mills laughed. "Son, if you don't know how that works, you have bigger problems than I thought."

Jerry smiled. "I know how it works. What I'm asking is did you breed her?"

Mills stiffened. "Of course I did. What do you

think, it was immaculate conception?"

The man was lying; he could feel it. "She was in heat when you were here. That's why you were keeping her in the camper."

Mills shifted in his seat. "That's right. You don't know what kind of mutts are lurking around a campground. I wanted to keep her inside until I could get her to her stud."

"I'm not buying your story, Mr. Mills. Your wife was ill. Correct me if I'm wrong, but I believe it was cancer. And because of that, you decided not to breed Lady. You said it yourself: you were spending all your time caring for your wife, who I believe is now in remission."

Mills' mouth dropped open. "How'd you know that? We just got the word yesterday."

Jerry smiled. "I know for the same reason I know you are lying about breeding your dog."

"Jerry is psychic," April offered. "He knows things that other people don't."

Mills' face paled.

Jerry leaned forward and intertwined his fingers. "How many puppies did Lady have?"

"Two." The word came out in a whisper.

"Two very special pups. Or am I wrong?"

Mills shook his head. "No, you're not wrong."

"So special that you'd already decided to keep both pups before this one disappeared. You were going to make up a story as to why April couldn't have him. Tell me I'm lying," Jerry said coolly. It was a guess, but one that felt right.

Mills swallowed. "So you know the puppy is… what is he? My wife thinks he's some kind of shapeshifter or something."

Don't say it, McNeal. "Mr. Mills, the puppies are half ghost."

Mills laughed a nervous laugh. "How do you figure?"

"Because I can see spirits. I saw one in the camper that day and later saw the dogs in the act."

Understanding washed over the man's face. "You mean that's why you concocted all that pseudo K-9 arousal nonsense? My vet about laughed me out of the office when I mentioned it – said someone had fed me a line of baloney."

Jerry shrugged. "Sorry about that. It was the best I could come up with at the time." He decided not to mention the fact that Gunter was attached to him.

"Okay, I get that you're saying the puppies are ghosts."

"Half," Jerry corrected.

"Okay, half ghosts. But that don't tell me how you knew about them or how you ended up with him."

Jerry searched his mind for an answer. "The puppy came to me." Okay, it was mostly the truth – he'd just left off the part about Gunter being the father and bringing the puppy to him and nearly giving his mother a heart attack.

Mills sat back in his chair and linked his fingers together, tapping his thumbs. "Why you?"

"Because he knew I could understand him." Jerry resisted the urge to laugh. The real reason the puppy existed was because his ghostly K-9 companion was a horn dog. Though she hadn't admitted it, he now felt his grandmother had a hand in the puppy coming to him, especially since Mills hadn't denied changing his mind about April and Max getting one. "Ghost dogs are a special breed, Mr. Mills. They need a handler who understands that."

"His brother has been a handful. That's for sure. But I can handle him. I've raised German shepherds all my life."

Jerry locked eyes with the man. "Have you told anyone about the puppies?"

"No. My wife told me not to. I thought maybe we could get a lot of money for the pups, but then Edith told me not to tell anyone. She was afraid people would think us crazy."

"What are you planning to do with the pup?"

"Elroy? Why, we aim to keep him." Mills shrugged. "We've both become rather attached to him."

That was what Jerry wanted to hear. Now to scare the man into keeping his mouth shut. "Mr. Mills, if you want to keep him, then you have to make sure no one knows what he is. Anyone on the street must think he's a normal German shepherd. There are bad people in the world who would want him only for testing."

Mills nodded his understanding. "Like that kid in that Stephen King movie."

Firestarter. "That's right. Oh, they'd tell you that isn't the case, but in the end, they would use him for science experiments. Reporters would hound you and you would never get a moment's rest. That would endanger your wife's health, wouldn't it? Especially knowing the pup was being subjected to God-knows-what in the name of science."

Gunter growled. Jerry resisted looking at the dog.

Mills frowned. "Why Lady?"

"Excuse me?"

"Why did that ghost dog pick my Lady to do his thing with?"

Because she was in season and Gunter took advantage of the situation. Think, McNeal, you can't tell the man that. Jerry looked at April, hoping for some words of wisdom. He was met by a shrug. He turned his attention back to Mills. "Maybe it was because of me."

"You?" The word came out in a whisper.

"Think about it. Why else would the puppy have come to me? Maybe I was meant to have it all along. The ghost dog knew that and waited until I was around you before making his move." *Crap, McNeal, you really think he's going to fall for that?*

Mills nodded once more. "I guess that makes as much sense as anything else."

Wow, McNeal, you missed your calling. You'd make an excellent used car salesman. "So you're okay with us keeping Houdini?"

Mills laughed. "Why not? You've already paid handsomely for him. I do get to keep the money, yes?"

"You can keep it and spend it in good health, especially now that your wife is healthy enough to help you spend it. I just want you to promise me one thing."

Mills raised an eyebrow. "If I can."

"You need to head off whoever told you about April having the pup. Tell them you came to see for yourself and it wasn't the same puppy. If anyone else knows Lady had two pups, tell them the story you told April about the pup. Play up the fact that a hawk must have swooped down and carried him away. No one is to ever know otherwise. And promise me that if you ever find that you can't care for Elroy, you will reach out to either April or me. We will pay the same as what you got in your inheritance and see he is well taken care of."

"I can agree to that. But don't look for it to happen. As I said, the wife and I are pretty attached to him." Mills started to get up then reconsidered. "I was thinking. Maybe instead of a ghost, our Elroy is an angel. I say that on account of my Edith didn't start getting better until after the puppies arrived. The doctors didn't hold out any hope. The next thing we knew, her numbers were getting better. Now she's in full remission." He looked at Jerry as if hoping for validation. "What do you think, Mr. McNeal? Do you think he could have been sent here to help save her?"

Jerry smiled at the man. "Mr. Mills, that makes more sense than any reason I could come up with." Better an angel than products of Gunter's rendezvous.

"Then if anyone asks about Elroy, I will just tell him he is an angel sent from heaven. I hear people saying that all the time, but I don't think they mean it in the literal form. People will just think I'm one of those guys. They don't have to know he's the real deal."

"I think that is perfect," Jerry agreed.

"So do I." April sniffed.

"I guess I won't be taking up any more of your time." Mills pushed from the couch, started for the door and paused. "You know, I came here looking for a fight. What I got was the answer to my prayers. I thank you for that, Mr. McNeal."

Jerry reached and shook the man's hand. "Glad I could help, Mr. Mills." Jerry waited until the man left and locked the door behind him. He turned to tell

April that he thought the visit went much better than expected when he saw the bewildered look on her face. "April, are you alright? You look a bit odd."

"You're the mind reader. You tell me."

He started to remind her he wasn't a mind reader but thought better of it. If this was one of those woman things his buddies had warned him about, he didn't want to stir the pot. "I'm afraid you're going to have to give me more than that."

She stood her ground. "I was just wondering when you proposed to me?"

Jerry searched his mind for an answer and drew a blank. *Tread carefully, McNeal. You are getting ready to go out on the road. If you don't choose your words carefully, you might not have a home to come back to.* "April, did I do or say something wrong?"

April's mouth twitched ever so slightly. "Only if you didn't mean it. I mean, it is a small town. Mr. Mills obviously heard about Houdini being here from someone, so word is sure to get out."

Jerry swallowed. "Word? What word?"

April smiled the slightest of smiles. "When you were talking to Mr. Mills, you called me your fiancée. I need to know if I need to deflect the rumors. I would much rather tell everyone that Mr. Mills heard incorrectly than later have to explain why we broke up."

Jerry ran his hand over the back of his neck. "We are living together and are talking about building a house together. I just assumed that meant we would be getting married. We had this conversation. You said you saw us being together. Was I wrong?"

April's smile widened. "No, you're not wrong, but a girl still likes to be asked. You know, so I can fuss at you in the future about your missing the anniversary of the day you proposed to me."

Jerry blinked his surprise. "You mean that's a thing?"

April winked. "Depends on what kind of mood I'm in."

Chapter Fifteen

As Jerry traveled up the lakeshore, he called longtime friend and former boss Sergeant Brian Seltzer of the Pennsylvania State Police Department to tell him of his conversation with April.

"So, did you ask her?" Seltzer asked when Jerry finished relaying the story.

"Not yet."

"But you intend to?"

"Absolutely."

Seltzer chuckled. "Son, I don't want to tell you how to run your life, but are you sure that was the right play? Are you sure you have a home to return to?"

Jerry smiled. The man was like a father to him and always offered fatherly advice. "Things are good at home. I could have asked her right there and then, but it just didn't feel right."

"Can I ask why not?"

"Because she was expecting it and I haven't bought her a ring."

"Yeah, I think women expect that sort of thing. You going to get down on one knee?"

"I have over thirteen hundred miles to figure that out. Double that if you include the return trip."

"Sounds like a doozy of a trip. Where are you heading."

"Deadwood."

"Lucky man. I've been there. Make sure to stop at Wall Drug on the way."

"You want me to stop at a drug store?"

"Not a drug store, *the* drug store, and one of the most visited tourist attractions in the badlands."

"I'll google it and get directions to see if it's on the way."

Seltzer laughed again. "Don't bother. If you're driving to Deadwood, it's on the way. Don't worry about directions either. You'll see the billboards long before you get there."

"Must be some place," Jerry replied.

"You can count on it. What's got you running out to Deadwood?"

"The agency's sending me out to see if a fellow is off his rocker or if he saw a ghost."

Seltzer's chair creaked. Jerry could picture the man leaning back, his white hair standing out against his black leather chair. "Must be a pretty important fellow."

"So important, I was given the name Mr. X."

"Good to know they trust you."

Jerry grinned at the dash. Seltzer had always been leery of him working for Fred. Mostly because the agency was so locked down, he couldn't find anything about it, and partly because the man was a tad jealous of Jerry's newfound friendship with his new boss. Jerry winked at Gunter and grinned at the dash. "They trust me to do my job without needing to know every single detail, just like someone else I once worked for."

Seltzer's chair creaked once more. Jerry knew the man now was reaching for a piece of chewing gum. "You're not taking April and Max with you?"

"Thought about it, but Max would've had to miss school."

"I thought you said the agency has offered tutors to help with homeschooling."

"They have. We haven't taken advantage of the offer yet. April and I have discussed it at length and think it is best to keep Max's life as normal as possible."

"Max is a forensic sketch artist who makes more money a year than I could ever dream of. She's thirteen and sees and talks to ghosts. I am not sure most people would consider that a normal life."

"I didn't say normal. I said as normal as possible." Jerry sighed. "Listen, you're preaching to the choir. I know how mean kids can be and how difficult it is to live with this gift, but also know Max has something I didn't."

"Which is?"

"She's surrounded by people who believe in her. She also has people – both living and dead – who have taken her under their wing and are training her how to use and understand her gift."

"Dead?"

"My grandmother has taken her under her wing."

"That is some life you lead, McNeal."

Jerry thought of his family and smiled. "Yep. I'm a pretty lucky guy."

"Huh."

"Huh, what?"

"You actually sounded like you believe it."

"That's because I do."

"I still think you should've taken them along."

"You've known me long enough to know I work better alone. It's hard to pick up on things when I have people blocking the energy. Besides, I plan on pushing hard to get there."

"I hear ya. Don't want bladders to slow you down." Another chair creak. "Then again, it could be just because you're too used to being a lone wolf."

Jerry reached over and roughed Gunter's fur. "We both know my lone wolf days are long over."

"Because of the dog or the new family commitment?"

"Both. And it's 'dogs' now, remember?"

"Like I could ever forget that one. Any new development with Casper and friends?"

"Gunter is fine. He's riding shotgun. Houdini is home with the girls."

"They going to be able to handle him?"

"Oh, yeah. Houdini likes me but seems to know his job is to watch after Max and April. His training is going well, but he is still a puppy who likes to do puppy things. As long as they can keep him from walking through doors or eating shoes, they should be good."

"Did you ever find out if there were any more of those hybrids out there?" Seltzer asked.

Jerry slid a glance toward Gunter. "Knowing my partner, I'd place money on it, but I don't count on ever finding them. Houdini is the only one from this litter. Odd that there'd only be one puppy, but maybe it's just because of the breeding. I recall you telling me that there were only two in Gunter's litter." While Jerry trusted Seltzer with the knowledge, he didn't know who else was listening in on their conversation and hoped he'd gotten his message across.

"Baffles the mind how those things work," Seltzer replied without missing a beat. "How's the new ride? Bet it has a killer sound system."

Jerry smiled. Seltzer had not only picked up on his veiled message about there being two puppies, but he'd also answered in a way so as to let Jerry know he understood the need for secrecy. "The ride is fantastic. I might break down and read the manual they gave me at some point so I know how to work all the bells and whistles."

"I'm sure you'll have fun figuring them out."

"You can count on it." Jerry saw a man standing on the side of the road with his thumb out a short distance ahead. The second he saw him, the hairs on the back of his neck stood on end. "Hey, I'm going to let you go for now."

"Okay, son. You need anything – even someone to talk to so you stay awake – give me a call."

"Will do." Jerry ended the call and slowed. Only then did he realize the man had long left this world. Jerry eased up beside the man and lowered his window. "Need a lift?"

The spirit peeked in the window, shook his head, and promptly disappeared.

He looked at Gunter. "Think he was afraid of you or me?"

Gunter lifted his lips and smiled a K-9 smile.

Once on the interstate, Jerry was able to put some miles behind him. He'd seen the ghostly hitchhiker several more times, but each time, he'd been in the left passing lane with too much traffic to make his way over. He stopped at a gas station in Adrian, Minnesota, thinking of gassing up and getting back on the road, then realized he was too tired to continue.

He texted April to let her know he'd call in a bit and went inside. He took care of business, then grabbed a couple of bottles of water and headed to the checkout. The cashier appeared to be in her early forties and seemed to have no knowledge of the dark-haired gentleman whose spirit lingered next to her behind the counter.

While the woman looked to be in good spirits, the same could not be said for the apparition whose worried scowl watched Jerry like a hawk. Jerry slid a look to Gunter, wondering if the spirit was unhappy about the ghostly K-9's presence.

The cashier – whose nametag read Debbie – looked up as he approached and greeted him with a broad smile. "Honey, I hope you aren't planning on getting back on the road without some coffee. You look like you're about to drop."

"Nah, I thought I'd let my dog drive while I get some sleep," Jerry replied, looking at Gunter and wondering about the possibility.

Gunter looked at him as if to judge his sincerity, then yawned a squeaky yawn.

Debbie laughed. "I don't know what kind of dog you have, but he's probably a better driver than some I've seen. That'll be $3.72, sugar."

Jerry handed her some ones and returned the change to his wallet as she bagged his items. He'd originally thought to get back on the interstate and look for a hotel to spend the night, but the hairs on the back of his neck told him he should hang around for a bit. "Actually, I think I'll get a few winks in the parking lot if that's okay."

"Fine by me, darlin'."

Jerry thanked her and looked at the apparition, who now paced the area behind the counter as if waiting for something to happen. Jerry started to tell the woman he'd be outside if she needed him, then thought better of it. A comment like that could be taken the wrong way. He thanked her as he picked up his bag and gave the spirit a long look before heading outside. He drove the Durango to the far edge of the lot and backed into a parking space with the front of the Durango facing the building. He got out and leaned against the driver side door as Gunter went on a walkabout with his nose lowered to the pavement.

Jerry took out his phone, found April's number and pressed dial.

"I miss your voice," she purred into the phone.

Jerry smiled. "We talked the whole way across Illinois."

"And your point is?"

He laughed. "No point. It's late. You need to go to bed."

"I tried. I can't sleep without you here. It's crazy how quick I got used to someone sharing my bed."

"I miss you too."

"Are you stopped for the night?"

So that was it. She was worried about him staying awake. "Yep."

"Is your room nice?"

"I'm not getting a room. I'm going to sleep in the Durango."

"You have an unlimited travel budget, you know."

"I know," Jerry said, watching the spirit, who was now fully visible and staring out the window at him.

"Are you going to try out the tent?"

The tent April spoke of was a custom addition made to the back of the Durango, which turned the vehicle into a sleeping room. "No, I'm spending the night in a gas station parking lot. While they won't mind me sleeping in the back for a few hours, I doubt they would be happy with my turning the parking lot into my own personal campground."

"You're probably right. I'm glad you are staying at the gas station. It's probably safer than sleeping in a rest area."

"Maybe." He chose not to tell April that the apparition shadowing the woman inside the station seemed to think otherwise. "Listen, I'm good. It's late, and we both need to get some sleep. Double-check the doors and go to bed."

"Double check the doors? Are you getting a hit on something?"

Jerry chuckled. "Just because I'm psychic doesn't mean everything's a premonition. I'm not feeling anything but bone tired." Okay, it wasn't totally the case, but if he told her his inner radar was humming like an electrical cable, she would not willingly hang up the phone. He was just glad Max was already in bed, as she would know he was lying and call him on it. That she hadn't already called to warn him of something was a good sign, as it meant he himself wasn't in any danger.

"Okay, Jerry. I love you."

"I love you too, Ladybug." Jerry disconnected the call before she could say anything to draw him back into the conversation. While he enjoyed talking to her every moment he could, he hadn't been lying about being bone tired. If something was going down here tonight, he wanted to be refreshed enough to react. Besides, there was no reason for him to stay awake and keep the place under surveillance, as his ghostly K-9 partner had proven himself more than capable of watching his back. Having been killed in the line of duty in the prime of his life, the dog reappeared shortly after his death and attached himself to Jerry. Why Gunter chose Jerry instead of his former human partner had mystified him at first, but Jerry – who'd never owned a dog – had quickly come to enjoy the dog's company and count on his new partner's ghostly presence to help solve crimes and protect him from other unearthly threats. He'd later discovered his granny had had a hand in Gunter's earthly appearance – sending the dog to act as a barrier between Jerry and any spirits who might wish to cause him harm.

Jerry whistled.

Gunter instantly appeared at his side.

"I need to get some shuteye. You've got the watch."

Gunter disappeared and reappeared a second later wearing his K-9 police vest, something the dog often did to show he took his mission seriously. The appearance of the vest was also a cue that the K-9 felt trouble brewing.

Jerry scanned the parking lot for any sign of a threat. Not seeing anything, he unlocked the door and climbed into the back of the SUV. While the driver's seat reclined fully, he'd spent enough time in the chair for the time being. Gunter climbed inside after him. Jerry pushed the button to lower the back hatch as Gunter made his way into the passenger seat to keep watch.

Jerry rooted for the pillow, closing his eyes as he stuffed it under his head. Even though the car was parked and his eyes closed, he could still see the road passing in front of his eyes – something that often happened after driving for a long time. He did several deep breathing exercises and felt his body twitch as he began to relax. Finally, sleep came to claim him.

***

Jerry woke knowing something was very wrong. He opened his eyes to see a man hovering over him with a long-barreled pistol.

Jerry kept his eyes trained on the man. *Gunter, where are you?*

The man's lips parted, exposing rotten teeth, something made overly apparent by the putrid smell of the man's breath. The man's brow knitted as he looked Jerry over. "You're dressed a bit odd, but I know it's you. I knowed it the moment I set eyes on you."

Jerry struggled to keep his voice calm. "I don't know who you think I am, but I assure you we have never met."

The man laughed a cackling laugh. "Not since the last time. Only this time, I have the upper hand, and it will be you who gets strung up."

Strung up? What's that supposed to mean? Where the heck is Gunter? He's supposed to have my six. He's also supposed to be watching the gas station. Maybe something happened to call him away. Think, McNeal. How can I think with the man stinking the place up? Whatever the smell was seemed to be radiating from his pores. "When's the last time you took a bath?"

"None of your concern. Now get up. We're going."

Jerry knew better than to go anywhere with the

man. Best to be killed in the parking lot and have them find his body than be taken off somewhere, tortured, and left to rot in a shallow grave. At least this way, April and the rest would know what happened to him. Still, if he could pretend to cooperate, maybe he could make a grab for the emergency button. While there were multiple safety features installed in Jerry's equivalent of the Batmobile, the emergency button was the one feature he never thought he'd need. He'd been given instructions to only use it when he had no other option, as it would send a distress signal to every agency in the area. He'd only had the souped-up ride for a handful of months and had already used it once. While he didn't like abusing the thing, at the moment, he couldn't think of another alternative. "Back up so I can get up."

"I'll back up, but you'd better not start any funny business," the man sneered. As he moved back, the smell surrounding him intensified.

Jerry gagged and pulled himself to his knees.

"What in the devil is that smell?"

Jerry snapped his head up to look at the man. "What do you mean what's that smell? It's you."

"Are you saying I stink?"

The sound of a siren filled the air. Jerry wondered who'd called the police. "I'm saying you smell like you've been dead for a hundred years." The words had no sooner left his mouth than the man shot him.

Someone screamed.

Gunter's barks filled the air and Jerry realized it was the dog's barks, not sirens that he'd heard.

It was a dream. Jerry sat up, gathering his wits. The man, yes, but not the gunshot that woke him. Jerry grabbed his pistol and leaned forward, pushing the button near the rearview mirror, which connected him directly to the agency.

"How can we help you, McNeal?"

"Shots fired at my location. No further details. I'm heading in."

"Roger that."

Jerry exited his vehicle, pistol in hand, surveying the parking lot. With the exception of his Durango and two other vehicles, the lot was empty. Since one of the cars was there when he first stopped, he thought it safe to assume the second belonged to the shooter. He memorized the Illinois plate as he headed for the building.

The apparition appeared in the window, frantically waving him inside. Believing the spirit wouldn't call him in if the threat was still present, Jerry picked up his pace, holding back just long enough for Gunter to enter first. The K-9 stopped just inside the door, blocking Jerry's way as they both took in the scene.

A young kid who looked barely old enough to drive was on his knees in front of the checkout counter while Debbie stood behind it with a pistol aimed directly at the boy. She was shaking as tears trailed down her cheeks. "He has a gun. He tried to rob me, but I shot him first."

The spirit stood between them as if he thought his ghostly presence would protect them. The question was whether he was trying to protect the boy from further injury or the shooter from doing something she would have to live with for the rest of her life.

Jerry concentrated on Gunter, willing the dog to hear him. *Don't let her take the shot.*

Gunter gave the other entity a wide berth and disappeared behind the counter.

Though the kid's arm was bleeding, he didn't look in danger of dying anytime soon. The boy looked at Jerry. "She's lying. I ain't got no gun."

Jerry kept his pistol aimed toward the kid and spoke to the clerk. "I've got him covered, Debbie. You can put your gun down now."

Debbie held fast. "No. I'm telling you he has a gun."

The apparition nodded his agreement.

"It's okay. I've got him covered. He moves a muscle, I'll take him out, but there is no sense both of you going to jail."

"I won't go to jail if I shoot him. He threatened me first."

"You will if you take the next shot." While a

223

good lawyer might successfully argue that point in court, Jerry was dealing in the here and now and didn't have the luxury of debating with someone who appeared to be in shock. He needed to get the situation under control before the police arrived and their mere presence escalated the situation. "Put down your weapon so I can take care of the kid without worrying about you accidentally shooting me."

Debbie started to put the gun on the counter, then reconsidered and placed it on the counter behind her.

"Good. Now move down to the end so I don't have to worry about you."

As soon as she moved out of reach of the gun, Gunter made his way to the kid – teeth bared while standing so close to him that the boy had to feel something from the energy the K-9 was throwing. Knowing Gunter would do whatever it took to keep him safe, Jerry moved in to check the boy for weapons. He found a gun hidden between the boy's legs within easy grasp had he wanted to do the cashier harm. Jerry kicked the gun away, placed his own pistol in the back of his pants, then pulled the boy to his feet, checking him for other weapons, of which he found none. "You want me to take a look at your arm?"

"You a doctor?"

"Nope."

"Then why would I let you look at my arm?"

"Fine, have it your way. Sit with your back against that counter." Jerry waited until the kid was settled and kicked the pistol further from the boy's reach.

Gunter stepped up close to the kid and dipped into a bow. As he did, a rather unpleasant smell that Jerry recognized from his earlier dream filled the air.

The kid scrunched up his nose. "What the heck is that smell?"

Jerry stared at Gunter accusingly. *It wasn't the guy in my dream who smelled. It was you.*

Gunter lifted his top lip, showing a K-9 smile as the first police car rolled onto the lot.

Jerry's phone rang, showing Fred's number. Jerry answered it. "Yeah."

"Police are on the scene. I told them to hold clear until I cleared it with you."

"Send 'em in. The situation is under control." Jerry had no sooner given the word than the patrolmen entered the building and pulled the boy to his feet.

Jerry moved aside as one of the officers led the boy to the ambulance, which had just pulled into the lot.

"Only you, McNeal." Fred laughed into the phone. "You spend the entire day driving across the country and end up picking the one gas station on your route where there is going to be trouble."

Jerry watched as the apparition followed the boy

and officer from the building and sighed. "Yep. I seem to be lucky that way. Listen, I didn't get much sleep. I'd appreciate it if you could make a call and do that thing you do so I can get on my way."

"Consider it done," Fred replied, then ended the call.

Knowing there wouldn't be any chance of getting any more shuteye, Jerry walked to the coffee center and poured himself a cup. He looked for Debbie and saw her speaking with one of the officers. She looked up, saw him staring at her and smiled. There'd been a time when Jerry had questioned the purpose of his gift. But not this time, for he knew that if not for him being at the right place at the right time, two lives would have been destroyed.

He smiled at Gunter. *Good job, partner.*

Gunter lifted his head, emitting a single howl that only Jerry could hear.

Chapter Sixteen

The instant Jerry saw Max's number light up the dash, he knew that she knew something had happened. He pressed to answer the call. "I'm alright, Max."

"I know."

Jerry started at the dash. "You do?"

"Yep. Granny told me."

That he hadn't seen his grandmother's spirit while at the gas station didn't matter. He knew she was always near. "Good. Then you know I wasn't really involved in anything dangerous."

Max giggled. "Meaning you don't want me to tell Mom because she'll worry."

"You're one smart kid, Max." Jerry smiled. Smart enough to help him with his current dilemma. "Hey, did your mom happen to say anything about what she and I talked about before I left?"

"You mean about you not asking her to marry

you?"

Crap, Seltzer was right. "Is she upset that I didn't ask?"

"She was a little, but Carrie told her she could tell that you loved her and that you were probably waiting until the right time."

"Carrie's a smart lady too. She's right. Plus, I want to get your mom an engagement ring."

"Size six. Mom said to tell you nothing too gaudy. She said it's okay if they can see it across the room, but she doesn't want to blind the neighbors when she's outside doing yardwork."

Jerry laughed. "The two of you talked about it, did you?"

"She knew you would ask me what size you should get, so she wanted to make sure I had all the details."

"I guess I can add your mom to the smart lady list. Hey, have you ever heard of a place called Wall Drug Store?" Jerry asked as he took the exit to what looked to be a major tourist trap.

"Sure, I have. A couple of the kids in my class have been there. They had pictures of them sitting on a jackalope. That's a cross between a jackrabbit and an antelope."

"I'll have to look for it and get a picture for you."

"You're there? Lucky!"

Jerry shook off the pang of guilt. "Sure am. They also have an eighty-foot dinosaur," he said as he passed the green beast. "Listen, I'm going to let you go for now, but I promise to pick you up a souvenir. And I want it to be a surprise, so no getting inside my head to find out what it is."

"Okay, Jerry, love you. You too, Gunter."

"We love you too, kiddo." Jerry disconnected the call and followed the traffic through the already-packed streets. He saw backup lights and slowed, considering himself lucky to have found a spot right in front of the main building, which boasted a green sign with large yellow lettering saying the store had been in business since 1931.

As Jerry entered the building, he was met with the aroma of fresh donuts. He smiled as Gunter walked through the room sniffing the air. *Bide your time, dog. I'll grab us some before we leave. First, let's see what the rest of the place has to offer.*

Jerry soon came to realize the place was a massive indoor maze where the rooms led into each other. Once he finished walking the store, he walked through the hall, weaving in and around the crowd dipping into one specialty shop after another. Each time he turned, he saw something that reminded him of Max or April and soon accumulated so many small bags, he felt like a kid in a candy store with an endless supply of quarters.

Jerry saw the Hole in the Wall bookstore. The name alone made him want to go inside. He walked the aisles studying the selection on the shelves until he saw a book that caught his eye. Blue with a German shepherd on the cover with the title *Always Faithful*, it reminded him of his time in the Marines. Deciding to let Max and April flip a coin to see who got to read it first, he paid for the novella and stuffed it into the bags with the rest of his purchases.

Gunter followed as he went to see what else the building had in store.

The instant he walked inside the hat store and saw the assortment of cowboy hats, an image of the man he'd seen hitchhiking came to mind. Something about the guy's white hat felt familiar.

Jerry picked one out, tried it on for size, then replaced it and picked out a black hat that felt more his style. He looked in the mirror and realized how grungy he looked. He'd not cut his hair since leaving the Pennsylvania state police. Once clean-shaven with a razored scalp, his hair now flowed past his shoulders, and though he shaved his cheeks and kept his beard trimmed, it was thick and looked impressive under the low-slung hat. Having slept in his clothes lent to the authenticity of the look and had him considering purchasing the hat.

"Mister, are you a real cowboy?"

Jerry turned to see a small boy with brilliant red hair and bright green eyes staring up at him. The boy looked around six and appeared to have wandered away from whoever he was with. *The kid's lost.*

Gunter moved forward, sniffing the boy, then

disappeared, presumably in search of the kid's guardian.

The kid repeated his question. "Well, are you a cowboy or not?"

Jerry was just about to tell the boy he was when he saw a woman with matching hair storming toward them with Gunter at her side.

The woman clamped her right hand on the boy's shoulder and used her left to dry her eyes. "There you are. I've been looking for you everywhere. Don't you ever run off like that again. I thought someone had kidnapped you."

"But I wanted to talk to the cowboy," the kid said, pointing at Jerry.

The woman was in no mood for an argument. "He's not a cowboy. He's just a man in a hat."

The boy frowned and dug in his heels. "But he looks like a cowboy."

"No, he doesn't. He's not wearing cowboy boots." The woman grabbed the kid by the hand and led him away without a word to Jerry.

Jerry looked in the mirror and wagged his eyebrows. *I do too look like a cowboy.*

Gunter yawned a squeaky yawn and pawed at Jerry's foot.

Jerry's gaze trailed downward. *Except for the tennis shoes.* Jerry recalled the selection of cowboy boots he'd passed only moments before and smiled.

***

By the time Jerry found the jackalope, he looked and felt the part of a "real" cowboy. He'd opted to wear his new boots and had the saleswoman place his sneakers in the box. He'd also found matching cowgirl hats for April and Max and had the information where they could both order boots if they so chose. Having a couple of hours to spare almost made up for the fact he'd only gotten a couple hours of sleep during the night. He stopped at the statue and snapped a photo while Gunter sniffed the base. He didn't have to worry about the K-9 photo-bombing the picture. The dog was rarely visible in photographs.

"Want a picture of you with it?"

Jerry turned to see the boy's mother. Unlike the last time he'd seen her, she was calm. She smiled, and for the briefest of moments, he thought of his friend Patti, also a redhead, who'd met an untimely death at the hands of a serial killer that targeted redheads. *Take it easy, McNeal. The guy isn't a threat anymore.*

A blush tinged her cheeks. "I'm Kate. I wanted to apologize for my behavior back there. I was worried about my son."

Jerry extended his hand. "Jerry McNeal, and it's completely understandable. Especially with so many people in the area."

"It's my fault. He saw you walk by and wanted to see you. I was busy checking out and didn't realize he'd gone after you. My mother-in-law passed a few months ago, and my husband wanted to get away for a while. Ever since we learned we were coming out west, I've been reading Ethan stories about cowboys to help cheer him up. He was very close to her. He's also very impressionable. I told him you don't look like a cowboy." Kate nodded toward his boots. "I hope my comment didn't make you purchase those."

It did. Jerry shook his head. "Of course not. I came here intending to buy them. I'm heading to Deadwood and needed to complete my look."

Kate studied him briefly. "If it helps, you now look like the real deal."

Jerry laughed. "Thanks."

"Ethan is over there with his dad. After I take your picture, would you mind if he takes one with you?" She winked. "You're the first real cowboy he's seen."

Jerry placed his packages in a pile by the rabbit and handed her his cell phone. "Sure."

Kate frowned at his bags. "Aren't you afraid someone will steal them?"

The bags were six feet away with Gunter sitting next to them as if daring anyone to touch them. "Nope."

"You're a very trusting man, Mr. McNeal. I'm so paranoid, I always think the worst. That's why I got so upset when I couldn't find Ethan."

Jerry looked her in the eye and held her gaze. "That's called the gift of fear. There's nothing wrong with it. You get a gut feeling, you go with it. My granny taught me that, and it has served me well." He nodded toward the bags. "She also taught me how to shop."

Kate laughed and took several photos, including one of the supposedly unattended packages, before handing him back his phone. "In case you want to send your grandmother a picture of your haul."

Jerry started to tell her his granny was dead but decided against doing so since the family seemed to have their own spirit hovering near.

Appearing in the form of a woman in her late sixties, the woman reminded him of Easter, with chin-length pink hair, bright fuchsia lipstick, and blue eyeshadow. The body was plump yet agile as she held her arms out and followed Ethan – the two of which appeared to be pretending to walk a tightrope using the cracks in the pavement to stay on course.

Kate waved at her husband. The man called to Ethan and started toward them with the spirit in tow. Kate smiled at her son and motioned toward Jerry. "Ethan, I was wrong. Mr. McNeal here is a real cowboy. Would you like to have your picture taken with him?"

"Can I sit on the rabbit too?" Ethan climbed up the statue as his dad hurried to help him onto the rabbit's back.

Jerry hid his disappointment. Here he was looking like a wrangler straight out of the Old West, and he'd been upstaged by a giant horned rabbit wearing a saddle. Maybe if he told the kid he could see ghosts…

The spirit sprang forward until she was mere inches from his face. "You mean you can see me?"

Yes, Jerry replied, using his inner voice.

"How come you can see me, and no one else can?"

Just lucky, I guess.

"That's not the reason. Now tell me. I need to know," she persisted.

I'll talk to you when I'm done.

"Why can't you tell me now?"

Because people will think I'm crazy if I start talking to myself.

"Tell them you are not talking to yourself. You're talking to me."

Please give me a couple of moments. Jerry stepped to the side and smiled while posing for a photo with the kid—something he found difficult to do since the spirit was still invading his personal space.

"Okay, now look intimidating." Kate scowled to show him what she expected.

That look proved easier as he glared directly at the spirit, willing her to give him room. That was the thing about spirits: they were quick to believe everything should be about them. Jerry had learned long ago he had to set boundaries. It was bad enough they often invaded his dreams, but it was difficult to appear sane when arguing with someone no one else could see.

"Okay, Champ, time to go," Ethan's dad said, moving in and lowering him from the rabbit. Once down, Ethan made a beeline for the covered wagon on the other side of the courtyard. As his father watched after him, Gunter trotted over to the man and sniffed the guy's groin. Not realizing he was being scrutinized by an invisible entity, the man shoved his hands into his front pockets and adjusted his pants. He saw Jerry watching and blushed. "Thank you, Mr. McNeal. Ethan has had a rough go of it of late."

Jerry willed Gunter to hear. *Gunter, leave it.*

Gunter moved in for one last sniff, then returned to the packages and sat, scratching an imaginary itch.

"Kate told me your mother died. I'm sorry for your loss." Jerry glanced at the spirit and used his mind to speak to her. *Do you want me to give him a message for you?*

"Why on earth would I want to talk to him?" The spirit stuck her index finger in her mouth and then used it to tame the man's eyebrow.

The guy scratched the same area, then strolled

off without comment, heading toward where his son was talking to a little girl who'd just joined him on the front bench of the wagon.

Jerry moved closer to the spirit. *Because it might be the last chance you get to speak to your son. I thought that's why you were here.*

"That's the trouble with the living. They assume since you're haunting a family, you're attached to them."

Jerry looked at Kate, who appeared to be editing the photos she'd just taken. "Did they turn out alright?"

"Most of them. This one's a little blurry, though." Kate held out the phone for him to see.

Jerry looked at the photo in question. The blur Kate was talking about was actually the energy from the spirit, which had been standing between him and Kate. If the photo were to be blown up, someone might be able to see the ghostly apparition. "Yeah, I think that one needs to go."

Kate deleted it. "Oh, well, I think we got some good ones. Thanks again, Mr. McNeal." She pocketed the phone. "Maybe we'll see you in Deadwood."

"Maybe. Safe travels."

"You too, Mr. McNeal." Kate hurried across the courtyard to where her family was waiting.

Jerry turned his back to them and pulled his Bluetooth earpiece from his pocket. Though he never used it for its intended purpose, Fred suggested it could help Jerry look less crazy when talking to those only he could see. He made a show of hanging it on his ear and addressed the spirit. "So why are you haunting them? You are haunting them, aren't you?"

"Of course I am. I needed a vacation."

"You're dead. You're on permanent vacation."

The spirit glared at him. "Now that's just plain spiteful."

"So is haunting a family for no reason."

"Fine, I'll stay with you."

Jerry gave a nod to Gunter, who was now lying beside the packages, soaking up the sun. "I don't think my friend there would like that very much."

The spirit took a step back when Gunter opened one eye and snarled. "That…he's…the dog is with you?"

Jerry smiled. For some reason, other spirits weren't as eager to harass him when they learned Gunter was attached to him. Hopefully, now the spirit would leave him be. "He is."

"You're Jerry McNeal?"

Jerry instantly blocked the spirit from reading his mind and worked to keep his face unreadable. "I am."

She sighed a relieved smile. "Well, color me happy. It must be my lucky day. I thought I would have to go all the way to Deadwood to find you."

Jerry rocked back on his heels. "Are you telling me you were haunting that family to get to me?"

"I wasn't really haunting them. I was just hitching a ride. I haven't mastered the art of … wait, I'm not supposed to talk about that."

Jerry ran a hand through his hair. "Care to tell me what you wanted to talk to me about?"

She shook her head. "I can't."

"You found me. I don't think the spirit code counts when it comes to telling me how I can help you."

She reached into her pocket and pulled out a lace handkerchief, and patted the moisture from her upper lip. "Oh, it's not about the code. I just forgot what I wanted to talk to you about." She laughed. "Don't that just beat all? I was forgetful in life, and it followed me to the great beyond. You'd think I'd have left that all behind. Why, I don't even remember my name."

Something about the ghostly visitor felt off. In his experience, earthly afflictions were just that – things that a person was affected by when they were living. In all his years of speaking with those who'd died, he'd never met a spirit who was weighed down by afflictions that had plagued their human bodies. Even Gunter, who had leapt in front of a bullet intended for his partner, thus ending the dog's life, showed no sign of being in pain. Jerry recalled the time the dog had appeared with all his battle wounds showing during a zombie run where the runners had dressed up. Even though the wounds were visible, the dog showed no sign of being in pain – actually, the opposite seemed true – leaving Jerry to believe the dog did it on purpose to gain attention.

Did that mean the spirit before him was lying about being forgetful? If so, to what end? He wasn't overly worried that she'd heard of him. It wasn't the first time something like that had happened. To her credit, the spirit appeared calm while he took time to process everything.

Then again, it might be because Gunter had rolled onto his back with his legs extending in various directions, letting the sun warm places that generally didn't see daylight. That Gunter didn't appear concerned about the ghostly visitor told Jerry the apparition wasn't a threat.

"Did you figure it out?" she asked after a moment.

Jerry furrowed his brow. "Figure what out?"

"What you're going to do with me? I presume that's why you're stalling."

That she knew him to be stalling was a good sign. At least she wasn't totally befuddled. "I need to be on my way. I have work to do and hadn't planned on being here this long."

She nodded her understanding. "Okay. Let's go."

"No. I'm going. You're going back to wherever you came from until you come up with an answer to why you needed to speak to me."

"How will I find you?"

"Now that you found me once, you should only have to think of me to find me again." Whether it was totally true or not, he hadn't a clue, but it seemed to be the way things worked. "And I think it would be best if you stop hitching rides with strangers. Hitchhiking is dangerous."

She screwed up her face. "You do know nothing can hurt me, right?"

Jerry nodded. "I'm not worried about you. I'm worried about the people you're riding with. The last thing we need is someone figuring out you are there and driving off the road."

"Are you sure I will be able to find you again?"

Jerry smiled. "You found me this time, didn't you?"

"Yes. Yes I did." She lifted a hand, blew him a kiss and promptly disappeared.

Jerry walked to where Gunter lay and began collecting his packages. Gunter took his time getting to his feet, then dipped into a low front stretch and groaned. Jerry laughed. "Come on, old man. I'll buy you a donut."

***

The spirit with the white hat was leaning beside the Durango when they exited the store.

Jerry looked the man over. "Is there something I can help you with?"

"In due time," the man said, speaking with a smooth southern drawl.

Obviously, the man wanted something from him, as he'd seen him many times over the course of the last two days. "Do you need a ride?"

"Nope. You're going the wrong way."

"Which way is the right way?"

"I'll let you know." The spirit tipped his hat and faded away.

Chapter Seventeen

Jerry drove past the turnoff to his hotel, opting to follow the invisible pull instead. Something about seeing the time switch to high noon just as he arrived in Deadwood gave him a chill. *Easy, McNeal, you've been watching too many old westerns.* Only he hadn't, not since he was a kid. And only when he could convince his grandmother to watch something other than *Murder She Wrote* or *The Rockford Files*. Still, as he drove under the arched sign telling him he was entering historic Deadwood, he had an intense feeling of deja vu. Just past the sign, he saw a white building on the right that looked like an old gas station, which now served as a wine-tasting venue. His thoughts went to April and then to Max a second later as he passed an impressive display of chainsaw wood carvings.

The town was busy with people milling about, but not overly so. One thing he hadn't expected was seeing the brick streets lined with motorcycles. He thought of Jonesy and realized he'd yet to check in with the man to let him know he was in town. Jerry made a mental note to call him and invite him out for a beer once he got settled into his hotel.

Jerry wasn't sure what he was looking for, but something was pulling at him. There wasn't anyone behind him, so he drove slowly, watching the road while sneaking curious glances at the brick buildings which lined each side of the street. The structures varied in height and displayed signs for saloons, hotels and casinos.

As he crept along the brick street, the bricks gave way to dirt as horses replaced the bikes. The sound of horses filled the air—lots of horses.

Jerry swallowed, watching helplessly as a stampede of black horses headed directly for him. No, not a stampede, but several horses hooked to a tall wagon.

That's not a wagon. It's a stagecoach!

Having no time to react, Jerry braced for impact as Gunter's woofs echoed throughout the interior of the Durango and shuddered as the ghostly mirage passed right through him. Instantly, motorcycles replaced the horses, and the dirt street was once more covered with brick. Strangely, the brick road now felt more alien than the dirt from his vision. He shook off the feeling of familiarity. How could things feel so familiar when he'd never been here before?

Gunter stood in the seat with his head pushed through the glass of the passenger side window, hind legs quivering. Jerry wondered if it was because of all the new smells or if he, too, now questioned his surroundings.

Jerry reached a hand to the dog's hindquarters. "You doing alright there, dude?"

Gunter pulled his head inside the cab, licking Jerry's hand, staring at him as if asking, *Did that really just happen?*

Jerry ran a hand over his head, torn whether to be happy the dog had experienced the phenomena with him or upset that Gunter seemed just as freaked out as he at the moment.

Gunter jumped across the console, pacing the cargo area as if looking for a threat.

Easy, McNeal, it's not a good idea to let spirits know they've flustered you. Jerry took a calming breath. *First rule of seeing apparitions is never allow the spirits to have the upper hand.*

Granny appeared in the seat Gunter had just vacated. "You just made that up."

A horn blared. Jerry looked in his rearview mirror, saw a yellow jeep, and realized he had his foot on the brake. He eased off the pedal and the Durango moved forward. Jerry spoke to her in excited tones while keeping his eyes on the road, watching for any other ghostly apparitions. "Did you see that? It was a stagecoach! I know it wasn't real, but for a moment… Even Gunter was afraid – that can't be good. I've never seen him get frightened."

Granny reached a hand to his shoulder.

While the deep inhale had not calmed him, his grandmother's ghostly touch instantly eased his anxiety. Jerry rolled his neck. "If I could find a way to bottle your touch, I'd make a fortune."

"Everyone has the touch."

"Meaning?" Jerry turned left, leaving the historic area, and stopped for the red light.

"Just what I said. Everyone is born with a healing energy, but most must be reminded of it."

The light turned green. Jerry made a second left onto the parallel street, which bypassed the historic district and had less foot traffic than the route he'd just traveled. He slid a glance toward his grandmother. "I don't recall you telling me that growing up."

"I didn't know."

"You've told me you aren't supposed to share stuff from the other side."

"No, I said I wouldn't tell you things that could affect your free will to make life-altering decisions. There is a difference."

"Do you know anything about the spirit that reached out to me earlier?"

Granny removed her hand. "You always have spirits around you, Jer. You're going to have to give me a bit more to go on."

"A woman who looked to be in her late sixties with pink hair."

"Oooh, what shade of pink?"

"What do you mean what shade of pink? Are you telling me you know more than one ghost with pink hair?"

"No. I was just curious."

He pictured the woman. "Rose pink. The pale ones – like the old-fashioned rosebush you had near the back fence."

"Oh, that sounds nice." She pulled down the visor.

Still rattled by the stagecoach, Jerry pulled into the visitor center parking lot. "I'm going to take a walk before I head to the hotel. Want to come?"

"No, I have something I need to do." She closed the sun visor and vanished without saying goodbye.

Jerry pulled on his newly purchased cowboy hat and stood feeling the energy. Something was in the air, but nothing like before. Gunter moved to Jerry's side as he crossed the road and made his way to the wood-carving display. He watched the chainsaw carver work on a three-foot bear and wondered if April would like one for the front porch. He admired the guy's handiwork as he passed eagles, Indians and tractors all carved out of logs. He spied a huge yeti over double his height and smiled. Gunter sniffed the base of the beast and started to lift his leg.

While Jerry had never actually seen a stream, he'd seen moisture rings on several occasions.

Don't even think about it, dog.

Gunter turned to look at him as if gauging if Jerry was serious, lowered his leg and moved on, sniffing a bench with a bust of Wild Bill Hickok. The back of the bench was made to look like playing cards, painted with aces and eights, the hand the man was reported to be holding when he was killed. The word DEADWOOD was carved on the upper back of the bench. Jerry used his phone to snap a photo, then sent the photo to both April and Max along with a message that read, *I'm here. I'll call in a few.*

He started toward the heart of town and instantly felt what he'd been searching for: the energy that had soared through him just before the stagecoach appeared. He looked back toward where he had parked the car, then pretended to watch the carver as he debated his next move. He recalled riding his bike after his dad had removed the training wheels. He'd nearly made it to the end of the street before wiping out. He'd wanted to go inside, but his dad insisted he get back on the bike and ride it home. Jerry had been sore at his dad, but to the man's credit, he pulled him aside later and explained that if he'd let the bike win, Jerry might never have had the guts to get back on. It was an age-old adage and one he'd heard a thousand times since, but at the time, he thought his pop to be the smartest dad in the world.

It was one of the few good memories he had of his dad before they'd drifted apart.

Jerry glanced up the street. *Come on, McNeal, it's just like riding your bike.* Only Jerry wasn't hurt, and it wasn't a bike that had unsettled him. It was the ghostly stagecoach and the man with the haunting laugh.

A Marine veteran and former Pennsylvania state patrolman, Jerry was no coward. While the streets of Deadwood looked peaceful and welcoming to those who didn't have the gift, the skin on the back of his neck was crawling, telling him something was lurking nearby.

Gunter must have felt his unease as the ghostly K-9 moved to his left side, acting as his personal escort the moment he stepped onto the brick street.

Jerry was grateful for the dog's presence as he quickly absorbed the anxiety that was threatening to send Jerry running back the way he came. An image of his sergeant came to mind. "I don't know what's got your panties in a bunch, but you need to suck it up, Marine."

Jerry pulled himself taller and walked up the slight incline with a purpose he hadn't felt before. He'd just passed #10 Saloon when the skin on the back of his neck began to crawl once more.

Gunter hesitated.

"I aim to kill you, Marshal!"

Jerry turned to see a man who looked as if he'd

just stepped out of a Wild West magazine standing behind him, his hands hovering over twin sidearms. Jerry looked the man up and down, noting the dust-covered jeans along with the spurs on the back of the man's well-worn boots.

Is this a joke?

Gunter moved in front of Jerry and bared his teeth.

"No joke. Call off your beast. You put a bullet in me once. Now it's my turn to return the favor." The man dipped a hand to his pistol.

Jerry reached for his gun, only to realize he'd left his pistol in the Durango. Just as quickly, it dawned on Jerry that he hadn't actually questioned the man out loud. *He's a ghost.*

A horn blared.

Jerry realized he'd been standing in the middle of the street. He lifted his hand and waved his apologies as he moved aside to let the vehicle pass. When the SUV cleared, the gunman was no longer there. Nor was the feeling of foreboding he'd felt from the moment he'd passed under the sign and began walking up the hill.

Jerry glanced at Gunter. *I think I need some sleep.*

Gunter yawned a squeaky yawn and stayed by Jerry's side as they returned to the Durango and drove the short distance to the hotel.

Jerry had been disappointed when he'd googled

the hotel where Fred had booked him and found out he wouldn't be staying at one of the many hotels located in or near the historic district. Now Jerry was relieved that his hotel was a short seven-minute drive from the heart of Deadwood's nightlife.

As the hotel came into view, showing luxury he hadn't fully appreciated when viewing the place online, Jerry knew why his boss had chosen the place. Fred Jefferies was a man who appreciated the finer things in life and expected those who worked with him to do the same. From its position on the bluff, to the sprawling footprint of the well-appointed craftsman architect, the Lodge at Deadwood lived up to that expectation.

Jerry took a left and smiled as the Hemi engine powered up the incline to the Lodge. He circled the lot before opting for his favored location and backed into a parking space with the rear of the Durango facing the road. He shifted into park, looked to the passenger seat, and felt his eyes bug.

Granny smiled a broad smile and patted her now pink hair. "What do you think?"

Jerry quickly blocked her from reading his thoughts. "It's a different look for you."

"Different good or different bad?" Granny disappeared when the dash lit up, showing an incoming call from Fred.

Jerry pressed to accept the call, welcoming the interruption, as it would give him time to search his brain for a tactful way to tell his grandmother she needed to ditch the pink hair. "Yes."

"Glad to see you made it. How was your trip to Wall Drug?"

That Fred knew he'd taken time to browse the stores didn't come as a shock. The Durango was equipped with many custom features, not the least of which was a surveillance system that allowed the agency to keep constant tabs on his whereabouts, a tool that was instrumental in saving him and others during a recent blizzard. "Interesting place."

"Speaking of interesting places, here's the deal. You're to check in to the Lodge under your real name. You have a reservation for a week, which can be tweaked in any direction needed. Tomorrow, you'll take one overnight bag and check in to the same place where Mr. X stayed while visiting Deadwood. I'll text you the information in the morning."

Jerry frowned at the dash. "So, I'm only staying one night here?"

"No, you'll have a room at the Lodge as long as needed. The other room is only for one night."

"Is not telling me the location part of the need-to-know?"

"Nope. I'm going to e-mail you some of the information about the assignment in the morning. Read it over and see if you get anything. We know what Mr. X said happened. I want to see what you get."

"What if I don't get anything?" Jerry wasn't worried about not finding a ghost. He was worried about finding the wrong ghost, especially since he'd already had a run-in with a ghostly stagecoach and a man who purportedly wanted to kill him. He decided it best not to share either of those details at the moment.

"The agency knows you're not infallible. With that said, I have faith in you, which is the reason I sent you. There are all kinds of so-called ghost hunters in the area. Heck, Deadwood is known for its hauntings. The last thing I want is to have some yahoo stick a blurred photo in front of my face and tell me it's a ghost."

Jerry thought of the blurred photo he'd taken with Ethan in front of the giant rabbit. "Sometimes blurred photos are all you get."

"If that's the case, I'll deal with it. But I'm counting on you coming up with a little more than that."

Gunter barked. Jerry looked in the rearview mirror in time to see the dog disappear. The ghostly K-9 reappeared in the parking lot in front of the Durango, stopped long enough to get Jerry's attention, looked at him as if to say, *Take your time – I have better things to do,* then took off toward the grassy hill.

Jerry glanced at the dash. "How much more?"

"As I mentioned before, the guy in question has his sights set on the Oval Office."

"And you want to make sure the man with his hand on the nuclear button isn't dangerous."

"Actually, Mr. X is the one who initiated contact with the agency. Seems his experience worried him enough to confide in his aide and ask them to reach out to someone who told someone until it reached our office."

Jerry chuckled. "So much for confidentiality."

"That we haven't heard anything on the news lets us know there are no moles in this guy's camp. Something like this were to get out, it would be the lead story on all the networks."

Unless they are saving it for a later date. Not your circus, McNeal. "If this Mr. X is so well known, why didn't anyone recognize him?"

"It's easy to fly under the radar if a person wishes. Check in under a fake name. Wear a hat and blend in. Don't do anything stupid, and you won't draw any attention to yourself."

The skin on the back of Jerry's neck tingled, leaving him to wonder if Fred had witnessed the incidents with the spirits in town. "Why do I feel there is a veiled message in there."

"Was I that obvious?"

"The only thing missing was the megaphone." *I'd better tell him what happened so he doesn't send someone out to investigate me.* Jerry yawned. *After*

I get some sleep.

"Sounds like you could use some sleep."

Jerry stretched and looked out the window, hoping to catch a glimpse of Gunter. "When I was in the Marines, I could go for days with little to no sleep. Between not sleeping last night and the time change, I'm beat. That or maybe I'm getting old."

"That's what married life will do to you."

"I'm not married," Jerry reminded him.

Fred chuckled. "It's only a matter of time."

"I am thinking of asking her when I get back home. We're talking about building a house."

"Going to stay up north?"

"Yep. It's safe up there. While I didn't like the leaving part, I felt confident knowing Max and April would be okay. Besides, they both have friends they care about." Jerry heard an engine gearing down and looked to see a large white tour bus with dark-tinted windows pull into the parking lot. The bus maneuvered its way close to the building. The hiss of the airbrake filled the air. A moment later, the bus's passengers filed from the bus. Jerry sighed. It didn't take psychic powers to know he'd missed his window of opportunity to check in without waiting. Unless the group of senior citizens were returning from a day trip, the front desk would be tied up for at least an hour. "Guess I'm going to have to wait on that sleep. A tour bus just came in."

"What about you?" Fred asked, ignoring his

statement. "Do you like living in Port Hope?"

"I like the laidback feel of the area. You know, I've never been one for crowds."

"And yet, you spent over two hours at Wall Drug."

"Does that bother you? Asking because that is the second time you've brought it up."

Fred chuckled. "That's because I made a bet with Barney." Barney, real name Barnaby Hendershot, was Alfred Jefferies' partner at the agency. Spending most of their careers using their given names, after the two were teamed together, a fellow agent jokingly referred to them as "Fred and Barney," and the names stuck.

"What bet?"

"Our tracking agent mentioned you'd been there for a couple of hours. I told him you were shopping. Barney disagreed – said you'd put your chair back and went to sleep."

Jerry yawned. "Tell Barney he lost."

"You just did," Fred said triumphantly.

"You shop like a chick," Barney grumbled.

Jerry smiled at the dash. "Sorry, dude. You should see me in thrift shops and yard sales. I can barter with the best of them."

Jerry heard Gunter bark and looked to see the dog running down the far hill. Gathering his feet under him, the dog reached out in long strides. Jerry craned his neck and saw Gunter being chased by a larger dog with horns. Jerry blinked. *No, not a dog. A big horned sheep.* Halfway down the hill, Gunter disappeared. Jerry laughed.

"What's so funny?" Fred asked.

"I think Gunter may have messed with the wrong guy." Jerry swiped his phone and snapped a picture of the ram, who'd stopped at the base of the hill and was currently pawing the ground. He sent the photo to Fred.

"Don't tell me Gunter..."

Jerry cut him off. "I don't know what he did to irritate the guy. All I know is the ram appeared to be chasing him down the hill."

"Do you think the ram can see him?"

"He was running the same path and stopped running shortly after Gunter disappeared." Jerry had no sooner finished the sentence than Gunter appeared in the seat beside him. The dog's tongue hung out the side of his mouth, and he looked every bit like a dog who'd just been chased.

"Riddle me this?" Jerry said, looking at the dog.

"Go on," Fred replied.

"How is it ghosts can get out of breath?"

"Okay, I'll bite?"

Jerry frowned at the dash. "No, I was asking you."

"Beats the heck out of me. You're the ghost whisperer."

"Except for the part where I have no clue how

any of this really works."

"You probably shouldn't say that to the man signing your paychecks."

Jerry stifled a yawn. "Feel free to fire me so I can go home and go to bed."

Fred chuckled. "Sorry, no can do. You'll have to rough it out in the Lodge for the next few days."

"Okay, it's your dollar."

"It's a little more than a dollar, but we've been happy with the exchange thus far. Now get some rest. The fate of the nation depends on it."

"Boy, and I thought Gunter was being dramatic. I didn't think the agency took political sides."

"Not taking sides, just leveling the playing field," Fred said sincerely.

"I'll call you when I get something." Jerry ended the call and leveled a look at Gunter. "I don't know what happened on the hill, but I'd better not hear anything about any bighorn sheepdog puppies romping around here after we leave here."

Gunter answered by lifting his top lip and smiling a K-9 smile.

***

While Jerry wanted nothing more than to grab a quick bite and go to bed, he decided he'd be better off pushing through and turning in a bit early to help combat the two-hour time change. He took his bag into the hotel and fell into the long line of senior citizens waiting to check in. Gunter sat and stretched a back leg to scratch his ear.

A man in a blue jacket approached them. "Mr. McNeal?"

Gunter jumped up and began sniffing the man's privates. The guy struggled to keep a straight face as he shifted from foot to foot, not knowing the reason for his sudden unease.

Jerry worked to ignore the display. "Yes."

"Mr. Jefferies has already seen to your registration." The man forced a smile and handed Jerry an envelope with his key. He made a quick adjustment to his pants, then pointed down the hall. "There's a beverage station right over there if you want coffee. We have two restaurants down that way, not too far past John Wayne."

Jerry turned, surprised to see a statue of the famous cowboy actor sitting on the back of a horse. Both man and horse looked to be true to size, leaving Jerry to wonder how he managed to miss seeing the statue when he came in. He decided to give himself the benefit of the doubt that the view of the horse had been blocked by the group of tourists milling about.

The man continued with the brief tour. "Deadwood Grill is a little more upscale with signature cuisine. Oggie's Sports Bar is right next door. You can still get great food. It's just a little more relaxed."

Jerry wondered if the guy gave everyone the

same introduction or if he was getting special treatment since it was rather obvious he hadn't showered since leaving home.

"There is a small gift shop just over there, and the casino is open twenty-four hours. Mr. Jefferies requested we put you on the first floor." The man pivoted in the other direction. He was calmer now, probably because Gunter had bored of the man and had moved on to the line of seniors. "You go down this hall, past the elevators, and take your first left. You're in a courtyard room halfway down the hall on the right."

"Got it. Thanks." Jerry was nearly to the elevator when Gunter appeared and walked at his side the rest of the way. Jerry opened the door to the king business suite, felt the coolness of the air and imagined the crispness of the sheets. It took a great deal of willpower not to climb onto the bed and give himself to sleep. *Not so fast, McNeal. You stink.*

Gunter stuck his head through the door leading to the courtyard and wagged his tail.

Deciding he was too tired to care what had captured the dog's attention, Jerry turned and headed to the shower.

Chapter Eighteen

"Mr. McNeal? Mr. McNeal, wake up! You're having a bad dream."

Jerry opened his eyes to see Granny hovering over him, wringing her hands. He blinked several times to get his bearings. *Not Granny. The spirit from Wall Drug.* "Go away!" Jerry groaned. "Or I'll have my dog bite you."

"I'm not stalking you or anything. I heard you call out and thought maybe you'd rather not be sleeping anymore."

"I don't remember any dreams." He looked at the clock. Two a.m. "Actually, I would prefer to be sleeping."

"It didn't sound that way. It sounded like you were about to get in a gunfight or something. Ya know, I have better things I could be doing than sitting here babysitting you. But no, I saw the way you acted after that fellow called you out on the street. I thought, there's a guy who needs to be looked after. Some thanks I get for that. I'm not sleeping, and yet you don't hear me complaining."

Jerry looked around the dimly lit room for Gunter.

"He's not here. I saw him wandering through the casino. That's why I was watching over you. I thought he was supposed to be protecting you."

So did I. "I don't need a babysitter."

"Oh, it's no trouble. Like I said, I really don't have anything else to do."

Great, just what I need: a spirit with boundary issues.

"Pardon me for caring."

Jerry blocked her from hearing his thoughts. *If she starts crying, I'm done.* "I'm sorry, but I'm okay, so you can leave."

"Are you sure?"

Positive. "Yes, I'm sure. The dog would be here if I was in danger."

"Okay, then. I guess I'll go get some beauty sleep. All these late nights do nothing for my wrinkles."

Jerry started to remind the woman she was dead. Sleep, or lack thereof, would do nothing for her wrinkles. He decided against telling her. She was willing to leave and that was all he was concerned about at the moment. He waved her away. "Take care now."

"You too, Mr. McNeal. Watch out for the foul winds."

Jerry started to ask what she meant by the comment, but she disappeared before he could ask. Gunter appeared in bed beside him. Jerry sighed. "Where have you been?"

Gunter lowered, groaning as he placed his head on Jerry's pillow.

"That's mine." Jerry pulled the pillow from under the dog's head, fluffed it and returned it to the bed, laying his head on top. He rolled over and looked at Gunter. "Those who stay out partying until all hours of the night don't get pillows."

The dog opened his left eye and growled a grumbling growl. A soft poot sounded. A moment later, putrid fumes filled the air.

Jerry pulled the pillow from under his head and turned away from the dog, using the pillow to block the smell. *How is this my life?*

***

April's ringtone filled the air. Jerry opened his eyes, groped for the phone and swiped to answer. "Hello."

"Jerry? You sound awful. Did I wake you?"

"I was just waking up," he lied.

"Rough night?"

"April, I don't know how to tell you this, but I met someone. She kept me up half the night."

"Want me to let you go back to bed?"

He frowned his disappointment. "I tell you that I met someone and you're not even the slightest bit upset?"

She giggled. "I would be if I thought I had something to be upset about."

Max. "Let me guess, Max already filled you in."

"Not on all the details, but she told me there's an old woman haunting you."

It wasn't the first time Max had picked up on something concerning him. "The woman's not that old."

"Really? Max seems to think so."

"Max is thirteen. Anyone over thirty looks old to her."

"So just how old is this woman, and what's she doing in your hotel room in the middle of the night?"

There it was. That tiny bit of reassurance letting him know she'd miss him if he didn't return. "She looks to be in her late sixties and I haven't a clue."

"She didn't say? Is that normal?"

"Nothing about this spirit seems normal." Jerry laughed and rolled over on his back. Have you ever watched *Bewitched*?"

"The television show? I've heard of it but haven't watched it. It was before my time."

Jerry decided not to remind her they were near the same age. "It was before my time too, but Granny liked watching the old shows, so I watched them with her. Anyway, there was a witch on there

– Aunt Clara – who had a heart of gold but was forgetful and always made a mess of things."

"So you think this woman is going to make a mess of things?"

I hope not. "No, but she's rather befuddled. She knows she wants something but doesn't seem to know what that something is."

"So you're saying it was random. No warning, she just showed up in your room?"

"I met her at Wall Drug. She was haunting a family. When I called her on it, she was surprised I could see her. Then she was surprised it was me."

"Why did that surprise her? Did the two of you know each other?"

"No. She said she'd heard of me and knew I would be in Deadwood, so she was coming to find me."

"I don't like it. Something doesn't add up. This has stalker written all over it. Can ghosts be stalkers? Wait, sure they can. Look at what happened to Max." April's voice softened. "Then again, if it wasn't for the spirit haunting her, we never would've met. Oh, my gosh, I'm such a bad mom."

"You're a terrific mom. Why would you even say that?"

"Because I just realized that I'm glad Ashley's spirit was haunting Max."

"That doesn't make you a bad mom. Because of Ashley, Max now has a terrific support group of people who understand her ability and will be able to help her along the way. She could have gone her whole life without finding that."

"I'm glad we both have you."

Jerry gripped the phone a little tighter. "And we're glad we have you and Max."

"I hope that 'we' you're referring to includes Gunter."

"Of course. How's Houdini doing without us there? Any trouble?"

"Nothing other than being afraid I'll trip over him anytime I move. He's been super clingy. The only saving grace is when Max is home, he transfers his attention to her. He also barks at every little sound. We are working on that, though, praising him in soft tones when he's quiet."

"Sounds like you have everything under control."

"We do on this end, but I'm still not on board with the woman visiting your room. Especially claiming she doesn't know what she wants."

Jerry had to admit the story sounded odd, even to him. "It's okay, April. Her spirit is just confused. I'll figure it out."

"You should have Fred look into it."

"I can't. Not without having the woman's name and something more to go on."

"Put me on speaker."

"Why?"

"Just do it," she said, firming her tone.

Jerry sighed and pressed the button. "Say what you have to say."

"Gunter. You watch over Jerry and don't let anyone hurt him. You hear?"

Gunter wagged his tail without opening his eyes.

"Did he hear me?"

"He wagged his tail."

"I'll make you a strawberry cupcake if you make sure Jerry comes home safe," April said, sweetening the offer.

Gunter lifted his head and growled his acceptance.

Jerry chuckled. "That woke him up."

"Okay, good, take me off speaker."

Jerry hit the button. "Done."

"You'd better be safe, Mr. McNeal. I don't want to become a widow before we're actually married."

"You know I haven't asked you yet," Jerry teased.

April laughed a seductive laugh. "Sure you have. You just haven't said the words, remember?"

Jerry smiled. "I love you, Ladybug."

"I love you too, Jerry. Hey, Carrie's here. We're meeting with the architect today to look over some floor plans. Are you sure you don't want to be here for this?"

"Nope. We've already discussed what we each want in a house. The rest is up to you. You know me, as long as the toilets flush and the roof doesn't leak, I'm a happy man."

"Okay, I love you. Gotta go," she replied and ended the call.

Jerry held on to the phone for several seconds after the call ended as if willing April to call back. She didn't, so he placed the phone on the nightstand and got dressed. He turned to Gunter. "I'm going to get something to eat. Are you coming?"

Gunter groaned, inched his way onto Jerry's pillow, and turned, sticking his legs into the air.

"Fine. Have it your way. I'll tell April you were too tired from roaming the halls all night to protect me."

Gunter opened his eyes, then closed them once more.

"Suit yourself." Jerry hung the "do not disturb" sign on the doorknob and left the room. When he reached the end of the hall, Gunter was waiting for him. Jerry grinned a wide grin – the dog might be a ghost, but he could still be bribed. "Come on, boy, I'll buy you a donut to hold you over until we get home."

Gunter licked his lips and fell in step beside him.

As they turned the corner, the skin on the back of his neck began to crawl.

Gunter alerted but remained at his side. A move that told him that while something hovered in the air, the energy didn't appear threatening.

Jerry slowed his pace, his eyes snaking from side to side, searching for what had alerted them. As he approached the elevator, he saw the wavering spirit of an elderly man wearing a faded red flannel shirt. Dove grey suspenders held his pants in place, and his boots were well-worn and caked with dried mud. The gentleman didn't pay them any mind, as he was too busy assaulting the elevator doors with a small pickaxe. The man was working in the ghostly realm, his efforts producing no sound and leaving no marks.

Jerry wouldn't have felt the need to stop if not for simple curiosity as the man was joined in the hallway by an equally old gray donkey. The donkey wore a leather strap with two leather satchels draped across his back. Both packs appeared full of gear. Several burlap bags were tied on each side while a shotgun and shovel lay across a sleeping roll, which was also strapped to the animal's back.

Aware of the cameras that lined the hallway, Jerry pretended to make a call while lowering the volume and sticking the phone against his ear. "You okay there, old timer?"

The man used a hanky to wipe his brow, then eyed Gunter as he patted the donkey on the behind. "Better keep that dog away from Matilda's back legs. She's likely to kick him ifin he gets too close."

"I appreciate the warning. You lost?"

"Nope. I ain't claim-jumpin' neither. I staked

this claim in '53. Got the paper to prove it." The guy opened one of the pouches and removed a yellowed piece of paper. He unfolded it and pointed a gnarled finger at the lettering. "See, it's got my name written right there. Benjamin Worthington. That's my mark down there at the bottom."

Jerry saw both and noted the date on the claim to be 1853. He raised an eyebrow and glanced at the gold elevator doors. "You've been mining here a long time."

The man smiled and bobbed his head. "Arrived nearly a year before they named the town."

Jerry shook his head. "1853, that's hard to believe."

The man narrowed his eyes. "You better believe it. It says it right there on the paper. It sure wasn't 1753. I'm old, but I'm not that old."

"I wasn't saying I didn't believe you. I just find it interesting." Jerry debated asking the man if he knew he was dead and then decided it would be best to tell him in case he wasn't aware of his passing. "Do you know that you're dead?"

"I figured it out some time back when all at once, I realized nothing hurt. At first, I was a little lost, then old Matilda showed up, and things were like they used to be; well, almost so. Now the mine has doors made of gold. I've been trying to carve off a hunk for years but have yet to get me a piece." Benjamin winked. "I don't mind. I've got nothing but time these days."

Jerry started to tell him the elevator doors weren't made of real gold and stopped. *The man's happy. What could possibly be gained by taking that away from him? He isn't bothering anyone, and it's doubtful he will be able to put a dent in the doors.* The elevator dinged. "Good Luck, Mr. Worthington." Jerry lowered his cell phone and turned to leave.

"You take good care, Mr. McNeal. There's a foul wind out today."

Surprised the spirit knew his name and used the same phrase as the other spirit, Jerry pivoted. The elevator doors slid closed. Both Benjamin and the donkey were gone.

Gunter yawned a squeaky yawn as a chill ran the length of Jerry's spine. As they passed the coffee station, he overheard two women talking.

"I could have sworn I felt someone in the elevator with me earlier. Do you think the place is haunted?"

Her friend laughed a cackling laugh. "It's Deadwood, darling. Everything is haunted."

***

When he first saw the agency's tech crew had installed a laptop in the Durango, he thought it a waste. Jerry McNeal was a lot of things, but computer savvy was nowhere near the top of his list. And yet, here he sat in what proved to be a practical makeshift office, listening to "Down Around My Place" by John Hiatt and Joe Bonamassa while using the laptop to read up on the case files Fred had sent. The files had been sanitized, leaving in things that could not tie Mr. X to his real identity – at least for most people. Jerry wasn't most people – while Fred had told him the name was only a placeholder. Jerry already knew the person to be a male. He also knew if he wanted to, he could easily use his gift to find out the real identity of the man.

According to the report, Mr. X had a few drinks in one of the downtown bars and walked back to the place he was staying alone. A few hours later, he was visited by a woman, and according to Mr. X, the two had been intimate. Those things were not up for debate. What Mr. X was unsure of was who the woman was and how she got into his room. He was worried that perhaps he'd been drugged and, if so, to what purpose. Further, he was afraid there may have been someone else in on the ruse who would produce photo proof of his infidelity at a time when such a leak could prove detrimental to his political career.

Fred's voice boomed through the speakers, silencing the music. "Getting anything?"

Jerry knew the Durango was a one-of-a-kind prototype built specifically for him by tech agents that would not divulge the vehicle's capabilities to any outside source. While he knew he was under constant surveillance and the SUV had buttons he could push to bring help without making a call, this feature was new to him. Jerry stared at the dash, knowing he had neither initiated nor answered a call. "Either I'm getting a divine message, or this is a vast invasion of privacy." Jerry looked at Gunter when the music resumed. "Tell me you heard that too."

Gunter woofed his response.

Jerry reached over and scratched Gunter behind the ear. "Since I don't speak dog, I'm going to take that as a yes."

The dash lit up, showing a call from Fred. Jerry pushed the button on the steering wheel to connect the call. "Decided to go old school, did you?"

"You seem to be uncomfortable with change."

"I'm uncomfortable living in a fishbowl. How many times have my conversations been monitored?" It was a rhetorical question. Jerry knew, firsthand, the agency to be more than capable to listen to any conversation most people thought private. He also knew the agency was not limited to using cell phones, computers, or televisions to glean confidential information.

"Do you want me to tell you the truth or lie to you?"

Jerry decided to ignore the comment. "I just finished reading the file on Mr. X. The file doesn't mention ghosts, so why not just send someone to investigate what happened?"

"We did. His name is Jerry McNeal." Fred continued before Jerry had a chance to respond. "There are cameras all around Deadwood that corroborate Mr. X's account of things. The same footage shows no one followed him to his room. So the threat could have come from within the house."

"Meaning a ghost."

"Or, whoever owns the property. Either way, we could only get you under the roof for one night. It's tourist season, so we were lucky to get that."

"There is more to this than you are saying. Why does the agency care if one man gets his career ruined? It happens all the time."

Fred sighed audibly. "Mr. X sits on several advisory committees that make some rather important policy decisions. We need to make sure there is nothing out there that can be used to blackmail Mr. X into voting against his conscience."

"It happens all the time."

"I'm sure you're right about that, but this one is on our desk. *Capisce?*"

"Enough to know you're telling me to stay in my swim lane. I also know you well enough to know that you don't like yes men, so don't expect me to follow blindly if something doesn't pass the smell test."

"You're saying you don't think Mr. X is on the level?"

"No, I'm saying I'm not going to sugarcoat

anything if I find he's not."

"Wouldn't have it any other way." There was a long pause. "So what's the plan?"

"Since you want to keep this investigation low-key, I'm going to wait until after dark to check in to the next place."

"Check-in is at three p.m. Why the delay?"

"You picked me for a reason, so trust my instincts on this. If someone did set him up, there's a chance they'll be expecting some kind of investigation. Since the place has a keypad check-in, I won't be dealing with an individual. I'll keep a low profile when I check in and scan the place for hidden cameras and bugs once I'm in. If this is something supernatural, it shouldn't take long to find that out. If it's not, then we'll start looking elsewhere. We won't need to be inside the house for that. If I'm wrong, you'll work your magic and get us back in."

"I wish I had time to send in someone to watch your back. Say the word and I'll pull the plug until we can work something out."

The case must be important. It was not like Fred Jefferies to be this wishy-washy. Then again, if he'd seen footage of the incident on the street, it could be his boss was having second thoughts on his decision to send Jerry in to work on such an important case. Jerry worked to sound confident. "I appreciate the sentiment, but you know I like to work alone."

Gunter growled.

Jerry reached a hand to the dog's head and mouthed the word "sorry." "Besides, you're forgetting that Gunter has my back," Jerry said more to appease the dog than remind Fred.

"We should all be so lucky," Fred agreed.

"Hey, listen, I'm going to leave the Durango here and take the trolley into town. If there are eyes on the place I'm staying, it's better not to draw attention to it. Same with the parking garage. Not that I get a bad feeling about it, but at least here, it will be under the surveillance of the hotel cameras." Jerry's gaze traveled toward the secret compartment above his head. "Ordinarily, I wouldn't worry, but someone decided to hide a small arsenal inside my ride."

Fred chuckled. "I don't recall hearing any complaints when you took possession of them."

"Not complaining at all. Just letting you know in case you see the Durango parked here and wonder why I'm not where I'm supposed to be." Jerry realized it was he that now sounded paranoid. He didn't like holding things back, and planned on having a conversation about the ghostly gunman eventually, but not until he could fully explain what was going on and assure Fred that he had the situation under control. The stagecoach didn't bother him – not anymore. After he'd had a chance to analyze what happened, he knew it was just a matter of being in the wrong place at the wrong time and further obvious that if he hung around town long enough, he was sure to see it again. Since he wasn't sure how often the stagecoach came to town, he planned on proving his assumption by having a conversation with his friend Jonesy. He didn't need to ask if Jonesy was still in town; he already knew the answer, as he'd felt the man to be close. He also knew Jonesy had a touch of the gift – nothing like Jerry had, but he could see spirits and that was enough for Jerry at the moment, as there was a good chance Jonesy had seen a few of his own. One thing was certain, for the first time in his life, Jerry McNeal was not only interested in hearing ghost stories, but also eager to swap a few of his own. "If it makes you feel better, I plan on having a conversation with a buddy of mine. If I need someone to have my back, Jonesy will step up."

"I don't want any outsiders in on this!" Fred's tone was unusually short.

Sheesh, what was that about? I'm not stupid. It's not like I planned on telling Jonesy why I'm in town. Jerry opted not to escalate matters. "Easy, boss, it was just a suggestion. You know me and know I would not do anything to compromise the mission at hand."

"You can talk to your friend, but he is not to know why you are there."

"Roger that, boss."

"Got to go. Check in when you get something," Fred said, ending the call.

Jerry looked over at Gunter. "Is it me, or is the boss acting weird?"

Gunter growled a deep rumbling growl.

"Glad to see I'm not the only one who thinks so." Jerry drummed his fingers on the steering wheel. *Fred must have someone breathing down his neck. It's the only explanation for the way he's acting.*

Jerry leaned into the dash and spoke in clipped tones. "No problem. I'll have a quick drink with my friend to catch up and then you and I will get to work." Jerry slid a glance to Gunter, who looked at him as if to say, *Yep, that didn't sound staged at all.*

Chapter Nineteen

Current day…

Tyler moved around the upstairs apartment with the ease of a man with two good legs. He wrapped the cord around the vacuum, then returned it to the closet and walked to the front window and looked out over the tops of the buildings, visualizing the town below. *You're one lucky man, Jonesy.*

As he stood there, he gave thanks for allowing him a second chance at life and for all that had happened in the year since arriving in Deadwood.

"Has it really been a year?" Lillian asked, appearing beside him.

Tyler nodded. "A year and twenty-nine days, to be exact."

Lillian turned and walked from the window, her long skirt rustling as she moved. "Time is all the same to me."

Tyler sighed. "It doesn't seem fair you have to

spend your days inside the house when there are so many spirits walking about the streets." The room grew cold, and he knew he'd made a mistake. The woman did not like to be reminded she was dead. He hurried to change the subject. "I'm glad you live here. If not for you, I wouldn't have made it past that first night without being booted to the street."

She turned, narrowing her eyes into a mysterious glare. "You give me too little credit, Mr. Jones. You would never have even stayed here if not for me. Juanita was ready to dismiss you without even giving you a chance. I was the one who pushed the button that allowed you to come."

Tyler placed his hand to his chest. "Pardon me for not giving you your full credit. I am eternally grateful for your good judgment." He removed his hand, placing both in his front pockets. He swallowed then lifted his gaze. "I don't know why you are here, but I think maybe you were sent here to help me. I was lost when I arrived. I didn't want to be here – I didn't want to be anywhere. But you refused to allow me to get lost in my self-pity."

"We are all afforded some self-loathing from time to time. It is when you wallow in your self-pity and forget to live your life that it becomes a problem," she reminded him.

"Thank you for pulling me out and helping me see that life is worth living. I honestly don't think I would have found happiness if not for you convincing me to stay."

"The mind is a wonderful tool, Mr. Jones. Meet each day with a smile and moment of gratitude, and the darkness will soon fade away. If you believe yourself to be happy, your soul will see it so."

"You are an amazing woman, Lillian Cramer."

Lilly beamed under the praise. "I was always good at getting people together – sometimes to my own detriment. It cost me dearly on account of I'd see the way a fellow would look at one of my gals, and I'd know I had to bring them together. Oh, I could have made a small fortune if I'd kept my mouth shut, as the man would have paid dearly to be with his love each night. But I'd remember the way my husband cherished me, and I'd feel the need to give them what I never had."

Tyler pulled his hands from his pockets, walked to the table, pulled out a chair and sat, giving his hip a rest. "You've told me this before but never said why you didn't love him."

"Oh, I loved him," she corrected. "But my father taught me never to fully trust a man. Mr. Cramer was the only person I ever told what happened to me. He knew I could not share everything. I gave him what I could and he told me it was enough. I didn't want that for my girls. I would rather see them stay with me than to go with someone who would do them wrong. I had to be sure that the man I chose for them would not be cruel to them. True love is a gift you give to each other. I find it is better to be alone and love yourself than be with someone who does not cherish what you have to give. Maybe it was because of what was done to me that made me a better judge of character than most because all of my girls went on to lead happy lives."

"You said you're the one who pushed the button allowing me to come. You had not met me. How did you know I was a good man?"

"I didn't." She laughed an easy laugh. "I said yes entirely on your looks."

"Which I lied about." He pulled his hand from his pocket and traced the length of his scar. "Did you have any regrets when you saw me?"

"Wrinkled sheets make the bed, Mr. Jones. In my profession, I had to learn to look past physical flaws. I quickly learned a person could be beautiful on the outside and ugly on the inside. That works both ways. I found some of the gentlest lovers to be outwardly flawed."

"No, by then, I could feel your soul and knew you to be a good man worthy of love. You knew it too; you just had to be reminded of it. There was a sadness in your eyes the first time I saw you, as if you'd forgotten how to smile. A wise woman once told me, meet each day with a smile and a moment of gratitude, and the darkness will soon fade away."

Tyler started to respond and realized she was no longer there. He was about to get up when his cell rang. He pulled it from his pocket and grinned as he took the call. "McNeal, buddy, it's been a long time, brother. You calling to check up on me?"

"Nope, I'm in town and wanted to check to see if you're free for dinner tonight."

"Aw, man, I'd love to, but we've got other plans. I'm free tomorrow or can spare an hour or so early this afternoon."

"This afternoon works. Where are you living?"

Tyler started to tell him and reconsidered and looked at his watch. "I'm not too far from town. How about I meet you at Mustang Sally's at 12:15?"

"I think I saw it when I drove through town. It's on Main Street, right?"

"Yep, that's the place. They have Bud on tap."

"My kind of place. See you in a few."

Tyler had just ended the call when he heard footsteps coming up the inner staircase. He pocketed the phone and pushed from the chair as Juanita entered the room.

She saw he'd been sitting and frowned. "Are you alright?"

"I'm fine. I was talking to Lillian when my phone rang. Remember my friend Jerry I told you about?"

"The psychic?"

"That's him. He's in town and wants to have dinner."

Juanita's eyes went wide. "Tonight?"

"Relax. I know better than to bring him here

without clearing it with you first. I'm going to meet him in town in an hour."

A frown flitted across her face and Tyler grinned. Juanita was deeply ensconced in writing her novel and had been stressed about getting the apartment ready for tonight's house guest. He spread his arms toward each of the outer walls. "All done."

Juanita's frown lifted. "Really? I was just coming up to see if you needed any help."

Tyler shook his head. "Nope. Our house guests were tidy. I finished a few minutes ago. Did you finish your chapter?"

Juanita moved to where he stood and rewarded him with a wide smile. "I'm so close. I'll be finished with the whole thing tonight. I was feeling bad for asking you to clean the space by yourself, so I took a break to see if you needed any help. Thank you."

He wrapped his arms around her and kissed her on top of her head. "I'm happy to have helped."

Juanita looked about the room and lowered her voice to a whisper. "Do you really think your friend could help Lillian?"

They had had this discussion before. Tyler had offered to call Jerry to see if he'd be willing to find out why Lillian was stuck here. "He's done it before."

She bit her bottom lip and nodded. "Okay. If you want to ask him, I'll agree."

"Do you want to run it past Lillian first?"

"No. If we tell her, she might not show herself. Tomorrow, okay?"

Tyler nodded. "I wouldn't think of bringing him here tonight. You've dreamed of this moment for so long. I'll meet with him and be back before Davie gets home from school. Trust me, I have your back on this. I wouldn't do anything that would jeopardize your finishing your book tonight."

Juanita's shoulders relaxed as she looked toward the door. "Do you want to use the outer stairs?"

The outside stairs were less steep than the inner stairs, which gave him trouble if he was having a bad hip day, which today was not. He shook his head. "No, I'm good today. Lead the way, Mrs. Jones."

***

Jerry had a bit of time to kill, so he dipped into a souvenir shop hoping to pick up a couple of things for Max and April. Gunter stayed at his side as he found them each a sweatshirt with Wild Bill on the back, picked up a shot glass and a couple of souvenir magnets, then made his way to the checkout located in the middle of the store.

The clerk smiled and began ringing up his purchases. "Find what you were looking for?"

"I did, thanks." Jerry watched as Gunter rounded the corner of the checkout counter and pretended not to notice when the clerk sucked in a breath. It didn't take a rocket scientist to know that Gunter was intruding on her personal space. She gave him his total, and he tapped his card on the device and slapped his left leg to get Gunter's attention while he signed for his purchase with the right.

The clerk leaned forward and peeked over the counter.

Jerry shrugged. "Gnats."

The woman lifted an eyebrow. "I thought maybe it was the dog. You really should keep him on a leash."

Jerry rolled his neck. Either the woman was messing with him or didn't realize Gunter was a spirit. "I don't own a dog." Technically, it wasn't a lie.

"He came in with you."

Jerry smiled a sheepish smile, took his bag and walked to the door with long strides, relaxing once he got outside. The time on his phone said it was 11:57. He looked both ways and stepped off the curb to cross the street.

"McNeal!"

Jerry recognized the voice as belonging to the gunfighter who'd called him out the day prior. Jerry sighed. Over a hundred people, but none were paying him any mind at the moment. Probably because he wasn't the only long-haired, bearded guy wearing a cowboy hat. *Maybe if I ignore him, he'll go away.* As soon as the thought came to him, Jerry knew he was wrong. This was the nightmare that had been haunting him. He suddenly recalled the dream in vivid detail. Only, in the dream, Jerry hadn't fared so well. *Don't freak out, McNeal. Spirits can't hurt you, especially with ghostly sidearms. Just keep walking.* That comment was meant for Gunter. Jerry froze when he realized the dog wasn't by his side. *Okay, this isn't good.*

"Come on out, or are ya too yeller?"

Jerry rolled his neck, glad his ghostly nemesis couldn't see the pistol tucked in the back of his jeans. He lifted his hands, started to walk to the center of the street, and decided against it upon seeing a line of cars heading his way. He spoke to the spirit using the power of his mind. *You're not going to shoot an unarmed man, are you?*

The gunman narrowed his eyes. "Do you honestly think I'm worried about my reputation? Besides, I wasn't armed when you finished me off, so why should it bother me?"

Jerry firmed his chin. *You're lying.*

The gunslinger flexed his fingers, hovering them over his holster. "You're saying I won't shoot an unarmed man?"

Jerry shook his head. *Nope. I'm saying you're lying about not wearing your guns when you were shot. If that were the case, your holsters would be empty. That means you deserved what you got.* Whether or not it was true, Jerry didn't know, but it felt right to say it.

The gunfighter kicked at the bricks with his

boot. "I've been dead a long time. How is it you still walk the streets without looking any different?"

Probably because I'm not the guy you're looking for. I suspect that person is long dead and chooses not to spend his eternity fighting battles he cannot win.

"What do you mean he didn't win? I'm dead, aren't I?"

You are. But I don't think that matters to you. I think if you actually did find the man you're looking for, you'd still call him out every time you see him. Tell me you haven't relived this day a hundred times before?

The gunfighter frowned, and Jerry knew he was getting to the guy. He shrugged. "It ain't like I got nothing better to do."

The bad thing was the spirit was probably right. If he had been gunned down in the middle of this street, it was likely he was stuck in a trauma memory. Unless the spirit was able to let go of the anger he felt, he was destined to spend eternity trying to right the wrongs. It didn't matter if he'd deserved the death he got. In his mind, he was wronged, and he'd spend eternity trying to make it right. Jerry felt the skin on the back of his neck begin to crawl. A second later, the gunfighter disappeared. Brick faded to dirt, and the sound of horse hooves filled the air, pounding the dirt as the stagecoach raced through the center of the street.

"Whoa!" the stagecoach driver called to the horses, pulling the team to a halt just down the street.

Jerry watched in awe as one of the drivers jumped from his bench seat and opened the door for those inside. The second man stood and started tossing bags from the top of the coach. The man on the ground caught the bags and lowered them to the ground, turning just in time to catch the next one heading his way. When the top was unloaded, the man climbed from the wagon, and both men moved to the rear and began untying a large trunk. A leg snaked out from inside the coach, turned, then was followed by the rest of a body. The man wore a dark suit and his boots had silver caps on the toes. As he turned, Jerry could see pearl-handled pistols beneath his coat. Once on solid ground, the man offered his hand to someone inside.

Jerry's breath caught as a woman in a long burgundy dress stepped down from the coach. Her hair was piled high on her head and her skin was so pale, it looked almost white against the richness of the dress. He knew her to be a spirit, but felt that had nothing to do with the color of her skin. No, this was a lady who'd rarely felt the warmth of the sun. She looked his way, staring directly at him with nary a smile. The man who was helping her down glanced to see what had caught her attention. He leaned in, and whispered something in her ear, and the woman's eyes grew wide as she opened a parasol and held it over her head. The gentleman splayed his hand on the small of her back. The couple took three steps and disappeared. A second later, the stagecoach too was gone.

Jerry realized he was standing in the street and looked to see if anyone was watching. While there were people milling around, none seemed to be paying him any attention other than the occasional glance. Gunter moved up beside him as he made his way across the street and to the retro-looking white and teal building.

The inside looked nothing like he'd expected. Tyler Jones sat at a booth near an inside brick wall. His eyebrows lifted as he waved to Jerry, welcoming him inside the spacious room.

Gunter jumped onto the bench seat and lowered into a crouch as Jerry slid into the booth across from his friend and placed his cowboy hat on the bench. While Jonesy's rugged exterior had shocked him the last time they'd met, the man's long hair, tattoos and scars seemed fitting in his new environment. The thing that looked oddly out of place was the shiny gold wedding ring that now encircled the man's left ring finger. It dawned on Jerry that with the exception of the wedding ring, scars and tats, the two could be brothers.

Jonesy looked at both Gunter and Jerry and grinned a wide grin as he leaned back in his chair. "Dang, brother, I thought I was looking in the mirror for a moment."

Jerry shook his head. "Nah, you're much prettier than I am."

Jonesy chuckled and ran a hand through the length of his hair. "There was a time when I might have agreed."

The waitress approached and handed Jerry a menu. She smiled at Jonesy. "The usual?"

"Yep." He glanced at Jerry. "Deluxe burger, fries and a Bud."

"Make that two." Jerry handed the menu back, waited for the waitress to leave and nodded toward Jonesy's wedding ring. "You look good, brother. When we last spoke, you were coming for a visit. Looks like you found something to keep you here."

Jonesy bobbed his head. "Did I ever."

Jerry draped his arms over the back of the bench. Gunter moved into a sit, conveniently maneuvering his head under Jerry's hand. Jerry absently scratched the shepherd's head as he spoke. "You move quick. You didn't mention coming here to visit anyone, so I gather it was love at first sight?"

Jonesy laughed. "Not hardly. Nita's a wildcat. Made her so mad the first time we met, I thought she was going to scratch my eyes out and send me packing."

"You seemed to have tamed her."

Jonesy shook his head. "She's still a wild one, but we were able to work out our differences with a little help."

Jerry cocked his head. "Counseling?"

Jonesy appeared to consider this for a moment. "More like divine intervention. What brings you to town?" he asked, changing the subject.

"I'm here on assignment."

Jonesy raised an eyebrow. "What kind of assignment?"

"Government work. Here to check out a jobsite." Not a total lie; more like a workaround of the truth.

"Where are you staying?"

"The Lodge." *Mostly.*

"Nice place. I wish I'd known you were coming. You could have stayed at our place."

Jerry shrugged him off. "I wouldn't want to impose on the newlyweds. Besides, I put everything on my expense account."

"I figured. We have an apartment that we rent out for short-term vacation rentals over the summer months."

The skin on the back of Jerry's neck began to crawl, and instantly, Jerry knew why Fred had been so terse at the mention of asking his buddy for help. "Booked up for the summer, are you?"

Jonesy shook his head. "We are. We have a guy coming in overnight and then we're booked for weeks at a time from here on out for the rest of the year. That's how I met my wife. I rented the apartment upstairs. That's what I was doing when you called, cleaning the place and getting the room ready for this afternoon's guest."

Tread carefully, McNeal. "I suppose you'll need to get back to let him in."

Jonesy shook his head. "Nah, we have one of those keypad thingies. We send them a code and they can check themselves in."

"You don't worry about strangers in the house?"

A sly smile crept over Jonesy's face. "Nope. We have a security system that sees everything."

Jerry's heart sank. He'd come here to visit a friend, not have the guy sent away for invasion of privacy and whatever other charges Fred could tag on. *Easy, McNeal, or he'll catch on that you know.* The waitress returned with their order. Jerry was glad for the interruption, as it gave him time to get his emotions under control. By the time she walked away, he'd decided the best course of action was to change the subject. He took a long sip from his beer glass and asked the question that had been pressing on his mind ever since he arrived in Deadwood. "How often does the stage come through?"

Jonesy slapped his hand on the table. "Hot dog, I knew you'd see it."

Gunter growled.

Jonesy threw his hands in the air and mumbled his apologies to people sitting near enough to have been startled by the outburst. Jonesy curbed his enthusiasm, leaning in so that only Jerry could hear.

"Every day, right around noon. The first time I saw it, I nearly wet myself. After that, I took to positioning myself so I could be in town when it arrived. Did you see the dandy and the woman in red?"

"Burgundy," Jerry corrected. "I don't believe I've ever seen skin that white."

Tyler grinned and bobbed his head. "That we can agree on. Have you met Larry yet?"

"The outlaw who wants to call everyone out?"

Tyler pointed a fry at Jerry. "He's not real."

Jerry stopped chewing midbite. "I know he's not alive. But he's real enough to make me glad I didn't have my pistol with me when he drew on me."

Tyler dipped a fry in ketchup and pointed it. "He's a ghost alright. It's the outlaw part that's a lie."

Jerry took another sip of beer. "Back up and explain yourself."

Tyler leaned back against the chair. "After about the fifth time the dude called me out, I decided to have a bit of fun with the guy. I came downtown and moved downwind from where he usually stands and waited for him to call someone out. He doesn't key on everyone – just seems to like people who look like they could play the part. You and I both fill the bill on account of the long hair and beards. The hats work too, but I've had him call out to me even when I wasn't wearing one. Now, most of the time, people go on about their way because they can't see or hear him. But on occasion, he finds one that has the gift, and he really puts on a show. So this one day, I snuck up on him and told him I had a gun pointed to his back. He got all weepy and told me that it wouldn't be right to kill an unarmed man."

Jerry tilted his head as if doing so would make it easier to comprehend what Jonesy was saying. "Wait, that doesn't make sense. Are you saying he don't know he's dead?"

"He does and doesn't. He's playing a role. Deadwood has long played host to reenacting gunfights to please the tourists. According to Larry, his claim to fame is being one of the original actors to walk the dirt streets and get shot by another man who played the marshal."

Jerry drew in a breath. The guy had been haunting his dreams for weeks and he wasn't even a real gunslinger. "So, he's just playing a part?"

Tyler chuckled. "Poor guy, playing the best role of his life and doesn't even get any applause."

"I've got one for you. This morning, I saw a miner using a pickaxe on the elevator doors at the Lodge."

"Seriously?"

Jerry ran his finger around the rim of his glass. "Apparently, the hotel sits right on top of the man's claim. The elevator doors are gold-plated, and the man thinks he's found the biggest gold strike in

Deadwood history."

Tyler arched a brow. "Did he say how he plans to get it out if he dismantles it?"

"I didn't ask. But I assume he'll put it on his donkey with the rest of his gear."

Tyler stopped chewing midbite. "He has a donkey in the hotel?"

"Yep. According to the claim stake he showed me, he's been working the same area since before the town was even here. I wonder if there are any stats on the ghosts said to haunt this town. Could be he's one of the oldest ones."

Tyler had been in the midst of taking a drink of his beer. He set down the glass and stared at Jerry as if he had something to say.

Jerry beat him to the punch. "Something on your mind, brother?" Jerry hoped that was the case. If Jonesy were to confess before charges were leveled, it could be used as leverage to get a better deal.

Tyler used his right hand to rotate his wedding ring. "I want you to meet my wife. Come to dinner tomorrow night."

Jerry smiled to hide his disappointment. "I'm not sure I'll still be in town tomorrow night."

"Come on, McNeal. I don't see a ring on your finger. What's so important you can't hang out another day?"

Because I don't want to be here when they arrest you. Jerry kept that thought to himself. *Maybe I'm wrong about the guy*. Only he wasn't. Jonesy was hiding something and that something was connected to the case. Of that he was certain. *Maybe his wife isn't in on it. Maybe he's asking me to dinner so that he can tell us both at the same time. Plus, I owe it to him to check out the room tonight just to make sure I'm not missing anything.* "Okay, brother. I'll hang out for another day."

Tyler grinned. "Good deal. I can't wait for you to meet the family."

"Family?"

"Juanita and Davie, my wife's kid from a previous marriage, and Grandma Lilly. She's had a rather colorful past. You'll like her."

Gunter's ears perked.

Jerry scratched Gunter behind the ear. "He misses Max."

"Max?"

Jerry caught the waitress's attention and asked for another round of beers, then settled into the chair to tell Tyler about his life over the last few months. He would leave out working for the agency and being guardian to a half-ghost puppy. Just two friends catching up on life. Everything else could wait – at least for the time being.

Chapter Twenty

Jerry said his goodbyes and walked across the street like a man on a mission. Halfway across the street, Gunter growled, and Jerry felt the skin on the back of his neck tingle.

"Fill your hands, McNeal!"

"Give it a rest Larry. I'm not in the mood," Jerry said without stopping.

Gunter barked and looked over his shoulder as if saying, *Yeah, what he said.*

Jerry made his way to the visitor center, intending to take the trolley. By the time he got there, he discovered he'd missed it, and the next wasn't due for another ten minutes. Jerry took off his hat and rolled his neck. *Not happening.*

Jerry replaced his hat, opting to walk back to his hotel. He wanted to call Fred but knew he needed to calm down before making the call. The last thing he needed was for Fred to fire him and make him find his own way home, though at the moment, that was the least of his worries, as Larry was following him up the hill.

"Go away, Larry."

"How'd you know my name?"

"So it's okay if you know my name, but I'm not allowed to know yours? Why have you been haunting my dreams, Larry?"

"She told me to."

Jerry stopped and turned to face the man. "She who?"

"I don't know."

"This she? Is she a spirit?"

Larry nodded.

"What does she look like?"

"I'm not supposed to tell."

Jerry motioned to Gunter, who moved in front of Larry and bared his teeth.

Larry faded in and out.

"Better tell me, Larry. The dog's a ghost. You disappear, and he'll follow you."

"I don't know her name. I only know she has pink hair." The instant he said it, he disappeared.

Gunter looked at Jerry as if asking if he should follow the spirit into the unknown.

Jerry shook his head, took off his hat and ran a hand through his hair. He looked at Gunter. "Do you know anything about this?"

Gunter yawned a squeaky yawn.

***

Jerry had nearly reached the driveway to the Lodge when the trolley drove past. Between his discussion with Larry and going over everything he planned to say to Fred, the walk had done nothing to curb his anger. He continued to his room, changed into his running clothes and retraced the path he'd just come. He ran through town and curved his way around until he'd reached Mt. Moriah Cemetery. He paid the dollar admission and walked up the hill with Gunter at his side. He visited the graves of Wild Bill and Calamity Jane, and while he saw a few spirits walking among the graves, he didn't see any that resembled the cemetery's most famous inhabitants. A part of him was relieved, as he might have felt the need to seek them out and speak to them, but that wasn't why he was there. Most people get freaked out in cemeteries, but Jerry often found comfort within the stones. Unfortunately, that was not the case today, as his mind wouldn't relax enough for his anger to dissipate. Frustration mounted as he left the cemetery, running down the hill, as if hoping to outrun his thoughts. He'd nearly reached the bottom when he realized he was being followed. The energy behind him felt ominous. He slowed and turned to face his would-be attacker, only to find several of the spirits he'd seen milling about within the gates of the cemetery. Jerry sighed. "What do you want from me?"

The spirits all turned and looked at each other. One stepped forward. "Nothing. The way you ran from the graveyard, we thought there was trouble. We didn't know what it was, but knew if you didn't want to be in there, neither did we."

Jerry ran a hand over his head, picturing the scene in *Forest Gump* when he turned and saw everyone following him. Jerry forced a smile. "There's no trouble. I just want to go home."

As the spirits started up the hill, Jerry pulled the phone from his pocket and dialed April's number. His call went straight to voicemail. It didn't matter; the sound of her voice was all that was needed to rein in his emotions. "Hey, Ladybug. Just wanted to hear your voice. All good here. I'll give you a call later. Love you, bye." He ended the call and started the long walk back to the hotel.

***

By the time he'd showered, he was calm enough to make the call to Fred. Jerry went to the courtyard to make the call, heard a couple talking nearby, and decided to take his call further away from the building and to the far end of the parking lot before pressing send. "I quit," Jerry said the moment Fred answered.

"Cool your jets, McNeal." That he hadn't asked why let Jerry know he'd been expecting his call.

"Oh, I'm cool," Jerry replied. "I was wondering why you'd sent me before having someone else investigate. You should have told me Tyler was involved. That way, I wouldn't have been blindsided." Jerry watched as Gunter took off up the hillside and disappeared from view.

"So you're saying he is?"

"Don't toy with me, Fred. We're way past playing games. You know good and well Mr. X rented the room from Jonesy and his wife. That's why you sent me. A pretty rotten thing to do if you ask me, sending me here to pull the rug out from under my friend." That was the bugger of it; he'd visited Jonesy shortly before the man had set out for Deadwood, and while he said the right things, Jerry could tell he was a shell of his former self. But now, the man was so full of life, he hadn't even mentioned losing his leg. "I don't want to destroy his life."

"I'm not asking you to."

"The heck you aren't."

"I didn't send you there to sell out your friend, McNeal. I chose you because I knew you were the one person that would be in the man's corner. Anyone else would look at this as an open and shut case. All the evidence points to someone trying to blackmail a person with incredible pull. I knew you would look past the obvious and use that gift of yours to prove the man innocent, provided that is the case. I also know you well enough to know that you won't sweep this under the rug if he isn't. You met with the man today. What is your gut feeling telling

you?"

"That if you'd sent anyone else, Jonesy would be in handcuffs right now."

"So you think he's guilty?"

Yes. "No. I think he said some things that have me concerned."

"He mentioned Mr. X?"

"No. He said his security system knows everything that goes on in that house."

"Sounds damning."

It didn't sound promising, that was for sure. Jerry sighed a resigned sigh. "I'll be heading over to the house as planned. If he's got the place wired, I'll find them."

"Does this mean you're rescinding your resignation?"

"It means I don't want to see an innocent man go to jail."

"You have to consider the possibility that he's already onto you and has removed any cameras that were there."

"I know. He invited me over to dinner tomorrow night. If I don't find anything, I'll come right out and ask him. If he's lying, I'll know."

"This is your investigation. I'll leave it in your hands. I have to remind you that this is still a classified mission. The agency will neither confirm nor deny being involved."

"Roger that, sir." Jerry ended the call. He thought

about whistling for Gunter but knew the ghostly K-9 could take care of himself and was more than capable of finding his way home. He glanced up the hill then went back to the room. He didn't plan on checking into the secondary location until after dark. Once there, he didn't intend to get much sleep, and he was already sleep-deprived. He kicked off his shoes and stretched out on the bed. An hour later, he was still staring at the ceiling. Not able to get his friend out of his head, Jerry decided to head to the rental earlier than previously planned. Things were what they were, and he was ready to get everything out in the open either way. He twisted his hair under a ballcap and took his backpack and left the room via the courtyard door. The trolley was just pulling to the front of the building when he rounded the corner. As he slid into an empty seat, Gunter appeared by his side. Jerry smiled and slid closer to the window to give him room.

They exited the trolley at the visitor center, opting to walk the rest of the way. Jerry took a right at the parking garage and made his way up the stairs. He was surprised how far up the hill the stairs went. As he climbed, he recalled his visit to Indianapolis to visit Jonesy. At the time, the man was physically unable to comfortably grab a beer out of the refrigerator, much less tackle stairs of this magnitude. That he'd even considered it showed incredible courage on his part. *Come on, Jonesy, you've made it this far. Please don't let me down.*

Once he reached Williams Street, Jerry stopped and looked at Gunter. "Wait here until I get inside. I may be able to sneak in without him realizing it's me, but not if he sees you."

Gunter sat as Jerry pulled the ballcap lower, dipped his head and started up the concrete steps to the house, diverting to the side of the house before he neared the porch. He kept his chin close to his chest as he climbed the outside stairs. He thumbed in the code on the keypad and opened the door. Stepping inside, he pressed into the doorway, checking the area around the landing for cameras, only to find none. Odd, as one would think a Marine would want to know the face of strangers entering his home. Not convinced, Jerry took off his ballcap and stepped onto the landing. If there were cameras, this simple act would have Jonesy reaching out to inquire why Jerry hadn't been forthcoming about his visit.

Jerry went back inside, pleased to see Gunter waiting for him. He smiled at the dog. "I need to know if there are cameras. Search!" An ordinary dog might have stood there staring at him. Gunter was far from ordinary and understood things far beyond what even the most highly trained dog would. He placed his nose to the ground and began his search. That Jonesy hadn't made an appearance led Jerry to believe the search would be unproductive. He walked to the window debating his next move. Mr. X had said a woman came to visit him in his room and had no clue how she entered. Jerry locked the outer door then double-checked the door to what he assumed were inside stairs. *Locked from the inside.* Jerry considered this a moment then pulled out his cell phone and called Fred.

"That was quick. Did you find the cameras?"

"Nope."

"Maybe you missed them."

"I wasn't the one searching."

"You trust the dog."

"Yes, and so do you. Now, let's play a game of what if."

"I'm listening."

Jerry held the phone away, snapped a photo of the stairway door and sent it to Fred.

"It's a door." Fred sounded unimpressed.

"A door that is locked from the other side. You haven't left anything unturned. What does Jonesy's wife look like?"

"She's a nice-looking lady."

"Nice enough you wouldn't kick her out of bed?"

"If I wasn't married."

"But you are. Stay with me a minute. What if Mr. X did have a visitor during the night? What if that visitor came up this set of stairs and let herself inside the room? Jonesy himself said his wife was a wildcat. What if she is the one who entered the room.

Jonesy looked good, but what if Jonesy can't keep his wife happy, and she uses this as a way to relieve tension? Mr. X admitted she showed up in his room without knowing how she got here. He'd been drinking and something happened. A lot of men have done worse and still ended up in the Oval Office. What if this is all a smoke screen to save his marriage in case the pictures do materialize? Someone accuses him of infidelity and he can say, 'Oh no honey, I was drugged. Look, see, there was this whole investigation on it.' And what if Jonesy didn't know a thing about it?"

"Pretty thin, McNeal."

"Thin, yes, but not out of the question."

"So, is this a theory you can prove?"

Jerry sighed. "Only if Mrs. Jones needs some stress relief tonight."

"So the plan is to wait there until she shows up."

"Nope. The plan is to go to town and knock back a few beers at the #10 Saloon. Mr. X was supposedly drunk when the visit took place. Maybe that's her M.O.; she only comes up when she thinks she has a chance. You wake up with a beautiful woman being nice to you, are you going to kick her out or chalk it up to drinking and continue the hallucination?"

"The question is what will you do?"

"I'm here to do a job, not make house calls," Jerry said dryly.

"Good. Keep your wits about you. Your friend's

counting on you."

"Yeah, If I'm right, I get to ruin his life either way."

***

Jerry spent the better part of the evening sitting at the bar and nursing beers at the #10 Saloon. Over the span of three hours, he'd been approached by several women, a couple of them spirits. He'd hoped to see Wild Bill, whose spirit was said to haunt the town, but apparently, the man had better things to do, as he never showed. While Jerry had been cordial to all who approached, he stuck to Mr. X's script, telling the women he was married. A few had questioned his lack of wedding ring. He'd lied and told them he'd forgotten it at home. He returned to the apartment at two in the morning, the same time Mr. X claimed to have returned to the room. The only difference, Gunter escorted him home.

Jerry relieved himself, then went to bed, keeping his jeans on, thinking to stay awake and wait for his visitor. Sometime later, Gunter growled a low warning, and Jerry knew they weren't alone in the room.

The covers lifted and he smelled the sweet perfume as someone climbed into bed beside him. How many times had he wished for an experience such as this? A few months ago, he might have waited to see how things would play out. That was before April.

Jerry rolled to the other side of the bed, thinking to turn on the light, and somehow he got tangled in the sheets and landed on the floor with a thud. By the time he freed himself from the sheets and turned on the light, his visitor was gone. The only proof it wasn't a dream was the fact that Gunter stood in front of the stairway door wagging his tail.

Jerry stomped across the room intending to pound on the door. He raised his fist, ready to do just that when he remembered Jonesy telling him his wife had a son. *No use getting the kid involved.* He lowered his fist and went to the nightstand to get his phone. He looked at Gunter. "I'll call him. If the kid wakes up, not my problem."

Before Jerry could make the call, someone pounded on the outside door. Jerry smiled. "Guess the little vixen knows she's busted." Jerry crossed the room and yanked open the door, expecting to see Jonesy standing there. Instead, he saw a woman that barely reached his chin. Wearing a pink robe that matched the color of her cheeks, her eyes were narrowed, and she appeared ready for a fight.

She pushed her way into the room. "Mr. Hendershot, I'm Juanita Jones. We have rules in place for a reason. My son sleeps below this room. I see you have two good legs to hold you up, so there are no excuses. I know you are only here for one night, but that doesn't give you an excuse to get drunk and flop around on the floor like a fish waking my son."

Jerry, who'd been thrown off by her calling him by a different last name, found his voice. "Well, Mrs. Jones, I wouldn't have been floundering like a fish if you hadn't snuck up the stairs and tried to have your way with me."

She stood there blinking as if he'd slapped her.

"That's right. I'm onto your little hanky-panky pastime. Coming up the stairs and climbing into bed with men who rent your room. Well, some men might like that sort of thing, but others..." Her shoulders began to shake. Jerry knew she was about to cry and was determined not to let her tears get to him. *Where's Jonesy? Wait, is she laughing?*

She was and doing a mighty fine job of it. While there were tears, they seemed to be tears of finding something outrageously funny.

Jerry used his cop voice. "Mrs. Jones, I assure you, attempted sexual assault is not a laughing matter."

Juanita grabbed her stomach and continued to laugh. So much so, she actually snorted.

Jerry slid a look to Gunter, who appeared to be just as confused as him. *A lot of help you are.* Jerry turned his attention back to the woman. *Maybe she's mentally ill. Yes, that has to be it. She has a medical condition that causes her to ...to what, McNeal?* "Are you ill? Is that it? Were you sleepwalking and just happened to find your way into my bed?"

Before she could answer, the door opened. Jonesy stepped inside the room, took one look at his wife doubled over in what looked to be pain and came rushing at him. Jerry ducked out of the way just in time to avoid a right hook to the jaw.

Gunter moved in front of Jonesy, blocking another assault. Jonesy cocked his head to the side. "McNeal? What are you doing here?"

"Keeping you out of jail." Jerry nodded to Juanita, who at least had the decency to stop laughing. "I'm not sure I can say the same thing about your wife."

Jonesy looked to his wife for an explanation.

Juanita smiled. "Mr. Hendershot."

"McNeal," Jerry said, cutting her off.

"Mr. McNeal got a visit from our friend."

"Our friend?"

She nodded to the doorway. "Yes, our friend."

Jonesy's eyes widened. The skin on the back of Jerry's neck began to crawl.

Gunter whined.

Jerry turned to see Gunter lying on the floor, staring up at a ghostly figure in a long black dress. While Jerry couldn't see her face, the woman's figure was rather impressive.

"Show yourself, Lillian," Juanita said firmly.

The ghostly figure morphed into a voluptuous woman – at least from the neck down. She smiled a wrinkled smile. "It's nice to officially meet you, Mr.

McNeal."

Jerry slid a glance toward Jonesy and his wife and smiled his understanding. "Grandma Lilly?"

Jonesy grinned. "I told you that you'd like her."

***

Juanita set a cup of coffee on the table in front of him. "I know you are tired, but I appreciate you taking a few moments to speak with us. I'm sorry about the chill, but it always gets like this when Lillian is confronted."

"She knows she is dead," Jerry said, wrapping his fingers around the cup. "She did seem surprised when I told her there was no reason she couldn't leave."

Juanita frowned. "We don't really want her to leave. We just didn't want her stuck here."

Lillian materialized beside the table. "You mean you didn't bring him here to force me out of my house?"

"No!" both Jonesy and Juanita said at once.

"Then why is he here?"

"Hello, handsome, here for a good time?" Charlie called from the other room.

"Be quiet before you wake up Davie," Juanita said, shushing the bird.

Jerry stifled a chuckle. "I think the bird knows more than anyone wants to admit." He went on to tell them an abbreviated version of why he was there under an assumed name.

Juanita's face paled as she looked at Lillian. "You mean this isn't the first time you've visited one of our guests?"

Lillian smiled a seductive smile. "I can't let you have all the fun."

Juanita gasped. "But you're old!"

"Technically, it's just my face that's old. I have the body of a thirty-year-old," Lillian corrected.

Jerry lifted an eyebrow. "She's not wrong."

"You're welcome to stay here if you behave. We can't have you ... well, we just can't," Juanita stammered.

Jerry took a chance. "Maybe if you feel the need for a visit, you can visit one of the local hotels so that you don't draw unwanted attention to your family."

Lillian's energy brightened, and the house instantly warmed as a smile transformed her face. "I wouldn't mind taking a stroll every now and again."

Jerry pushed his coffee cup aside and resisted proclaiming his work here to be done as he stood. "I think you can handle things from here on out. I need to go back to the hotel and get some rest."

"You sure you don't want to sleep here? We don't need to clean the room for a few more hours."

Jerry shook his head. "Nope. When I crash, I plan on sleeping for at least twelve hours." He slid a look to Lillian. "Twelve uninterrupted hours."

***

"It's four in the morning. This better be good," Fred grumbled.

Jerry lowered the visor and looked at his reflection in the mirror. "I haven't slept in three days."

"We pay you good money not to sleep."

"I can't argue with that. I'm in the Durango. I didn't trust myself to go inside. Once I do, I am turning off the phone and going to sleep."

"Understood. So what's the deal? Are we going to arrest the husband or the wife?"

"Neither."

"I'm not following you."

"The woman who visited Mr. X was a spirit."

"Can you prove it?"

Jerry laughed and looked at the dash. "You're kidding, right?"

"So I'm supposed to just call this guy and tell him he had a playdate with a ghost? You think he or his people are going to believe that?"

"Probably not."

"Maybe we should bring Max in on this."

"For what purpose?"

"We get her to sketch a picture of this woman, and we can prove to him it was a ghost."

"Or he'll see the picture and think Max drew a picture of a woman who he is going to want prosecuted. Besides, there's a bigger problem."

"Which is?"

"The woman's like a hundred and fifty years old."

"She's a ghost; she's supposed to be old."

"I'm serious. From the neck down, this woman is incredible. From the neck up, she looks two days older than baseball. I can't imagine it would please the man to find out he made out with his great-grandmother."

"Probably not. You got any other ideas?"

"Tell him it was all a dream. Work your magic, doctor a lab test or something. Have the doctor call him and tell him the report had been delayed, that someone slipped him a mickey, and it was all just a bad dream."

"Think he will buy it?"

"I think he'd be so happy to have this behind him without any future fallout that he'll make himself believe it."

"So what about the ghost? Did you do anything to help her?"

"I tried. She's not stuck in the house; she just doesn't like change."

Fred chuckled. "Sounds like someone else I know. So you weren't able to help her?"

"Yes, and no. She knows she's dead but doesn't like to be reminded of it."

"So she's going to continue haunting them?"

"They all mutually agreed she can stay. She's part of the family."

"She's dead."

Jerry shrugged. "No one seems to care."

"Hey, while I have you on the phone, someone on the surveillance team showed me a video of the day you arrived in town. He said it looked like you were having a nervous breakdown or something."

"What'd you tell him?"

"I told him if there was a problem, you would have called."

The line grew quiet, and Jerry wondered if Fred had fallen back to sleep. "You still there, boss?"

"Yep, I figured if I waited long enough, you'd tell me your side of the story."

Jerry smiled. "Can you wait until I have time to figure out what that's going to be?"

Fred chuckled. "Get some sleep, McNeal. I've got another assignment for you the day after tomorrow."

So much for heading for home anytime soon. Jerry sighed. "Where am I going?"

"San Antonio."

"Texas?"

"Yep. Unless you have any objections, I thought maybe I'd send the jet to pick up Max and April and have them meet you there. We have a house in the area, and there's plenty to keep them busy while you're doing your thing."

"Thanks, Fred." Jerry sighed a weary sigh and ended the call.

Gunter, who'd been curled in the passenger seat beside him, lifted his head and gave a single yip.

Jerry looked to see the man in the white hat standing beside his driver side door. He powered down his window. "I'll be heading to Texas in a couple of days. I'm assuming you'll be needing a ride?"

The spirit reached out a hand and tipped his hat. "Since you'll be going my way, I'd be much obliged." Just before he disappeared, Jerry noticed the silver star fastened to the man's shirt.

"Oh, goody, I just love road trips."

Jerry glanced in the rearview mirror to see the lady with the pink hair grinning back at him and closed his eyes, hoping it all was another bad dream.

Jerry opened his eyes, and the spirit was gone. He looked over at Gunter. "Please tell me that was a dream."

Gunter growled a deep growl.

Now available for e-book preorder
Coming August 25, 2023:
Join Jerry McNeal and his ghostly K-9 partner as they put their gifts to good use!

Star Treatment – book 14 in The Jerry McNeal Series

About the Author

Sherry A. Burton writes in multiple genres and has won numerous awards for her books. Sherry's awards include the coveted Charles Loring Brace Award, for historical accuracy within her historical fiction series, The Orphan Train Saga. Sherry is a member of the National Orphan Train Society, presents lectures on the history of the orphan trains, and is listed on the NOTC Speaker's Bureau as an approved speaker.

Originally from Kentucky, Sherry and her Retired Navy husband now call Michigan home. Sherry enjoys traveling and spending time with her husband of more than forty years.

Made in the USA
Las Vegas, NV
24 April 2023

71059415R00184